SHOWDOWN IN THE ARCTIC

Mac was on his feet in a split second, bringing the Sten up in the same motion. All he had going for him was surprise . . . and he used it. In a flash, he tore open the nearest Nazi's head with two 9 mm bullets from the silenced barrel.

Wingate didn't pause to admire his handiwork. He pivoted and raked the opposite wall with lead. He kept his finger tight on the trigger until the click of the firing pin on the empty chamber was audible to all . . .

MAC WINGATE

6
MISSION CODE: SNOW QUEEN
BRYAN SWIFT

A JOVE BOOK

MISSION CODE: SNOW QUEEN

Copyright © 1982 by Ejan Production Company

First Jove edition published February 1982

First printing

Printed in the United States of America

Jove books are published by Jove Publications, Inc., 200 Madison Avenue, New York, NY 10016

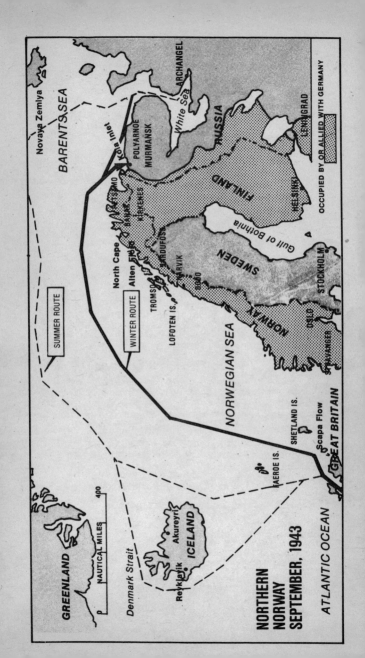

MAC WINGATE
MISSION CODE: SNOW QUEEN

"The *Tirpitz*—the "Lonesome Queen" as the Norwegians called her—lay at Alten fjord, greatly affecting the Allied convoys. She had escaped a series of attacks until the winter of 1943. On September 22, in broad daylight, a midget submarine surfaced inside the torpedo nets . . ."

British Military Journal
November 11, 1943

CHAPTER 1

Halfway out of town, and his head already felt like the inside of a camel's mouth. And Mac Wingate knew what the inside of a camel's mouth looked like. He had started officially fighting the war in North Africa as part of General Patton's forces. Before that, he had done some unofficial work for the Presidential Advisory Organization—the PAO—in the South Atlantic when the United States had not yet joined the war effort. That kept him away from camels' mouths for a while, but not from that pulpy, mealy, mucus-laden feeling that he had come to know so well. Only after he had the delightful distinction of staring into a camel's chaw was he able to make the comparison.

Another way of describing Mac's state of mind was that of a brain prepared like oatmeal. He felt something white and lumpy swimming inside his cranium, making the seemingly simple exercise of thinking an effort worthy of the Nobel prize. Wingate bounced around the back of the British truck in a sitting position, doing his best not to ruminate on anything.

He didn't think about the last time he had gotten a good, home-cooked meal. He didn't think about the last time he had gotten a good night's sleep. He didn't think about these things because, if he did, he'd probably have to realize that a good meal and a good rest was the only sure cure for his befuddled brain. And he wasn't likely to get either a thick steak or a long nap for some time to come. The way things were going, he'd be lucky to get some year-old rations and a sly wink from his fellow truck travelers.

Slowly, he became aware of one of those other men standing above him. He looked at two booted feet seemingly moored to the rocking metal floor on either side of his. He looked up into the face of a young British soldier wearing a beret.

"We've come a long way," said the young man casually. "Just a spot farther to go, Captain."

Wingate nodded, then returned to try and contemplate nothingness. It was too late. The soldier's words had forced thoughts upon his consciousness. They were not images of piping hot meals or soft, warm beds. They were visions of sand and rock, of bullets and blood. He had come a long way, all right. Both that night and in the months previous. But contrary to the Englishman's belief, he still had a hell of a way to go.

Less than a year before he had been in Africa. Patton and Montgomery were chasing the desert fox, Rommel. Operation Torch, the invasion of North Africa, had been a resounding success. The Allies were poised on the brink of victory in North Africa, and Wingate wanted to be part of it.

But just at that time, Mac was pulled out. He was pulled out under the thumb of one Colonel Olaf Erikson. It seemed the Norwegian officer had better things to do with the American. It seemed that Wingate had talents the hierarchy found very appealing.

First, he was both partly Norwegian and German himself, having been born Peter Magnussen Wingate to a farming family in Wisconsin. From his Nordic father, with German on his grandmother's side, he learned three languages: those of his heritage and that of his home. His mother threw some pepper into his lineage stew, for she was an original American, descended from the Ojibway Indian tribe. Together, his two heritages worked in harmony on both the mental and physical planes.

From his mother he got his straight, dark hair, dark eyes, and strong bones. From his father he got his strong, somewhat stocky build and his love for the natural order of nature. He became strong, resilient, and individualistic. Shunning team sports, he'd usually find challenges that tried him personally. Soon, anything that he could throw or shoot, usually hit its target.

He had sealed his wartime fate by entering the University of Wisconsin with a major in engineering. There he took to the craft of mining and the explosives that made it work. He

2

had been in the Brazilian jungles, blowing holes in a mountain, when the Japanese were in Hawaii, blowing holes in Pearl Harbor. The news was slow in getting downriver but Wingate was quick to respond.

It was then only a matter of time before the brass discovered his talents. Taking it all into careful consideration, they decided Mac was too good to crawl into battle and kill the enemy with thousands of other men. He should crawl into battle and kill the enemy *alone*.

So, for close to a year now, Mac had been hurled from Casablanca to Poland, from Poland to Albania, from Albania to places all around the Mediterranean, each place involving an extremely delicate, extremely dangerous mission he usually couldn't understand until it was all over. In the process he learned that his was definitely to reason why, then quickly do and try not to die.

So far he had been successful. When stuck in the worst positions, Wingate desired not to die, but to kill. It was with this attitude that he suffered the abysmal plane trip to London. He had gotten off the crummy plane after a rocky ride to find waiting orders for a meeting with Erikson. Immediately. So he hoisted himself onto an ancient truck for a bumpy ride into the suburbs.

In one respect he was dog-tired and about as personable as a Tasmanian devil. But, in another way, he was quietly exhilarated. He had known the job was going to be dangerous when Erikson first demanded that he take it, and he admitted to himself that he'd be a hell of a lot more irritable had he been sitting at a desk or sinking in a sodden foxhole for the entire war.

This realization was not enough to counteract his irascibility, however. Even the soothing effects of the beautiful English countryside normally seen out the back of a truck couldn't help, because the rolling hills and quaint villages were not to be seen. Not only was it the middle of the night, but Great Britain was gripped, as it had been every night since September 7, 1940, with the Nazi plague.

The Blitz had stopped in the summer of 1941, but the raids continued. No matter how skilled the British pilots, no matter how effective the newly developed radar, the English soldiers couldn't be everywhere at once. The crusty, solid English civilian took up the slack by "blacking out" almost the entire country.

Lights went out, shades were pulled, glass was painted black; a dark blanket seemed to cover the country every sunset. And what the German bombers couldn't see, Wingate couldn't see, either. His other senses had plenty to do in the meantime, however. He got to smell the musty oil and gas fumes in the back of the rickety vehicle and listen for any air raid sirens, the first sign of a Nazi attack.

Mac pulled his regulation army jacket around him. It was an English September, bringing with it a damp chill that usually didn't hit Wisconsin until a month later. Just as he got a bit more comfortable, the truck came to a grinding halt.

"That's it, then," chirped the young soldier. "Slough Station. Your stop, Captain."

Wingate looked up, his irritation coursing down from his brain and out of his mouth. "Slough? That rhymes with plow. I'm suppossed to have a meeting in Datchet, which rhymes with hatchet."

"Yes, sir," the soldier said solemnly. "I know, sir. But headquarters could not provide a personal carrier for you, sir, so they hitched you a lift with this personnel carrier."

Wingate said, "So?"

"So," the soldier repeated. "We have some personnel to carry back to London. In Maidenhead. We have to drive on."

Wingate digested this information sullenly, then painfully hauled himself to his feet. It was just like the whole damn war, he thought: I have to do everything myself.

"How do I get there, then?" he asked the Englishman.

The soldier pointed out the back of the truck. "Go right up past the hotel and onto Route 53. You'll go straight down that for about three miles and there will be Datchet Green. You can't miss it. It's right on the Windsor train line."

"No chance the Windsor train will be running, is there?" Wingate inquired.

The soldier smiled. "None at all, sir."

"All right." Wingate gave in, moving toward the rear of the truck. "Have a good trip, then."

"Yes, sir," the soldier replied as Mac hopped down to the street. "Thank you, sir."

Mac looked around quickly, spying the white stone hotel

4

up on a little knoll to his left. He started in that direction until he heard the British soldier call out.

"Oh, sir!" Mac turned around. "You might be needing this," said the Englishman, throwing something at him underhand. Mac caught it. It was a helmet. "You never know," was the last thing the soldier said before his truck rumbled off into the night.

Mac grinned at the worn, bumpy, obviously abused American helmet. He was right, Wingate thought. You never know. He held the headgear under his arm as he went in search of Route 53. He cast an envious glance over his shoulder at the picturesque inn as he found the road right where the soldier said it was. He bet there were comfortable beds inside. And a warm, cozy kitchen with a ruddy-faced cook who could rustle up a steak and kidney pie for him. There might even be a maid or two to take the chill off a cold English autumn.

Wingate forcibly wrenched his mind off such matters as he looked at the hotel. It was a two-story, white stone structure with two one-story additions built on either side of it. In the back was a small parking area in front of an even smaller garden dining area. It looked a bit overgrown with weeds, but even so, there was a nice feeling of simple serenity about the place. It was not the peace of death. It was a comfortable quiet hostel. One that belied the fact that less than five hundred kilometers to the east was a country intent on enslaving the world.

Mac shoved his hands in his coat pockets, adjusted his grip on the helmet, and turned his back on the inviting hostelry. As he took his first step on Route 53, the sirens started.

It was a faraway, low wail, seemingly muffled by the dark English night. Because of that, Wingate couldn't be sure which direction it was coming from. He looked up quickly. The sky seemed the same as always. Thankfully it was fairly cloudless, so he could see the stars. The stars were very important. They were good for more than just telling sailors what direction they were going in. They were good for telling Mac what direction danger was coming from.

Above his head, to the right, a few stars winked out. Then they appeared again. A second later, Wingate heard the thin, piercing whistle a heavy falling object makes. He raced off the road and behind the first thick tree he came to, just as the front of the white stone hotel blew out.

5

The Nazi bomb slammed into its roof like a blackjack smashing onto someone's skull. For a split second before the charge was detonated, the roof collapsed in around the bomb. Then, as the explosive ignited, the plaster, wood, and metal screamed up and out, splattering the second floor across the grassy knoll.

Another explosion to the right of the damaged hotel immediately followed, sixty feet in front of the tree Wingate was behind. A spinning metal shard and hunks of dirt and rock splashed against the bark as he huddled in a ball behind the trunk. The next explosion blasted a car parked on the street farther to the right. The auto slammed to the street, then bounced and spun as the small amount of rationed fuel in its tank whooshed out with the German explosive.

The explosions continued in a line farther down, then left off. For Wingate, the immediate danger was over. It was as if a tornado had touched down on the street and ripped a single line in front of where Wingate was now standing. In the sudden silence, he surveyed the damage. Some property was blown to hell, and the hotel was now on fire.

Then he heard the scream.

The clear night air disclosed the direction immediately. It came from inside the shattered, inflamed hotel. Wingate threw the worn helmet onto his head and ran to the small backyard dining area. To his right he spied a door with broken windows. Gray smoke billowed out from the holes in the glass. Immediately, he kicked the portal open and dived in.

Contrary to what others might have done, Wingate didn't charge into the flames without thinking. Wingate never did anything without thinking. He may have acted instantaneously, but he liked living, and doing dangerous things without thinking was an open invitation to an early funeral. The gray smoke told him there was a fifty/fifty chance he wouldn't be char-broiled as soon as he entered. White smoke, he would've sped in without a second thought. Black smoke, he would've waited for the fire department, scream or no scream.

He heard the call again. Peering through the artificial fog, he pinpointed the sound from another room to his left. He saw a fairly well-supplied kitchen all around him. He was moving to the left of a big wood-topped table and a Dutch oven. To his right was a long sink that covered the length of

6

the wall. Next to it was a swinging door. The majority of the smoke was pumping out from under it.

Wingate checked the ceiling. It showed no signs of extensive damage. He didn't want it falling on him before he got out. As he checked, he reached into his jacket and pulled a Browning 9 mm automatic from his shoulder holster. Getting close enough not to miss but far enough away so a ricochet was not likely to take off a hunk of flesh, he shot off both jambs on the kitchen door. First the bottom, then the top.

Even as it was falling, Wingate had slipped the weapon back under his jacket and grabbed the wooden rectangle by both sides. He knew it wouldn't fall forward with the pressure of the fire and smoke pushing it back. But he didn't know how much fire there was, which was why he shot the door loose in the first place. He used it as a shield against a possible wall of flame. Thankfully, the ends of his fingers which were wrapped around the front of the partition were not charred off immediately, so he hazarded throwing the door forward.

It fell on a carpet in the middle of the small hotel's lobby. To the right was a smoking stairway up to the nonexistent second floor. To the left was a broken entrance to the bar. Directly in front was an anteroom and the front porch.

Wingate heard the scream again. It was more desperate this time, a cry combining sobs of fear with yells of pain. It was coming from behind him. Wingate turned to the wall next to the kitchen door. In the middle of it was an open space leading to the cashier's and manager's offices. He looked inside. It was a disastrous sandwiching of both the upstairs and the downstairs. The bomb had blasted a hole in the upstairs floor, hurling guest furniture down into the administration area.

Through the belching fire and smoke, Wingate saw a lone figure pinned under both a bed and a file cabinet. It was a dark-haired girl in a blue sweater and dark skirt. Her clothes were ripped, her face was cut, and her fingers were bloody. She was clawing at the stuff that was pinning her down as her hair was smoking. The large hole in the ceiling above created a sort of blast furnace effect. The fire raging upstairs would occasionally belch down like the breath of a mythical dragon.

Wingate vaulted the hotel counter and ran to where the girl lay, just as another flame swooped down. He felt the fire lick at his head and shoulders, the jacket and helmet providing just enough protection. He quickly reached under the bed. It was heavy, but his leverage was good. With the adrenaline racing through his veins magnifying his normal strength, he hurled it aside. But the file cabinet was another matter. Made of thick, green metal, it was filled with papers, making it much heavier and more awkward than the bed. When Wingate couldn't lift it, he slid it off the girl's body.

She did not look good. Her torso and sweater were torn, the cloth and flesh mingling. Wingate assumed there was internal damage as well as broken ribs. Normally he wouldn't have moved her. But lying under furniture in a disintegrating hotel was far from normal circumstances. But what struck him most as he slid his arms under her knees and shoulders was the expression on her face.

Wingate had seen many wounded and many dead men. But this look on the girl's face he had not seen before. In addition to the shock that would naturally accompany such an injury, there was a look of confusion, surprise, and anger. In a strange way, it looked as if she were angry because she hadn't been prepared for the explosion—the possibility that out of all the people in the world, the ceiling would fall down on her.

Wingate couldn't understand it. Her wounded expression lacked any understanding of what had happened to her. Maybe he was reading too much into her look because he was so tired. Maybe he was being sardonic because he knew the Nazis had dropped over 200,000 pounds of bombs on England already. What right did this girl have to be uncomprehending? But still, her expression disturbed him. He looked away from her as he picked her up and hustled back into the lobby, through the kitchen, and out the back door.

He kept his speed up even outside. He couldn't be sure that the weakened wall wouldn't fall over onto him. He kept trotting until the smoke cleared and the parking area yawned before him. A crowd of authorities and civilians were already gathered there. A soldier took the girl from his arms. A crowd of people broke off from the main throng and huddled around her as the Britisher laid her down.

Wingate didn't hear a specific voice. He heard an accented babble. A muddled conversation of concern which mingled with the roar of the fire and the noise of the fire fighters. He looked around. One lone engine to the side was pumping a steady stream of water onto the hotel blaze. It was like spitting into Hades. The hotel was unsalvageable. Even as he watched, the first floor collapsed completely. What had been a warm, safe-looking hotel was now a blazing pile of thick kindling. Shaking his head, Wingate marveled that it was the thing he had just run into.

He felt a tug at his sleeve. He looked over and down into the face of a middle-aged Englishman in dark trousers and a frayed, buttoned sweater.

" 'E said you were the one,'' the man said with a coarse cockney accent, motioning with his head back at the crowd around the girl. "The one 'oo ran in to save me girl.''

Wingate looked at the crowd. The only man looking in their direction was a fire fighter. He nodded at Wingate. Wingate nodded back, then returned his attention to the short Britisher next to him.

"That's right,'' he said. The father wasn't smiling in gratitude or frowning in worry. His mouth was open and his eyes looked bloodshot. His brow was puckered, his lashes curling up on either side of the bridge of his nose. He looked pitiful, so the American turned to watch the fire. "What was she doing in there, anyway?'' he asked.

"Well, she 'ad to work, now, didn't she?'' the man answered, also looking at the fire. "I got a call. Whole new load of boarders comin' in tomorrow. Needed a cleanin' right away. Wanted me Sal to do it. Well, she 'ad to. Needed the money. Made her walk. No other way at night, y'know.''

The man needed to talk, but Wingate didn't want to hear it. The girl's expression stayed with him and he didn't want to hear her father's excuses. He wouldn't be the father's buffer against her probable death.

"Yeah,'' he said. "I know. Tough luck.'' Wingate hunched his shoulders, stuck his hands back into his coat pockets, and walked away.

"Guv'nor,'' the man said after him. Wingate waited, but he didn't turn around. "Thank you.'' Wingate nodded slightly, then continued walking. He stopped next to the fireman who had nodded at him.

"Any chance?'' Mac asked.

"Not unless a doc arrives soon. Sorry.''

"It happens,'' Wingate said flatly. "I'll see what I can do.'' He headed back toward 53.

"You've done enough," the fireman said.

"Not enough," Wingate called back without turning. "Not yet."

He *was* tired. The mental cobwebs had all but disappeared, replaced by a murky, hollow cave where thoughts echoed and magnified louder and larger until bare ideas were warped exaggerations. Wingate walked along Route 53 for about an hour, empty fields on one side and house-dotted forests on the other. After a while, it seemed as if the raid had never happened.

He thought about the girl's expression and why it bothered him. He decided it was the look of the home-front victim that he had never before seen. Up until then, he had seen the faces of soldiers and innocents in the middle of intrigue-laden war zones. They had looked horrified, pain-ridden, and shocked, but somehow there was always a vestige of expectation, of prior knowledge. They had all been aware of the possibility that death might happen.

That was what had been missing with the girl Wingate had pulled from the inferno. She never thought that several hundred pounds of well-packed death would fall on her. It simply was not in the vocabulary of her existence. That bothered Wingate because his business was delivering those same parcels of death to the enemy. He knew all there was to know about them. He prided himself on it.

He wasn't sure whether running into the girl made him more angry or sad. Almost as soon as he had sorted his feelings out, he buried them. They were the thoughts of a poet or conscientious objector. Neither had any place in his mind at the moment. He capped his mental explorations with the thought that finding someone who didn't suffer from the war would be some trick. There was no one.

The soldier in the truck was right. Finding Datchet Green was easy. It was an oblong bump running alongside Route 53. As the road veered off on either side of the wide, flat lawn, Wingate took the less traveled road to the right. It took a sudden turn farther to the right at a corner. At the end of it was a railroad crossing and a circle of stone townhouses. Mac continued down this road, stopping only momentarily at the train tracks.

Looking in the direction of Slough, he tried to see some hint of the Nazi air attack. He could no longer hear the fire or even the warning sirens. And all he saw in the distance was Windsor Castle, the historic sight a town away from Datchet. The ancient, majestic structure was at odds with the evening's experience, so Wingate walked on to the two-story house just outside the deserted train station.

He opened a wrought-iron gate that came up to his hips, walked up the stone steps to the thick, windowless door, turned the knob, and went in. Those had been his instructions.

The brightest artificial illumination he had seen in thirty-two hours assailed his eyes as he quickly closed the door behind him. He stood until his eyes adjusted somewhat. The scene he took in gave some credence to Windsor Castle's existence in the scheme of things.

The entryway Wingate was standing in was sumptuous. It was Mac through the looking glass and into Buckingham Palace. Making the situation all the more incongruous were an extremely good-looking Wac sitting at an oak desk on one side of the hall and a male valet in a tuxedo sitting on a Louis XIV love seat across from her.

The Wac had been typing when Mac came in. Both she and the butler looked up as he stopped stock still in the middle of the foyer, the door clicking shut behind him.

"Captain Wingate?" the beautiful Wac inquired.

Mac nodded, more interested in hearing the woman speak than himself.

The Wac looked down at some papers next to her typewriter. She was a brunette according to the severely bunched hair wisps leaking out of the bottom of her perfectly positioned military cap. As she leaned forward, Wingate couldn't help noticing how well her shirt, jacket, and tightly knotted tie fit.

"You're a little late," the Wac commented, her lips pouting. "I'll see if Colonel Walters is busy."

She rose, an accomplishment Wingate was tempted to applaud when he saw the figure it revealed, and disappeared through a door to the right of her desk. The butler also rose and approached him. His expression was one of slight revulsion.

"May I take your . . . your helmet, sir?" the man slowly pronounced. He looked pointedly at Mac's charred jacket.

Mac glanced up. He saw the rim of the battered helmet just over his eyebrows. He reached up, pulled the metal dome off, and handed it to the white-gloved servant.

"Thank you, sir," the butler said carefully, masking all

but just a hint of distaste, and walked away, holding the helmet before him.

As he disappeared to the left, the Wac reappeared to the right, smiling broadly. Her smile was the second brightest illumination Mac had seen in thirty-two hours.

"Very good," she said pleasantly. "They are waiting for you. Colonel Walters will see you now. Follow me."

Wingate resisted saying, "with pleasure," but moved behind her swinging hips with the same aggression with which he blew up planes. The Wac passed through the same door she had before. Behind the door was a room whose size rivaled many baseball fields Mac remembered from Wisconsin. But in decoration, the room had it all over the Oshkosh Bar and Grill.

There was a long marble table in the middle of the rectangular, high-ceilinged space. Along one side sat two men. A third was standing on the other side, in front of several maps and charts stuck up on a bulletin board. Between the three men on the table was a silver tea set and delicate-looking china cups filled with the smoking rose-colored liquid. The only other things smoking in the room were a cigar in an ornate ashtray and Wingate's jacket.

"This is Captain Wingate," the Wac announced, then backed out, closing the door behind her.

The man standing looked at the one of the men seated with his back to Mac. "This is your best man?" he said incredulously.

Wingate saw the seated man wince before he rose and turned to face him. It was Colonel Erikson. The Norwegian seemed to have changed a little, even though they had been apart for only a couple of weeks. There were some new lines in his face. But he was still a smidge shorter than Wingate, much blonder, and a little thicker set. While Mac could chop wood, Erikson looked like he could rip it apart by force of personality. The clear blue eyes in that resolute face took Wingate in.

The difference in their appearances was striking. Erikson did not look out of place in the opulent room. As usual, his uniform was impeccable. Wingate looked like a chimney sweep who stumbled into the wrong house.

"Captain," Erikson said simply.

"Colonel," Wingate replied, saluting.

"What happened to you?" his superior inquired in total seriousness.

"A Nazi plane from the Reich conspired against me," Wingate answered, with the same seriousness. Exhaustion and irritation were tricky emotions when dealing with superior officers. Mac walked the tightrope between wit and insubordination.

Erikson nodded as if Wingate's explanation was more than enough and made perfect sense. He turned to the other men in the room. "Colonel Walters," he said toward the standing man; "Colonel Tyler," he continued, head moving vaguely in the direction of the seated officer; "Captain Wingate," he almost finished, looking back to Mac, "one of our best men in the field."

Mac realized why Erikson had cringed when Walters had initially spoken. He hadn't wanted Mac to know that he had called him his best man. So the "one of our best" part of the introduction was for his benefit and the "in the field" part was for Walters.

Catching his official faux pas, Colonel Walters boomed out a friendly greeting, sweeping his hand toward a chair. "Wingate, eh?" he asked in cultured British tones. "Not related to Major General Orde C. Wingate, by any chance?"

Mac moved over to the delicate-looking chair the English colonel pointed out. "No, I don't think so, sir."

"Too bad," Walters snorted. "Quite a shame. Smashing fellow. Doing a bloody good job in Burma. Have a seat, Wingate."

Mac looked at his own scruffy pants and the soft brocade-work of the obviously expensive seat. Thinking better of it, he said, "I'll think I'll stand, sir. If you don't mind."

"Suit yourself, suit yourself," Walters huffed. "Cup of tea?"

Something in Walters's tone and manner set Wingate on edge. It was more than the fact that he seemed to have stolen his entire personality from Ralph Richardson. He seemed irritated that Wingate didn't sit down. He seemed to have geared his entire presentation on getting Wingate in a chair with a cup of tea. He wanted Wingate comfortable. Mac found that when superior officers wanted him comfortable, it was usually because they didn't want him to suspect that he was about to be cut off at the knees.

Wingate didn't like the whole setup. He was fatigued, but more than that, he was a professional. He didn't want and really didn't have time for mollycoddling. His job was helping the Allies and killing the Axis. He wasn't interested in jockeying for position about it. But like it or not, Walters had rank on him and Walters seemed intent on setting the stage. The sooner the better, as far as Wingate was concerned.

"Yes, sir," he said. "Thank you, sir."

"Excellent!" Walters said. Wingate was satisfied he didn't say, "Smashing." What the colonel did say afterward was, "Dickie, old boy, would you pour Captain Wingate a cup?"

Mac shrugged mentally. He couldn't avoid the "old boy" cliché. Well, one out of two wasn't bad. The seated colonel, however, did not seem happy about the situation. He bristled when Walters called him, and with only the greatest reluctance leaned forward toward the tea service.

"Smashing," Walters commented as the tea was poured. So much for wishful thinking, Mac thought. "Sure you won't have a seat?" Walters asked as the cup was handed to him by the sullen Colonel Tyler.

Wingate looked at the antique again. Anything to get on with it, he thought. "On second thought, I think I will," he said pleasantly. "Thank you, sir." He sat easily, glancing at Erikson as he did so. He wasn't sure, but he detected some slight commiseration in those blue eyes. Oh well, he tried to answer silently, it's your chair.

The effect of his sitting was rewarding. Walters straightened up and seemed to cheer considerably. He had Wingate where he wanted him, so he plunged right in.

"Captain Wingate," he intoned, "Colonel Erikson tells us that you are an expert in demolitions."

Walters paused. Wingate had already understood that the Englishman was expecting an answer, but he was just tired enough, just dirty enough, and just plain pissed enough to make the meeting harder. He took a sip of his tea, then seemed suddenly to notice the silence.

"Yes, sir. Of course, sir."

Colonel Tyler certainly seemed to find the silence awkward, for as soon as Wingate had finished speaking, he asked a question of his own.

"And you've taken the SBS underwater demolitions course?" His voice had a slight mid-American drawl.

Before Wingate could reply, Walters cut in. "Of course he did. Our reports show that."

"And that's all they showed," Tyler shot back. "We don't know whether he passed or what he excelled in or anything of that nature."

"I assume he passed," Walters replied with elaborate patience. "Why else would they include the information on our reports?"

"To make him look good," Tyler answered with some disgust. "That sort of thing is rampant all over the department."

"I beg your pardon?" Walters boomed indignantly.

"In answer to your question! . . ." Wingate shouted. His voice bounced off the walls in the cavernous room. The two colonels stopped their argument and looked at him in surprise. "Sirs," Wingate continued, now that he had gotten their attention. "I passed the Special Boat Section's course. Is there anything specific you would like to know about it?"

The look on Walters's face turned from surprise to a touch of shame for getting into an argument in front of a lower-ranking man, then to anger that the lower-ranking man had pointed it out to him. Wingate recognized all the expressions and really didn't care. He was there because they needed him, and if he left the room a corporal, it made little difference in the long run.

Colonel Erikson seemed to agree with him, for as soon as Wingate had finished his question, the Norwegian took over the meeting.

"That isn't important, Captain," he said pointedly. His underlying meaning to Mac was, "Forget the question was ever asked." Wingate centered his undivided attention on his immediate superior, who was moving around the table toward the bulletin board. "We need to know some things," Erikson continued, his voice casual. Mac knew that game as well. Erikson was going to edge around a subject, extracting as much valuable information as possible without revealing the direct purpose of the interrogation. The brass called it a "contingency weaponry discussion," utilized for security reasons. Mac called it a cat-and-mouse game played for the joy of the sport. It was time to pin the tail on the mission.

He heard Erikson speaking with his back to him, supposedly examining the charts on the board. "What do you feel is the best waterproofing for standard heavy demolition explosives?''

Mac leaned back in the dainty chair. He felt Walters and Tyler eyeing him like a pair of starving wolves. With an effort, he searched the encyclopedia part of his brain for the most concise answer possible.

"Well, sir, gas-treated canvas is good enough for outside weather, but certainly insufficient for submerging.''

"What do you mean?'' Tyler wanted to know.

Wingate wanted to say, "What do you mean, 'What do you mean?' " because he felt the answer was obvious enough, but instead he managed to elaborate effectively. "Underwater you need one hundred percent efficiency. The slightest leak may ruin the material.''

"Of course, of course,'' Walters blustered. "What about C-2 plastic, Captain?''

"What about it?'' Wingate replied dryly, unable to eliminate all sarcasm. "C-2 hasn't been waterproofed yet to my knowledge and just because it's plastic doesn't mean it'll hold out underwater. Direct contact with water, petrol, or any other corrosive will shortly render it useless. Its advantages are its power and flexibility, not its insolubility.''

Mac's speech had the effect he had hoped for. His extensive knowledge of a singular material thrown at him impressed the collected colonels. For a moment, Walters was rendered speechless. Wingate saw Erikson smile behind the Britisher's back for a split second before resuming.

"Captain, given a supply of C-2 plastic explosives, could you pack it in a light, waterproof casing?''

Mac was not quick to answer. All too often, gung ho officers would promise the brass anything to get ahead, only to get their asses wiped when it came time to deliver. In Wingate's business, a hasty answer could be the final line on a death certificate.

"Yes,'' he said. "I suppose I could.''

Tyler was again primed by his initial silence. "Could you set it off with primacord?'' he asked quickly.

This time Mac was sure and answered just as quickly. "Yes, but I wouldn't know its effectiveness without quite a lot of experimentation.''

"No good,'' Tyler mumbled. "We don't have time.''

"Time is irrelevant,'' Walters hastily announced.

"What are you talking about?" Tyler demanded. "The whole point . . ."

"I said time is irrelevant!" Walters nearly shouted purposefully. He stressed each word with greater emphasis until his meaning became clear, probably even to the Wac out in the hall. Tyler had slipped some solid information into the supposedly hypothetical questioning. That was not part of the rules. Wingate was beginning to feel truly sickened by the whole routine.

"If you're thinking about blowing anything really heavy," Mac said, letting his exhaustion come into his voice, "you'll need a shaped charge. And according to my information, you'll need a very heavy casing for such a charge . . . need a whole damn submarine for that. Or a friendly whale."

Wingate looked around the room. His attempt at levity fell on deaf ears, if Walters's face was any example. His Adam's apple was bobbing, while his eyelids narrowed. The American decided to press on before anyone could react.

"Colonel Erikson may be able to back me up on this, but I'm told the Norwegian group has come up with a limpet that has a special detonator on it." He looked at Erikson, but the colonel didn't look back, so he continued. "The entire section is encased in a ring of salt. Once you stick it to the hull of anything and get it wet, a half hour later the salt's eaten through and the firing pin is released. Try to take it off and it'll take you off."

Walters leaped on that. "Can a single man carry it?"

"Not unless he's got 'Super' as a first name," Mac told him, his face and tone expressionless.

"Captain Wingate," Erikson sighed. "A simple 'yes' or 'no' would suffice."

Mac slowly, and seemingly painfully, turned in his seat to face the Norwegian. "Begging your pardon, sir, but I don't enjoy being the man in the middle. It's never easy second-guessing anyone, but when you're talking about explosives, these mind-reading games can get dangerous. Heaven help some poor jackass who gets even the slightest bit of errant information. One wrong decision in battle and he'll be splattered all over it. I don't relish being responsible for that because I couldn't answer with the exact information you wanted."

Wingate sat back in a silence that Tyler didn't dispel.

Walters didn't look happy about the turn of events but he couldn't fault the captain's logic. At least he didn't to Wingate's face. It was Erikson who finally replied.

"Are you finished?" he said.

"Yes, sir," Wingate replied.

"No more speeches?"

Mac inwardly seethed. Trust the Norwegian to put him in his place with a callousness as cold as his country. "No, sir."

"Very well," Erikson sighed. "How would you cut through an A/T net?"

Wingate answered flatly with no embellishment. "Depends on the mesh gauge. Usually, I'd use an electrical torch, but you need a large generator on the surface for that. But I've often thought it would be possible to make a series of small bottle units for an entire underwater team of divers."

"What . . . ?" Walters began, but Erikson cut him off with a sharply upraised hand. "Elaborate," Erikson demanded softly.

"All right," Wingate agreed. "Let's say each man had enough fuel to cut ten links. Then the size of the team would vary with the size of the hole you wanted."

"Interesting," Erikson mused. Sufficiently chastised, the other pair of colonels waited for the Norwegian's word. It was not long in coming. "Thank you, Captain Wingate. You will wait outside until necessary."

Mac knew a dismissal when he heard one. Also sufficiently reprimanded, he played his exit by the book. Simply saying, "Yes, sir," he got up and walked out.

The Wac was still there, still typing, but the butler was nowhere in sight. Wingate supposed the man had been waiting for him and once he had arrived, there were other duties elsewhere in the mansion. Mac slipped off his coat and threw it on the love seat opposite the Wac's desk. The woman looked at the khaki garment dubiously. She didn't consider his putting it there the most sophisticated of moves. Wingate didn't much care. He had more on his mind than impressing the finest hunk of army flesh he had seen in months.

Dressed in a simple, severe shirt devoid of military awards or tie, he slowly approached the desk and deliberately gripped the edges. He eyed the Wac's rank insignia as well as several other parts of her uniform. She blushed under his scrutiny.

"Sergeant," he said. "Sergeant . . . ?"

"Porter," she said demurely. Wingate grinned. He knew he was considered attractive and the war hadn't completely destroyed his style.

"Sergeant Porter, could you please locate the nearest army doctor and send him to the hotel in Slough at the mouth of Route 53?"

It was not what the Wac expected. But rather than follow orders because of the captain's charm, she fell back on regulations.

"Did Colonel Walters have you ask me?"

"No, Sergeant. He was more concerned with other things. It is important, however."

"I have no doubt of that, Captain, but Colonel Walters has specifically instructed that there be no personal calls out of Operational HQ."

"This is not a personal call," Wingate contended. "There's a wounded girl . . ."

"A girl?" The Wac interrupted. "A civilian?"

"A girl wounded in a Nazi air raid."

"The regulations are quite specific on such matters, Captain," the Wac sniffed. "Without the authorization of Colonel Walters, no military personnel may be utilized for nonmilitary purposes . . ."

"What are you babbling about?" Wingate exploded. "A girl may be dying! Will you get on the horn . . . !"

"Captain Wingate," said a cold voice behind him.

Mac turned to Colonel Erikson.

"What seems to be the problem?" the Norwegian asked quietly.

Harnessing his impatience, Wingate explained the situation more fully. When he finished, Erikson pulled a jacket out of a well-disguised closet opposite the meeting room, shrugged it on, and brushed by Wingate to the desk.

"Sergeant Porter, please contact a medic and get him to the hotel as soon as possible. Will you do that, please?"

"Certainly, sir," the Wac replied, again all business. She got on the phone immediately.

"Come with me, Captain," Erikson instructed, moving toward the door.

Mac hastily picked up his jacket and looked down the hall for any sign of the valet and his helmet. Erikson seemed unconcerned about Wingate's borrowed headgear and opened the front door. "Are you coming?" he commanded more than asked.

Wingate chalked the helmet off. It had served its purpose. He followed his superior. As he passed the desk, he heard the Wac whisper, "You could've told me."

Mac whispered back. "Sorry. It's been a long day." Sergeant Porter favored him with a dazzling, honest smile that made him wish he visited Datchet more often.

"The doctor is on his way, Colonel," she called to Erikson.

"Thank you, Sergeant. Wingate? . . ."

Mac never saw the Wac or his helmet again. He walked out into the English night with Erikson. It had only gotten darker and colder since he left it. Blue, wispy clouds had covered up the stars. The two military men walked back to Datchet Green in silence. Once there, Erikson staked a claim on one side of a handy bench. Mac stood, looking down Route 53.

"Worried about that girl?" Erikson asked.

Wingate shrugged but didn't turn around. "I pulled her out. Would be a shame if she died anyway. Terrible waste of army personnel, as Walters might say."

"Don't like him much, do you."

It was a flat statement. Wingate saw no reason to reply.

"Well," said Erikson, "you have more important things to worry about than a civilian girl."

Wingate whirled at that. He stalked over to the bench, staring down at the stocky superior. Half of his mind wanted to tell him what he thought about the entire night and the colonel's bloodthirsty apathy, while the other half couldn't help but agree with Erikson's cruel statement. What was one innocent girl on the face of it? What were dozens? On the one hand, they were everything—they were what he honestly fought for. On the other hand, they were meaningless—ultimately expendable. That, in a nutshell, was the insanity of war.

"Colonel, what the hell are we here for?" It was not meant as a rhetorical question and it was not taken as one.

"Captain, we are here waiting for a ride back to London Airport, where you and I will take a little ride up north. To Scotland. From there you will be put on a boat I wouldn't trust to get across the Thames, to travel over eight hundred kilometers across the North Sea. You are going home, Captain. Unfortunately for us both, however, you are going to my home, not yours.''

"Norway?" Wingate blurted. "What for?"

"That is classified information."

"Excuse me?" Wingate asked incredulously.

"All I can tell you is that you will be leading a mission of vital importance to the Allies," Erikson explained, his legs straight out on the grass, his hands in his pockets. "And that you were not chosen by having your name pulled out of a hat."

The disclosure was of little comfort to Wingate. He had gone into missions blind before, but never this blind. Erikson seemed to sympathize with the captain's stammering amazement.

"I wouldn't worry," he said as the dim headlights of their transportation appeared down Route 53. "Your mission contact will be Colonel Walters. And that 'poor jackass' in battle will be you."

CHAPTER 2

Scalloway was beautiful that time of year. In winter, there was little daylight. In summer, there was daylight round the clock. It was fall, so things were fairly normal, day-and-night-wise. The thermometer hovered somewhere in the low forties. The rough, white tips of the choppy Atlantic Ocean waves seemed to be snow-capped.

Mac surveyed the Scottish village's barren beauty from the deck of an Allied transport. He saw deeply cut cliffs rising from the base of the sea. He saw lonely-looking lighthouses amid lushly growing fields. He saw long-wooled sheep and small herds of cattle grazing inland. The only human activity he could spot was on the extensive dock which the transport was approaching.

Surprisingly the trip from London was far better than he had expected. Perhaps it was because Wingate was in the company of Erikson. It was well known that the Norwegian gave the orders that the American followed, so maybe the rest of the soldiers respected that power. Whatever the reason, the carpet was as red as it could get in wartime.

The plane ride to the mainland of the Scottish Orkney Islands was smooth enough for Mac to catch some much needed sleep. When they got on the ship to traverse the one hundred miles to the Shetland Islands, Wingate was well rested and fully aware. He was aware that he was about to embark on a mission that would be more dangerous than giving Hitler a hickey. Erikson's silence attested to that. The fact that the Norwegian wouldn't or couldn't fully delineate the situation only served to concern Mac more. It meant that there were greater powers than the colonel at work.

But rather than get an ulcer, Wingate spent the remainder of his travel time plotting out a variety of war scenarios. He attempted to imagine every possible mission Allied HQ might want him on. That way, no matter what happened, he would be prepared for it.

He considered and eliminated several possibilities. They really didn't need him to blow the U-boat pens at Swinemünde. The Allied Air Command was doing a good enough job on the German Navy by themselves. The fuel depots at Rotterdam needed a good blowout, but that was in the other direction. Even HQ couldn't be stupid enough to send him to Holland by way of Norway.

As he was thinking, Erikson joined him on the deck. Both men wore fairly light coats, both having come from nearly Arctic childhoods. The Wisconsin winters could rival the Nordic season from the middle of the country on down. Wingate couldn't guarantee that he wouldn't need gloves above the Arctic Circle, however.

"The remaining ride shouldn't be too bad," Erikson commented, looking toward the dock. "The air boys have been making dogmeat of the U-boats. Forty-one in one month alone."

"That was last summer, Colonel," Wingate replied tersely. "Since then, the Nazis have used 'radar foxers.' "

"The Jerries call it 'Black May,' Captain," Erikson answered with no little relish. "Forty-one of their subs located and destroyed in the North Atlantic. The krauts are frightfully behind us in radar technology. And their subs are slow, blind, clumsy, and have very little endurance."

"And occasionally deadly."

Erikson shrugged. "I wouldn't worry. Its only a matter of time before we sink them all. A short time. The German Navy is the weakest link in the Nazi chain."

"That's easy for you to say. You're not going."

The Norwegian's voice suddenly became hard and bitter. "I assure you, Captain, if there were any way I could replace you on this mission, I would. If there were any chance, nothing would stop me from going myself."

Wingate turned to his superior for the first time during their daylight trip. Erikson's face was set in lines that combined a seething inner rage with a horrible pain. As Mac watched, the

23

colonel controlled his emotions, and his expression settled into the placid professionalism it was known for.

The American remembered all their previous conversations. Norway was Erikson's home. He had grown up there, becoming one with his environment as Wingate had with his. Erikson had worked as a lumberjack there. He had married and raised a family there. He had found a happiness there that so far had eluded Wingate. But Wingate was the luckier man. Having nothing, he had nothing to lose. Mac did not have everything he cherished destroyed by a war.

Wingate had lost his parents in a car accident shortly after Pearl. His brother, Erik, and his sister, Berta, were far away from the Nazi terror, safe in America. Erikson's mother was sent to a concentration camp. His youngest sister's fate was even worse. She was sent to a breeding camp. His father went out of his mind. His son was shot down in the street by the German conquerors. His wife and his nine-year-old daughter might still be alive. That was the worst torture of all. He didn't know.

The American could think of a lot to say. But nothing would've been right. The only thing he could do would be to keep doing what he had all along: follow Erikson's orders and do the best damn job he knew how. Winning the war was the only revenge Erikson could achieve.

"Believe me," the Norwegian said with conviction. "You are the best man for the job."

"Yes, sir," Wingate answered simply.

The ship docked alongside the ornate wooden facilities. A variety of military men, in various uniforms, secured the lines. Standing away from all the activity, but seeming to be part of it nevertheless, were colonels Walters and Tyler.

Mac groaned inwardly. Although he was fully prepared for more verbal fencing, he never looked forward to it. As a means of further preparation, he went belowdecks and collected the materials he was able to bring along. Hauling the large, heavy duffel bag onto his back, he joined Colonel Erikson for the disembarkation.

The three high-ranking officers were in uniform. Mac was the odd man out again, wearing his outfit-in-the-field, consisting of a plain shirt, pants, boots, and jacket devoid of military cut or any insignia whatsoever. His 9 mm was in the triple-draw holster under his left arm, his hunting knife with the

24

black-painted blade and black-tape-covered hilt was in its scabbard on his right calf, and a collection of number 27 MkI detonators were in various places on his coat. All was right in his world.

"Captain Wingate," Walters began almost as soon as they had touched terra firma, "I don't believe we have been properly introduced. I am Colonel David Walters, of the Admiralty's Operational Intelligence Center. This is Colonel Dickie Tyler, United States Army Air Corps."

Tyler stuck out his hand. "Richard Tyler," he said. "Call me Richard."

Mac shifted the sack on his back and took the fellow American's proffered hand. Tyler's fingers were lanky, just like the rest of him. His grip was steady but not strong. He looked like a distant relative of Jimmy Stewart. While that might have been initially comforting in Wingate's subconscious, the active part of his brain warned him that Tyler might stick out like a sore thumb in Norway.

Walters seemed to feel left out of the chummy first-name-basis the American colonel had introduced, so he captured Mac's attention by booming, "Yes, yes. And you should call me Davey. Never could stomach any of that Colonel Walters crap. You're the leader here, Captain. You're the boss. Shall we go?"

Without waiting for a reply, the Englishman set off with brisk strides toward the other end of the dock. Wingate took a second to look at Erikson and then heavenward. If Walters didn't get off his cliché kick soon, Wingate was afraid he might drown the mission contact midway through the trip.

The Englishman led the group toward the opposite dock, which held three different sea craft. "Have you ever ridden the 'Shetland Bus,' Captain?" Walters inquired.

"Can't say that I have," Wingate replied, purposely leaving off the customary "Sir." If he was, indeed, the leader of this mission, he was going to act like one.

"Stunning success!" Walters retorted. "Been setting up a regular commuter service between Scotland and Norway. The SOE, with information supplied by the NID, sends out his own private navy to bring in materials and SIS officers for the OIC."

Mac decided to get the mission off on the wrong foot.

"Excuse me, Colonel, but could you translate what you just said?"

"What?" Walters said incredulously as he stopped short. "Don't you know?" The Englishman responded to Wingate's question with a certain small triumph rather than hurt insult. "Explain it to the man, Tyler," Walters pronounced, moving on down the dock.

The American colonel appeared at Wingate's side as they followed Walters. Erikson brought up the rear, his hands behind his back, his lips pursed, and his eyes taking in the dock's planking.

"These escape and entry ships, disguised as fishing boats, are supplied by the Special Operations Executive and utilize tactical information from the Naval Intelligence Division," Tyler told Mac. "SIS and OIC stand for . . ."

"Secret Intelligence Service and Operational Intelligence Center," Wingate finished for him. "I know. All just frosting on his conversational cake, huh?"

Tyler nodded. Mac sighed and shook his head. The whole group stopped in front of the three floating crafts, where four more men were waiting for them.

"Captain Wingate," Walters said, "may I introduce your fellow mission members? They will be under your direct supervision and should supply all the manpower you will need. They were specially picked for this assignment."

Wingate didn't much like the sound of that. It gave the impression that these four men and these four men only would listen to his commands. As far as Walters was concerned, he was still head honcho and Tyler still a member of the colonies. In reply, he put down his duffel and nodded. Walters, having offered to make the introductions, then didn't seem, on second thought, to consider the job worthy of him. He nodded at Tyler, who wound up doing the honors.

"Captain, this is Sergeant Bruce Biggins and Corporal Michael Sumner from the Australian Independent Company."

Wingate was pleased to see the two. The Independent Company was well known to him as a justly famous bunch of commandos who knew how to take orders and deliver on them. The taller of the two moved forward, a big, wide-faced, ruddy man with a stomach bigger than his chest. But the belly had the hard look of muscle, not fat. He put out—and Mac took—his thick, callused hand.

"I'm Biggins, Captain. Boys call me Breaker."

"Breaker," Wingate acknowledged. "I'm Mac."

The second man came up. "Mike, Captain," he said.

Wingate shook his hand, taking in the young, angular, almost boyish face, as well as the well-shaped hand with wide veins that denoted lithe strength. These looked like two men he could depend on for a change. Every Aussie he had worked with in the past had come through for him with flying colors. The final members of the mission quartet looked no worse in terms of dependability.

"These two are from the Canadian First Special Service Force," Tyler explained, sounding fairly awed by it himself. "Eugene Baker and Donald Neill."

Baker was a thin, curly-haired Canadian with a lot of French blood in him. If Walters was Ralph Richardson, Baker was David Niven with a dash of Charles Boyer. He seemed raffish and just a touch elegant. It wasn't in the way he looked so much, as in his attitude. His lips were thin and even now curled in a crooked grin. Still, he looked capable.

"*Bonjour*, Captain," he said, his handshake solid. "My nickname is Candy."

"I'm not surprised," Wingate replied, getting a throaty laugh from the Canadian.

The final member of the team barreled forward. Neill was short and wide, looking like a oil drum with legs. He was completely bald except for a half-circle of white hair on the back of his head. If Candy reminded Wingate of David Niven, among others, Neill reminded him of Popeye.

"Call me anything you'd like, Captain," he told Mac. "I don't have a nickname. I just handle the sardine scow."

He poked a thumb behind him as Wingate took his other hand. Mac looked over his head at the boat floating between the two others. The sandwiching crafts were well-outfitted, powerful ships. The one in the middle looked like it could barely float. It must have been SOE's or Walters's idea of a typical rustic Norwegian fishing trawler. In other words, it was an atypical rust trap. Wingate turned to Erikson.

"Couldn't get me a submarine chaser, could you?" he said wistfully.

"The Yanks couldn't spare one," Erikson said. "Besides, they're all crewed by Norwegians with Royal Navy and RAF support. You could barely escape notice with that kind of cover.''

''We might not be able to escape notice with this tub, either,'' Wingate noted.

''What do you mean, Captain?'' Walters demanded to know. ''My men spent hours dressing this ship down. We took pains to look authentic.''

Wingate glanced at the ship again. The basic structure was correct. The hull was simple and stout with a small cabin and bridge near the rudder. Directly behind that was the mast with a small, four-cornered steadying sail. Near the front was another mast, attached to the back one by a system of ropes.

But the additions to the basic works were meaningless. Oil was slopped everywhere. The paint was flaking. The wood creaked. There were holes in the bridge windows. The sail was tattered.

''Colonel,'' Wingate said patiently, ''the Norwegians are a seafaring race. They've been living off the ocean for fifteen hundred years. The most important things in their lives are their ships. Once we reach port, this tub will stick out like Goebbels's clubfoot. What did you use as a model? A Burmese tramp steamer?''

''Captain,'' Walters replied icily, ''we don't have to fool the Norse. They are on our side. We have to fool the Germans. And I say we have a better chance, looking like this!''

Wingate didn't bother answering. Instead he turned back to Neill. ''Can this thing make the trip?''

''They ruined the outside, but didn't touch the engine, thank God,'' the short Canadian reported. ''She'll get there. I can't promise much about the return trip, though.''

''Neither can I,'' Wingate told him. ''First things first. Top speed?''

''Twenty-five knots on a clear sea.''

Wingate whistled. ''What's our destination?''

Neill looked helplessly at Walters. Wingate followed his stare in wonder. Walters clamped his lips shut.

''Nordmelan,'' Colonel Erikson said. ''Midway between Trondheim and Rorvik.'' Walters spun on the Norwegian officer. Erikson returned the man's angry stare dispassionately.

''We should make it in about a day, then, barring any major storm,'' Wingate figured.

"All ready, then?" Walters inquired impatiently, as if speaking to a schoolboy.

Wingate looked at him slowly, then snapped. "Let's see our supplies."

"That is none of your concern!" Walters nearly roared.

Wingate studied the flushed-faced colonel for a moment. Then he delivered a statement carefully but clearly. "I am about to venture into occupied territory, Colonel. We're going behind enemy lines. Into the lion's den, you might say. And if I am to lead this expedition and if we are spotted by the Nazis, I'll want to know exactly what I've got to get my ass out of there. In that eventuality, nothing is outside my concern. If you don't like it, replace me."

For a second, Walters's head looked like a tomato being pumped up with air. Then, suddenly, the storm passed and the Englishman folded his arms across his greatcoat. "Suit yourself, Captain," he said pompously. "But may I remind you that time is absolutely of the essence?"

"Nice of you to let me know," Wingate said pointedly. "Are you ready to cast off?"

"You'll find me on board," Walters answered. He motioned for Tyler to follow, then stalked past Wingate and the others toward the ship. A few perfectly uniformed men helped the colonels on board. The only colonel left on the dock was Erikson. He stood facing Wingate with his hands folded in front of him.

"Go through the stores," Wingate instructed the Aussies and Canucks. "Give me a rundown."

Candy was the only one who replied with a "Yes, sir," before the quartet of commandos followed the two officers to the ship.

Wingate eyed his superior. "Is this trip really necessary, sir?"

Erikson answered sharply. "I can only say again that this mission is of vital importance, Captain. You will get your instructions from Colonel Walters."

Wingate nodded. The brass cat still had the colonel's tongue. "Very well, sir," he said, snapping off a salute. The Norwegian returned it.

"Good luck, Captain."

"Thank you, sir." Wingate spun in his finest military fashion and marched to the end of the pier. He was expecting to hear the colonel call him. He was expecting the colonel to give him a little clue as to the mission's purpose. He was expecting the man to soften just a little bit because of all the times they had worked together and all the jobs Wingate had completed.

He didn't get what he was expecting. When he gave in and turned just before going on the craft, Erikson was already walking away. That, more than anything, bothered him. Mac went quickly on board before the Scottish air gave him a chill.

"Oh, Christ!" Neill exploded. Wingate heard him all the way on deck. He followed the sound of the Canadian's curse through the bridge, out a door in the rear wall, down a ladder, up a hall, and into the hold. "Jesus! Mother of mercy. Oh, my God!" Neill was holding his head in both hands over an opened box. Wingate leaned over and looked in. Candy did the same on Neill's other side.

"Holy sweet bejesus," Baker breathed. "Reising 50's." Inside the box were rifles that looked like the common hunting variety except for a blunt, wider barrel and a twenty-round magazine hanging down in front of the trigger guard.

"Enfield Mark 1's over here, sir," Breaker announced on the other side of the small, fairly empty hold. Wingate strode over to see the revolvers lying in the second box.

"That's it?" he wondered aloud. "What's in the crates over there?" He pointed toward where Sumner was standing.

"Foodstuffs," the Australian replied. "Canned goods."

"What is this?" Wingate marveled. "No back breathing gear? No diving dress? No electrical torches? No explosives?"

"Anything the matter?" came a cultured voice behind him. Colonel Walters was standing in the hatchway.

"I'd say so," Wingate snorted. "We're going to visit the Nazis with no bombs and some weapons that couldn't hit a house at fifty yards!"

"Careful, Captain," Walters warned. "Colonel Tyler and I supplied this material ourselves."

"Then what did you need me for?" Wingate exploded. "What was that song and dance in that Datchet Taj Mahal for? If you were looking for my blessing on your choice of weapons, you can forget it."

"Captain, this is not the time or place to discuss it," Walters said affably. "Won't you join me in my cabin?"

Wingate whirled back to the commandos. "Keep going through this stuff. I want an itemized list." He turned back just as Walters crooked a finger at him and walked away. Mac followed until they came to a sliding doorway on the right side of the narrow hall.

"Your quarters are opposite mine," Walters informed him. Wingate glanced through the open door of the cabin the colonel had indicated. The space looked barely large enough to fit the captain standing up. Walters's living space, not surprisingly, was a bit more spacious. He had two bunk beds along one wall and a tiny plank that attached to the other which served as a desk. Colonel Tyler got out of his way as the Englishman sat in the seat behind the board. "Is there something bothering you, Captain?"

Wingate had expected something on that level. He had pegged Walters as a master of understatement long ago. He had heard a lot about officers like the Englishman. Lonely, unimaginative men of good breeding who thought of war as some sort of exercise that they could try on for size. As a means of testing their mettle and business savvy. Where success didn't mean the number of battles won but the number of stripes on the shoulder. These were men who were born to command because they were too incompetent to follow orders themselves.

He had heard a lot about these men, but he never expected to be trapped aboard a sinking ship with one. "The question is not what's bothering me, Colonel, it's what isn't bothering me," Wingate said in no uncertain terms. "I've been officially assigned to lead this mission for several hours now and I still don't know what it's about."

Walters waved the question away. "I thought you had some complaint about the weapons."

"Weapons?" Tyler spoke up. "What's wrong with the Reising? The British bought them from us specifically for the Canadian Army."

"And that's why the Special Service boys reacted so badly," Wingate explained. "The weapon overheats, it jams, it gets dirty easily and when it's dirty the bolt never locks, its springs are weak and it's made to take a twelve-round magazine. At that, it's worse than my Browning handgun."

"Those are the American weapons," Walters interrupted.

31

"What about the British Enfields? It's what our boys in the field use."

"Only because they have no choice," Wingate spat out. "It's a heavy, violent weapon with the accuracy of tobacco spit. You can't cock it because the hammer spur was removed in 1938; the trigger mainspring is still fourteen pounds, cutting down the aim even more; the safety stop was removed in 1942, so the damn thing goes off every time you drop it. It makes any sort of accurate shooting impossible! If you wanted any revolver at all, why didn't you get the Smith and Wesson 38/200? It was made for the British."

Walters ruminated on Wingate's outburst for a few seconds, then decreed, "Might I remind you, Captain, that your own Browning is of English manfacture?" Wingate groaned aloud. "You find nothing wrong with that, do you?" Walters wanted to know.

"No," Mac answered, trying to calm down, "but the other men are not similarly equipped."

"They have weapons," Tyler offered. "They can make do."

"This has gone far enough." Wingate declared. "I'll tell you the truth, sirs. I don't like mystery missions. I don't like leading operations I know nothing about. It worries me. It makes me edgy."

Walters leaned back, seemingly considering Wingate's plight. Then he leaned forward, putting one elbow on his desk and rubbing his lower lip. Finally he put both hands on the surface in front of him.

"Now I'll tell *you* the truth, Captain," Walters said, steel creeping into his voice and his expression as placid as an undertaker's. "Your nervousness is your own concern. I am the advisor on this mission. I am your contact. And you will get your orders from me when the time is right and not before. Your immediate concern is keeping the four commandos in line. Do not concern yourself with Colonel Tyler or myself. That is an order. Do you understand?"

Wingate had become very quiet and very still. The Englishman had him. Erikson was not around to overrule Walters now, and there was little Wingate could do short of a court-martial offense. And a court-martial offense would not serve the mission the Norwegian considered so vital. Mac had no choice but to bide Walters's time.

"Do you understand?" the Colonel repeated.

"Yes, sir," Wingate said flatly.

"Get this ship under way then," Walters snapped. "I will reiterate that time is of the essence."

"Yes, sir," Wingate repeated, rising and turning toward the door.

"Oh, and Captain?" Walters called pleasantly. Wingate turned. "If you ever lecture me, or counterorder me, or overrule me, or embarrass me in front of anyone again, I will see to it that your balls hang over Datchet Green. Have I made myself clear?"

"Yes, sir," Wingate said for the third time, a taste of ashes in his mouth. He left quickly.

Wingate strode back to the hold. All of a sudden, he too was anxious to get out of port. More than anything, he wanted to get out onto the open sea where the atmosphere might be a little clearer.

"Well, sir?" Neill asked. "What about the Reisings?"

"With any luck you'll never have to fire them," Wingate snapped heartily.

Neill frowned. Candy scoffed. The Australians looked unconcerned.

"Let's go," Wingate ordered. "Cast off."

The air was much clearer at sea. After all, they were only four hundred miles from the Arctic Circle. Its cold but brisk, bracing air did much to improve Mac's mood. If he had ever doubted his Norwegian stock before, his enjoyment of the fishing boat's voyage dispelled it. The only drawback was that he knew he'd have to face the collected colonels again sometime.

It was all vindictiveness. Petty vindictiveness. Walters hadn't liked Wingate's attitude, knowledge, or expertise. So he was going to grind the captain any way he could. Mac had heard about the animosity between Ike, Patton, and Montgomery, but until he saw Walters in action with Tyler and himself, he couldn't fully believe it. He couldn't really comprehend that Allied generals would let their dislike for each other result in their men's deaths.

It was a little more realistic for him now. And he didn't much like the thought that he might be the underling who got caught in the vise this time. But until he had more to go on, he'd play the good little wooden soldier and prepare as best

33

he could. Pulling his duffel bag into the small, rectangular bridge, he set it down next to where Neill was standing and zipped it open. As the Canadian watched, Mac pulled out two rolls of black tape, a pair of all-purpose wire cutters, four Mark 11A1 American-made grenades, and several sections of a submachine gun.

"Been shopping?" Neill inquired.

Mac grinned, starting to put the weapon together. "You never know what you might need."

Neill eyed the six thirty-two-round magazines still in Wingate's pack. "Or how many rounds it'll fire," he commented.

Mac pulled the last piece into place. "The Sten Mark 2S silenced submachine gun. Fires 550 rounds per minute. Too many bullets are never enough."

It was an impressively simple weapon. Only thirty inches long, it looked like a tube with some bulbous growths. The stock was simply an elegantly bent steel band. The trigger was a metal shard that stuck straight down, protected by a square guard. The barrel spring could be clearly seen through the side. The magazine fit just in front of that, sticking out to the left.

"Impressive, truly impressive," the small, solid Canadian said dispassionately. "You always enjoy torturing people who have to use Reisings, don't you?"

Wingate grinned, hefting the seven-pound weapon in one hand. Its solid, steady· feel added just a bit to his mental security. The Sten and his Browning, along with all the other tricks of his war trade, had almost become extensions of his limbs during the past months of battle. He knew enough to get by without them, but just the same, he liked the extra edge a good killing machine gave him.

And the Sten was good. Designed by Major R. V. Shepherd and H. J. Turpin of the Chief Superindendent's Office, it was demonstrated in January 1941, officially tested in February, and delivered from the factories in June. It wasn't perfect—the magazine sticking out the side sometimes led to problems—but Mac hoped the two Aussies and Canucks were as dependable as it was.

As he thought of them, the other commandos straggled in from below. Candy didn't look happy, but the Australians maintained their languid indifference. They put down their own packs on the bridge floor.

34

"It's not very good, Captain," Candy reported. "Besides the Reisings and Enfields, there's ammo and enough food to make dinner for eight, but just barely."

Wingate swallowed what questions he had. He could have interrogated them for days, but he already knew what the answers would be. He didn't need to ask to know there were no high explosives, no C-2 plastic, no limpets, and no primacord aboard. What he really wanted to know now was *why*, and he doubted the quartet could tell them that. Only the pair of colonels could fill him in on that, and they were belowdecks practicing their Cheshire Cat impersonations.

Commandos, however, were notorious for learning things they weren't supposed to know. Wingate himself had made a wartime career of it. They had a lot of hours on the ocean to kill, so if Mac couldn't check the explosives, which were nonexistent, he could at least check out his operatives.

He started slowly, making an attempt at casual conversation. "Too bad there's no target I could test the Sten with," he mused, examining the weapon in his hand.

"You could strafe the hold a couple of times," Neill suggested.

That elicited a few chuckles from the gathered professionals, who had found places to sit in the small, rectangular control cabin. Breaker and Mike pulled their packs over to the left-hand wall, leaning and looking through the side windows at the rolling Atlantic water. Candy leaned forward over the bridge's one table to the right of his fellow Canadian.

"I wouldn't worry about those guns, me lad," Breaker announced buoyantly. "You Canucks can use all of them if you want. We have our own weapons. If one Reising fails, just pick up another one."

"And if that one fails?" Candy suggested.

"Use the Enfields," answered Sumner. "And if that doesn't work, take the bloody bullets out and throw them! The accuracy will be better than the pistol, and the power'll be better than the submachine gun."

Everyone chortled as if they were discussing a Sunday lark into the country rather than a mission in occupied territory. It was a good sign of growing camaraderie, but Wingate was more interested in something Biggins had said.

"You have your own weapons?" he echoed, looking at Biggins.

Breaker looked over the Sten in Mac's hand, then reached for his own pack. "Great minds work alike," he mumbled, pulling out a few familiar-looking metal pieces. Mike Sumner did the same and soon both Independent Company members had complete submachine guns in their hands.

Sumner had the Austen 9 mm in his grip, its barrel, body, and trigger copied from the Sten. In fact, "Austen" stood for "Australian Sten." Its bolt mechanism, however, was stolen from the Schmeisser MP-38 Nazi gun. Made in Melbourne, it was an effective if unexceptional weapon that looked a little like a handgun with delusions of grandeur. Its compact sleekness seemed well matched with the lithe Sumner.

The machine Biggins had put together matched his personality also: big, impressive, and just a touch strange. He proudly displayed the Owen Mark 1. Like Mac's weapon, it looked like a bunch of spare parts slapped together, only more so. Its barrel was thinner, its body was even less ostentatious, and it had a grooved grip in front of the trigger butt for steadier handling. And since the thing fired 700 rounds per minute, 150 more than the Sten and 200 more than the Austen, it needed that extra grip.

But the oddest thing about the device was its magazine. Rather than poking out the side, or hanging below, it rose out of the top of the weapon's body. It certainly seemed to make sense—the extra help of gravity would make the bullets feed easily—but it certainly looked funny.

"Merde," breathed Candy. "Did someone forget to tell us something or what?"

"First lesson in staying alive," Breaker said solemnly. "Never trust anything a superior says."

"Present company excluded," Sumner added, nodding at Mac.

Mac nodded back with a smile, then turned to the slightly dejected Canadians, whose expressions said that they were caught with their equipment down. "I'm as much in the dark about this as you are," he admitted. "They pulled me out of the Mediterranean for this little jaunt, then suddenly got a bad case of lockjaw. Anybody know what this is about?"

The commandos responded with almost a sense of relief. Each had been masking his own doubts about the mission through forced whimsy. Once they thought Mac wasn't holding out on them, they opened up.

"Damned if I know," Neill growled, still irritated by the lack of a reliable gun. "Since the Dieppe disaster, we've been crawling all over northern France and Sicily. When our commander asked if we'd like an easy time of it in Norway, we bit."

"Easy?" Wingate asked. That word was contrary to the build-up Erikson had given him.

"Well, compared to Dieppe, yeah," the helmsman said a bit less assuredly.

Dieppe was a disaster. It had been an Allied "test" to see if they could capture any Nazi-held harbor in the North Atlantic. Only this test was played out for real, using real Canadians. It was incredibly badly planned and the wonder was not that the raid failed, but that any of the commandos survived it. In August of 1942, five thousand North Americans went in. Half of them came back and much the worse for wear. Total German casualties? Six hundred. It didn't help Wingate's survival sense that the leftovers from that fiasco were sent to help him on this one.

"We've been scratching MacArthur's back in New Guinea." Breaker delineated the Australian background.

"He still wants to return, you know," Sumner cracked at Candy.

"Our boss said he thought we could use a little rest and relaxation, the pommy bastard," Breaker continued. "So here we are, freezing our bloody butts off. As to what we're doing and where we're going, I was hoping you'd tell me!"

"Isn't that just like the brass," Neill interjected, the growl back in his voice, his eyes straight ahead out to sea. "They never tell you enough. It's like they're afraid you'll survive."

"Yeah," agreed Sumner. "They figure it's better that you become a ghost and haunt them than become a hero and come back to bother them."

Wingate couldn't help but agree. Except in the extreme cases of safeguarding a "sleeper" agent inside enemy territory, he could never understand why his superiors consistently told him less than he needed to know to do a thorough job. It wasn't like he was a foot soldier whose responsibility was to shoot anything that moved. Still, that wasn't what he wanted to discuss. They had already established the fact that they all knew next to nothing. He needed some kind of clarification. Any kind.

"Forget hero," he said. "Let's just see if we can make this a round trip."

"According to our superiors," Sumner replied, "there should be no doubt of that."

"He made it sound like a bleeding vacation!" Breaker added.

"Not a chance," Candy said quietly, looking down at Neill's chart. Not surprisingly, everyone looked in his direction. He didn't need any further encouragement. He looked up slowly, a small smile on his face. "We're the last team. The backup squad. The final chance. There were two groups ahead of us who couldn't do the job."

The other four men reacted as if someone had just found a time bomb in his shorts. They didn't panic, but they didn't run around laughing hysterically, either.

"You'd better elaborate," Wingate recommended.

"Yeah, elaborate," Neill snarled at his countryman.

"I don't have all the details, Captain," Baker informed Wingate, "but on the eve of our departure here, I shared a glass or two with our commander . . ."

"Never let this man get you alone in a tavern," Neill warned. "He may look thin, but he's hollow."

"And . . .?" Wingate prompted.

"And I discovered that they've tried whatever it is we're supposed to be doing twice before and it failed both times."

"Target?" Wingate asked hopefully.

"Unknown," Candy answered.

"Casualties?"

"Unknown."

"Importance?"

"Unknown."

"What else do you know?" Wingate finally inquired in desperation.

"Only that we're cutting it close," Baker said. "According to the CO, if we blink on this one, we might miss it."

Wingate threw up his hands in exasperation. The only thing anybody had been able to tell him for sure was that time was of the essence. Add that to all his other information and it seemed that somebody was in a rush to get no place to do nothing.

"So what else do we know?" Wingate asked.

"About what?" Sumner asked.

"About anything," Wingate responded. "Let's grab at straws. It looks like they are all that's left us."

"Well, I know that if both the previous missions went to Norway by way of the 'Shetland Bus,' " Neill spoke up, "their chances were slight to begin with."

"What are you babbling about?" Biggins demanded. *"We're* on the 'Shetland Bus!' "

"Right," Neill continued. "Out of the thirty-seven trips from Scotland to Norway and back since last year, only nineteen were successful. And most of those were on submarine chasers."

"Heartening news," Candy commented.

"Ah, yes," Neill agreed, "but none of those sunken eighteen had me as the captain." The compact Canadian took a moment to pull out a cigar from his jacket pocket and clamp it between his teeth before returning his attention to the sea.

"More heartening news," Candy decided.

"Are you just saying that to prepare us for the inevitable," Wingate asked the white-haired helmsman, "or to give us heightened faith in your seamanship?"

"Like you said, Captain," Neill replied, "as long as there aren't any major storms or a sudden descent by the Luftwaffe, I'll get us there. Once we arrive, though, I'm not promising anything."

"I'll take it from there," Mac assured them. "Let's just arrive, all right?"

"You're the captain, Captain," Neill shrugged.

"Right," said Wingate, not really relishing the position. "If any of you can think of, or remember, anything that might give me a better idea of what we're getting into, let me know. In the meantime, do your best to prepare for our arrival."

"What would you suggest we do, Captain?" Breaker inquired with just a touch of sarcasm.

"Break out the stores," Wingate retorted sharply. "Find out who's doing the cooking around here. Prepare the weapons for easy access. Get your commando outfits on. Get some sleep. Do I have to do everything around here?"

"Yes, *sir!*" Breaker responded, snapping to attention and hurling a salute at his forehead. The big man let the side of his hand bounce off his brow, and wobbled as if he had been karate-chopped. Sumner and Baker laughed. Neill elaborately chewed his cigar from the left side of his mouth to the right.

Great, Wingate thought. A joker. The slightly forced humor was back. In the face of the unknown, Breaker was the kind of guy who'd whistle a merry tune. As long as he shot fast and straight, Wingate didn't care.

"All right," he said. "Get going."

The three commandos filed out to do whatever they could find that needed doing. Neill remained behind the fishing trawler's wheel, the cold, midmorning air creating a chill inside the bridge. Mac took up a position where he seemed to be poring over the charts. But he did not see the maps for wind and water currents, nor the various towns at the mouth of the Trondheim fjord. Instead he saw Erikson's expression as he sent the American back to his hereditary homeland. It was the face of a man shutting out all emotion. Like the face of an executioner who took pride in his ability but didn't like the job. A man who was doing what he felt he had to do.

"It's really too bad about the Reisings," Neill commented. His words broke Wingate out of his reverie.

"What?"

"The Reisings," Neill repeated. "Not good guns. Not good at all."

"No," Mac agreed, looking out at the rocky sea. "Hardly better than my Browning automatic. I told Walters so. He reminded me that the Browning was a British-made weapon."

"Like hell," Neill scoffed. Mac looked over at the little man. "It may have been designed by John Moses Browning, but it was developed by the Belgians. The blooming British had their chance to make them in 1941, but declined. The gun you've got, Captain, was probably manufactured by John Inglis and Company, Toronto, Canada."

"Well, hell," Wingate breathed, looking at Neill with new respect. He was impressed. And he was pretty sure he and the cocky little Canadian would get along just fine.

"Damn colonels don't know what they're about," Neill mumbled. "Neither of them. The 'British' Browning is made in Canada and the Yank air force trains in Canada. Who's fooling who?"

"Hold that thought," Wingate suggested. "If there's any trouble, get in touch with me on the horn." The captain pointed to the tube communications device attached to the side of the chart table. Neill nodded. "I'll relieve you come dinner time," Mac finished. With that, he moved to the rear door and went below.

He marched down the hallway and rapped on the colonels' door smartly. He was answered with a clipped, booming "Come!"

He entered to see the two superior officers in more or less the same position he left them. Walters was sitting at the plank desk and Tyler was leaning over his shoulder, looking at some papers clutched in the Englishman's hand. The only difference was that they were no longer wearing their coats. Both were in casual uniform.

Walters was quick to lay the papers face-down on the makeshift desk as Wingate entered. It was a casual, but fully considered motion. He wanted to make Mac suffer any way he could.

"Everything under control, I trust?" the British colonel inquired.

Wingate did not say what he wanted to. He did not say, "Sir, the men are a little worried. They've been on secret missions before, but this secret mission is a secret!" Instead, he had to play Walters's game again. He couldn't afford to antagonize the superior any more than he already had. So instead he said, "Yes, sir," and stood at attention in front of the Englishman.

Walters took it well. He smiled, leaned back, folded his hands over his belly, and commanded, "At ease."

Wingate planted his feet and put his hands behind his back. Walters mused at him for a few seconds.

"All right, Captain," he finally said, his voice melodious. "I suppose it is time to clear the air just a bit. Now that we are under way, it becomes important for you to know what you're dealing with."

Wingate said, "Yes, sir," and couldn't help but lean forward slightly in anticipation.

Walters also leaned forward, carefully assuming the position used by any wise, self-respecting, old war-horse when he wanted to get his men's loyalty. "We are going to Alten fjord in a minor, backup capacity. Our mission, at best, is a minor diversionary one that may not even be required. Until we know for sure, we are at the service of the Norwegian under-

41

ground . . . the . . .'' Walters paused while he checked the paper in front of him. "The Militow Organization."

The silence following Walters's short speech was deep, thick, and deafening. Wingate just barely kept from saying, "Is that all?" Instead, he tried to draw Walters out with an elaboration.

"Do you mean the Militoer Organisajonen, sir?" he asked.

Walters checked the paper again. "That's what I said, isn't it?"

"Begging the Colonel's pardon, sir, but is the Norwegian resistance force? They're called MILORG for short."

"Yes," Walters pronounced, still looking at the page. "Yes, that's right, Captain. It says right here: MILORG."

Wingate relaxed from his tight "at ease" position for a moment to scratch his head. He waited, but no more words of explanation were forthcoming. Mac refused to let it bother him.

"Very good, sir," he said and performed a sharp about-face in the cabin.

"Captain Wingate," Walters said to his back. Wingate turned, silent. The English colonel leaned over and pulled up a small sack which he plopped down on his desk. He undid the knotted corners and laid out a small block of C-2 plastic explosives, some various casings, and a short length of white primacord.

"I have those materials we talked about," Walters said. "The ones you needed for experimentation? I trust you will do what you can and report to me before our arrival in Norway."

Slowly, Mac approached the desk. Scanning the paltry materials, he was tempted to do just what Walters asked. Experiment detonating C-2 inside a waterproof casing with primacord. Setting off explosives on a ship whose first hole meant sinking. On a ship whose primary requirement was to be covert. Even if he could proportion the C-2 so it wouldn't be more powerful than a firecracker, setting off even firecrackers would be U-boat bait.

Incredulous, Mac collected the demolition supplies and strode out of the room. He closed the door to the colonels' quarters softly and carefully. Then he stood outside, breathing deeply. After a few seconds to calm down, Mac marched into his own room and dumped the materials on his cot. He stood over it, seriously thinking.

Everyone seemed to have different bits and pieces to the puzzle. Only each piece was completely different from the others and there seemed to be no way on God's green earth that they would fit together. Erikson's piece was that the mission was of the utmost importance. Walters's piece said the mission couldn't be less important. The commandos' direct commander's piece said it would be easy. Candy's piece said it was amazing they weren't dead already.

Somewhere, somebody was lying, and Wingate didn't like deliberating on just who that was. Because whoever it was, he was behind Wingate with both hands against the captain's back on the edge of a cliff. So decided, Mac emptied out his thoughts again. He simply opened the floodgates of his mind and let his concerns wash out. He knew his situation, now he had to deal with it. And in cases like these, there was only one way.

Mac turned into the perfect wooden soldier. If they wanted him to play it by the book, play it by the book he would. If they wanted a minor diversion, a minor diversion he would give them. If they wanted him to be at the beck and call of MILORG, than all MILORG had to do was bark.

Wingate sat down next to the C-2 and primacord. Somehow, its presence was comforting. He felt a little better knowing it was available for use. He felt the rhythmic rumbling of the trawler's motor below him, and the coarse rocking of the ocean. He thought about everything that had happened in the past few hours. And he realized that if he had the choice, he'd rather be back inside that burning English hotel than here.

CHAPTER 3

Things started to fall apart when they got within spitting distance of their destination. Dinner had been fine. It seemed as if the colonels had had a choice. They could supply K rations to the commandos and eat real food themselves, showing exactly how they felt about the men; or they could suffer the indigestibility of K rations themselves; or, finally, they could all eat relatively decent food. They all ate relatively decent food.

The remainder of the voyage had been fine. Wingate had relieved Neill right after dinner. The Canadian ate, then took an eight-hour rest. The sea was blissfully calm and Mac handled the wheel easily. They remained on course with no problem. And it all served to make Mac all the more tense. If a storm had kicked up, at least it would have allowed him to blow off some steam.

As it was, Mac thought about the Norse legends his father used to tell him as a boy in Wisconsin. He especially remembered the stories about "the Draug." It was a horrid, troll-like creature who sailed the Norwegian sea forever. The monster didn't have to do anything. Its very sight portended death to any seamen who glimpsed it.

The night and the sea played tricks on Wingate's eyes. There were always dark shapes out on the waves. Thankfully, he could make out no discernible beasts or anything that shot at him. But still his tension mounted.

Donald Neill returned right on time. The moon and the position of the stars told Wingate that. He didn't have to look at his wristwatch with its black band and brown-tinged plastic crystal. It was two o'clock in the morning. The pair stayed on the darkened bridge for a few more hours, sharing tales of their various seas. Before the war, Neill had traveled all the waters around Canada. He had shipped through Hudson and Baffin bays, sailed the North Alantic and the Pacific, and even reached the Beaufort Sea and the Queen Elizabeth Islands around the North Pole.

Mac talked about traversing the Great Lakes and some of his earlier wartime experiences in the Mediterranean. The outwardly calm, almost wistful, conversation managed to soothe him somewhat, but when Wingate went below, he couldn't help but liken the talk to ones resigned criminals had with priests just before they walked that last mile.

So it was no wonder that when the low whistle sounded in Wingate's cabin, he was instantly awake and fully aware. He reached up from his bedding and pulled out the hoselike communications device.

Mac pried off the metal cap with the tiny whistle in the middle, which was attached to the thick hose by a thin, short metal chain.

"Yes?" he asked softly but clearly into the opening.

"Better get up here, Captain," came Neill's muffled voice. "Ship in sight."

"Markings?"

"Can't be sure at this distance, but it looks like another fishing vessel."

"Roger," Wingate concluded, far from whimsically. He slapped the cap back on, stuck the hose back into its holder on the wall, and sprang out of bed, all in one motion. He had slept in his clothes and boots, so all he had to do was break out the cap and jacket he had packed specifically for purposes of disguise. The hat was a plain seaman's cap. The jacket was a canvas sort of thing with a hood that could fit over the cap. It was standard fisherman's gear.

He was pulling on the coat as he silently moved out of his quarters. Before going above, however, he stuck his head through the portal where the commandos were sleeping.

"Up," he said simply to see if they responded. All were awake. "It could be nothing," Wingate went on, "but be prepared anyway. Neill has spotted a ship. Listen for the whistle. If I blow once, we're clear. Twice, be ready for a fight."

Mac pulled on the cap as he trotted down the ship's hall.

45

He hauled himself up the steps to the bridge, feeling acutely the lack of his shoulder holster and Browning. If they were boarded for any reason, he couldn't chance the automatic giving them away before the commandos down below could do something about it. If they caught Neill and Wingate dead to rights, the others would be sitting ducks, no matter how well armed they were.

The new morning was impressive as Wingate stepped out into it. Off to his right, he could see the mist-enshrouded shores of Norway. At this distance, there was very little detail, but he could make out the barren coastline seemingly made up of one mountain after another. All around him was the olive-and-white sea, rougher than it had been for the entire trip. And right in front of him was the other ship—a small, solid fishing vessel with *"Varsø"* written on the front of its rounded wooden bridge.

A misting rain had kicked up, splattering the windows of Wingate's bridge, effectively blurring any other delineations. The sun had not completely risen, giving the ocean a gray-blue pallor that made vision all the more difficult. Mac couldn't see anyone on board the approaching trawler. The only good thing about that was that whoever was on the other ship probably couldn't see them very well, either.

Mac took up a position at the chart table next to Neill. "How long have they been coming?" he asked.

"Made a beeline for us as soon as sighted," the Canuck answered. "Not a good sign."

"Any other contact?" Mac asked.

"No," Neill replied. "In the colonels' infinite wisdom, they neglected to outfit this ship with a radio."

Wingate looked quickly around. He spied a bureaulike unit at the back of the bridge. He went over, crouched, and opened both small, swing-out doors. Inside were various trawler requirements, like a ship's log, various lengths and widths of rope, and, incongruously, a brass telescope. He pulled out the last item, opening it with incredulousness.

"What does Walters think?" he wondered aloud. "We're sailing into the nineteenth century or something?"

He walked to the right of Neill and the wheel to the farthermost window. Using one hand to pull the jacket's hood over his head and the other to undo the window's latch, he swung the glass partition back, and stuck his head out.

The telescope helped. With it, he could just make out a figure moving onto the *Varsø*'s deck. It was a wide, solid figure with a pair of binoculars. Mac couldn't make out his features, but he could make out the man's blue-and-white cap. It bore the unmistakable bird clutching the little round swastika insignia in its claws. It was the hat of a Nazi officer.

Wingate didn't immediately give voice to what he felt. If he had, he might have lost yesterday's meal, or turned Neill's ears blue. Between looking a mess, not having any major markings other than grease stains, and not having a radio, the 'Shetland Bus' had almost screamed for attention. Mac quickly pulled his head back inside, pulled in the telescope, and shut the window. He clamped his teeth shut. In case the German could see him through the military binocs, he didn't want to be spotted cursing in either English or Norwegian.

Quickly, he strode to the other side of the cabin, located the four communications tubes that led to his room, the colonels' quarters, the hold, and the engine room, pulled up the hold device and blew twice.

"What is it?" Neill asked, already expecting the worst, but wanting to know the details.

Mac looked over at the helmsman, his mouth opening. Then his mouth shut in surprise. Then it opened again and in spite of himself, Mac swore.

"Jesus fucking Christ," the American marveled. On Neill's otherwise unassuming jacket was the insignia of his outfit: the First Special Service Force. It was a beautiful thing, with a red Indian arrowhead and the letters USA emblazoned across the top and the word CANADA coming down vertically. Mac pulled up his pant leg, brought out his knife, and ripped off the patch with a swift, angry stroke.

He thrust the knife back in its leg scabbard and shoved the insignia into Neill's shocked hands.

"Get below," Wingate ordered. "Tell the men there are goddamn Nazis on the other ship. Tell the colonels nothing. I'm going to try to bluff them out."

Neill stumbled back, dropping the patch in the process. He bent and picked it up, apologizing all the while. "Hey, I'm sorry, Captain, I . . . I forgot all about it . . . my, uh, wife put it on during my last furlough . . ."

"Forget about it," Mac snapped. "Get below. If they make one move to board, I'll blow the whistle and you guys

47

get up here shooting. If I suddenly speed up, do the same. Got it?"

"Yes, sir!" Neill announced, disappearing out the door.

Wingate shook his head in wonder. On this trip, nobody could help being woefully unprepared. He squinted out the front window. It was still a dark, dank, gloomy morning, but there was really nothing he could do about the approaching craft. Even in the dark, he would still see the other ship, so veering off now would be suspicious. He had little choice but to stay on course and tough out the possible confrontation.

Wingate felt the constant thrum of the diesel motors beneath his feet. He saw the *Varsø* getting closer and closer. He heard his teeth grinding against each other. Mentally he boned up on his Norse dialects. He decided to use "Nynorsk," the language of the old Norse, rather than the more commonly used "Riksmaal," based on Danish forms. Even if the Nazi knew Norwegian, he'd still probably be confused by the ancient dialect.

The *Varsø* was getting close. Wingate shook himself and tried to feel unassuming. In an effort to create the proper mood, he quietly sang an old Norwegian song his father used to sing to him.

"Midnattsol, oh, midnattsol . . ."

As the other craft got closer, Mac could see the German officer more clearly. He was blond, with a mousey beard. He wore all the Nazi regalia, including a knotted tie. Only now, he had fellow soldiers all around him. Wingate saw four Nazi sailors wearing their dark, plain uniforms, folded caps, and life preservers which circled their torsos. To top it all off, each carried a Karabiner 98K, the standard Nazi rifle.

Wingate thanked heaven for little things. At least they didn't have submachine guns. With those five-round, bolt-action weapons, the commandos could make quick work of it in case of a firefight, but Wingate hoped it wouldn't come to that. The *Varsø* finally pulled alongside and idled its engine. Mac did the same. In order to talk, he had to go to the window opposite the door to below, as his ship was pointing east and the other craft was pointing west.

Mac pushed open the side window. *"Goddag!"* he shouted out across the waves. *"Kan jeg hjelpe Dem?"*

The Nazi officer reacted rather brusquely to Wingate's

"Hello, can I help you?" Instead of talking to him, the German turned to the *Varsø*'s bridge, shouting and gesticulating.

Mac saw the bridge window facing him open. A ruddy-faced, dark-haired Norwegian captain stuck his head out. He nodded at the Nazi, then called back to Mac in Norse.

"You are a bit far out for simple travel," he said, awkwardly translating the German's question. "It is still several months before the cod travel."

"There is still the *lodde*," Wingate called back, referring to the salmonlike fish in the Norwegian waters. "Besides, it is never too late or too early to sail. 'The land divides us, the sea unites,' " he concluded, quoting a well-known Norse catchphrase.

The other captain nodded, his expression saying he agreed with Mac. But rather than answering immediately, he yelled down a rough German translation to the officer. The Nazi barked back. Wingate pursed his lips. If only the Nazi wasn't shouting away from him, he could pick up the words before the Norwegian translated, giving him more time to create a reply. As it was, the wind blew the German words away from him.

"This is not a good day for sailing," the Norwegian shouted. "You would do better to repair your boat before sailing on such a hazardous morning."

Wingate saw visions of a throttled, impaled, bullet-ridden Walters in his mind. The Germans had picked up on the trawler's disrepair right away. About the only good thing about the Norwegian's new speech was that it seemed to be leading up to a curt dismissal and fond farewell.

"I will!" Mac shouted back. "I was planning to, but I needed to test her seaworthiness, and the ocean's beauty carried me away." In an American translation, the phrase might not have worked, but in Nynorsk, it was perfectly apt. The Norwegian captain's face told Wingate again that the old salt often felt the same way. And he told the Nazi that in words the Germans could accept and understand.

It seemed to do the trick, because right after, the *Varsø*'s engines roared into renewed life, gray smoke belching out the thin chimney next to the bridge. The German nodded and turned away. The Norwegian waved. Wingate waved back and turned to start his own engines.

He nearly walked into the still, standing figure of Colonel

Walters. The Englishman's appearance there had to rank with Mac's most shocking experiences during the war. Wingate literally stumbled back, his mouth working, his head minutely shaking from side to side. He acted as if he were facing the Frankenstein monster. As if the Draug had slipped aboard the ship and set up housekeeping on the bridge.

Because it wasn't just Walters's image that so surprised him. It was the fact that the Britisher was wearing his full Allied uniform. From top to bottom he appeared exactly as he had in Scotland.

"I'll take it from here, Captain," he said sharply.

In numb shock, Wingate suddenly realized how it felt to touch madness. He couldn't comprehend how Walters could do such an incredibly suicidal thing. Struck dumb, he managed to shake his head no.

"You don't understand, Captain," Walters said. "This ship is our contact. The resistance had promised to meet us with another trawler."

The explanation brought Mac back to this earth. He swung his head to look at the other ship. He saw one of the Nazis pointing at him. He turned back, put both hands on Walters's chest, said, "Not this ship," and shoved.

Walters fell on his back and the first bullet came through the bridge window at the same time. Walters stayed where he was, but many more bullets followed the lead of the first.

Colonel Tyler started to come through the open port at the back of the bridge. He managed to utter, "What is going . . ." before Mac put his hand on the American's chest and pushed him down the stairs.

Ignoring the storm of lead buzzing around the cabin, Wingate leaped back to the wheel, slammed the throttle down, and spun the wheel toward shore. He fell to the floor himself then, dragging the communications tube with him. Holding the wheel with one hand, he popped off the cap with his other thumb and blew long and hard, twice.

"What are you doing?" Walters managed to bluster, still flat on his back.

Wingate had no time for vindictiveness or sarcasm. "If we can make it to shore, run and keep running. If we can't, jump off and swim for your life."

As he finished, Wingate heard the stamping feet of the

commandos lunging up the steps. "Keep down!" he shouted. "We're under fire!"

The lithe, wiry Sumner came jumping through the door first. He slid all the way to the front wall of the bridge. Candy was next, wrapping himself around the curve of the opening and slinking along the back wall. Neill was third, clutching a Reising in one hand and an Enfield in the other, nearly tripping over Walters as he took cover next to the wheel. Finally, in came Breaker Biggins, standing almost full length, already blasting out the opposite window with his Owen submachine gun.

As soon as one Australian kneeled, the other was up with the Austen, sending out more fire. The Canadians responded in turn.

"Neill," Wingate shouted. "Take the wheel and keep this thing pumping toward shore! Baker, stay inside the bridge and cover him as best you can. Biggins and Sumner, fan outside and see what you can do. Use what cover you can without endangering Neill. He's our only chance to outrun them!"

"Captain," said another voice, "what about me?"

Wingate looked around to see Colonel Tyler laying on his stomach, just inside the door, cradling an American M3 submachine gun, otherwise known as "the grease gun," in his arms. Normally, Wingate wouldn't have used him, but when he was this angry and in this position, he refused to waste the manpower.

"Go with the Aussies," he said.

"No!" Walters shouted. "Tyler, get below!"

"Move out!" Wingate told the others. The American colonel ignored his British counterpart. When Biggins slid open the side door to the outside, Tyler went with them.

Wingate crawled toward the door down to the hold.

"Where are you going?" Walters demanded.

Mac turned. He saw the *Varsø* out the shattered windows opposite, chugging in pursuit. As it dipped in and out of sight because of the choppy waves, he also saw at least half a dozen Nazis near its bow, shooting at them.

"Stay put," he said by way of answering the Englishman. "With all the extra soldiers' weight on board the other ship, we may be able to outrun them. But I doubt it." Mac reached the back door, slid through, and stood on the third step.

"So what are you going to do?" Walters cried.

"Neill, Baker," Wingate boomed. "Get ready to abandon ship. When I say so, get out the door the farthest from the other ship and swim for all you're worth. Make sure the others do the same. No matter what happens, just keep going, underwater if possible. Clear?"

Both Candy and Neill answered, "Clear."

"But what about me?" Walters wailed.

"Do whatever you'd like," Wingate said, his back already turned, his feet already pounding down the steps.

He ran immediately to his quarters. Placing just one foot inside, he scooped up the block of C-2 and his two weapons. Then he marched toward the hold, the plastic explosives under one arm. As he went, he searched through the detonators in his coat until he found the one he was looking for.

Then he was in the hold, searching for the trapdoor to the engine. He found it below some empty cartons near the middle of the enclosure. Knowing it would be too dark for any delicate work down there, Wingate prepared the charge standing over it. He took the special detonator and buried it deep in the C-2. It was a "ring-pin" detonator, one that worked much the same way a grenade did. Once the little pin, attached to a ring, was pulled out, the priming charge would go off, detonating the larger bomb.

Wingate crouched down, opened the metal trapdoor, and dropped into the engine area. There was hardly enough room for one man to fit, so it was perfect to house the explosives. Wingate pushed the plastic stuff against the engine and hopped back into the hold again. As he raced back toward the bridge, he could hear the sounds of the battle grow more intense. Every few seconds, the bridge would reverberate with the sounds of hacking submachine guns. He climbed up the stairs and put his head just over the bottom of the door opening.

"Captain Wingate!" Walters exploded. "What is going on? What are you doing?"

"Captain," Neill called over the Britisher's complaints, "it's no good. They're more experienced in these waters than I am. And I can't do my best in this position."

Wingate empathized. Trying to outrun an enemy by shooting and steering at the same time in a crouched position was nearly impossible.

"How much longer can you hold out?" Mac asked.

"A couple of minutes, but then they'll be on us."

"All right," Wingate decided. "Candy, get over to the cabinet at the back of the bridge and get me some strong string."

Baker crab-walked back to the unit that Wingate had gotten the telescope from, and pulled out all the rope he could get his hands on, then threw the whole bunch at the back door.

"Take your pick," Candy said, keeping his eye on the pursuing craft.

Wingate collected all the strands and pulled the rope down with him. He returned to the hold where he propped open the engine area's trapdoor with some of the empty cases. Then, just to make sure it wouldn't slam shut, he put the commandos' jumbled bedding on either side of the opening. If it did try to swing closed with the wrong roll of the sea, the rolled-up blankets would keep it from cutting the lifeline he was planning.

Reaching down into the engine area, he tied one end of the cord he was carrying to the ring of the ring-pin detonator. Then, ever so gingerly, he tested its give. One tug too hard and the boat would blow with everyone still on it.

It was a situation that required finesse. He couldn't just attach the other end of the rope to the trapdoor so it would go off when the Nazis opened it. If he did that, they'd all be dead in the water by the time the Germans got around to searching the ship. He had to work it so the place would explode after they had gotten away, but before the Nazis could spot them and shoot them like ducks in a barrel.

Mac unraveled the coiled cord as he walked backward out of the hold. He ran it down the hallway. One length ran out at the steps, so he tied another length to it. He unraveled it up the steps. Then he stuck his head over the doorsill again.

The *Varsø* was coming up along the opposite side now. When Neill had turned toward shore, the other vessel had simply followed. It had been on the left side of the commandos' ship at first, but now it was gaining ground on the right side. It all worked perfectly for Wingate's plan. He crawled into the cabin on his stomach, pulling the cord along with him. Reaching the front corner of the bridge, he pulled the rope as taut as he dared. Then he tied it to a bolt at the base of the floor.

He reexamined his handiwork. It seemed to be perfect.

53

The rope was stretched across the bottom of the right doorway to the outside. If someone slid open the door without looking down and stepped in, they would kick or trip on the rope, which would pull out the ring-pin, which would ignite the detonator, which would charge the C-2, which would turn the trawler into matchsticks.

Not trusting Walters for anything, Wingate pronounced, "Don't touch the rope." Then he crawled to the left-hand door, slid it open, and shouted, "Get in here! Now!" He slid away from the opening as the three men charged back inside, looking none the worse for wear.

"Any damage?" Wingate asked everyone.

"Not in this bloody weather," Breaker reported. "They can't hit us with their peashooters, and our rounds are gone with the wind!"

"It'll get worse as they get closer," Sumner said.

"And they're going to get closer!" Neill promised.

"All right," Wingate interrupted. "It looks like we can't outrun them, and getting into a one-on-one firefight is too chancy."

"That's ridiculous!" piped up Walters. "Why, with our submachine guns, we can make mincemeat out of them!"

"And what if they turn tail and run?" Wingate demanded, forgetting all about the "sir" stuff. "We can't catch up to them and they'll have an armada waiting for us in the fjord. No, we've got to get them all in one fell swoop."

"What if they've already radioed for reinforcements?" Tyler suggested, breathing heavily. It was obvious he wasn't used to battle.

"I don't think so," Wingate reasoned. "We must look pretty minor to them. Just a couple of people returning fire against a larger group of Germans. I'm hoping the Nazi pride will make them remain silent until they mop us up."

"So what now?" Breaker demanded.

"I'm going to cut the engines and I want all of you to slip off the other side of the ship as one. Submerge as much as you can and swim as quietly as you can away from this thing."

"What about you?" Neill wanted to know.

"Don't worry about it," Wingate answered. "If this works, you'll see me soon enough. If this doesn't work, we're probably all dead anyway. Get ready."

Six men huddled by the door opposite the booby-trapped entrance. Mac held on to the vibrating throttle while he kneeled behind the wheel. He waited until he saw the very front of the *Varsø* out the rearmost window, then started to pull the throttle back. The ship slowed.

Mac turned and nodded at the colonels and the commandos. Sumner slid the door open silently and they all crab-walked out. The bridge effectively blocked them from the Germans' sight.

Wingate continued to slow the vessel. He saw the commandos tense. Colonel Tyler started to rise, preparing to dive in headfirst. Breaker Biggins pulled him down brusquely. Wingate checked the opposite window. It looked like the *Varsø* was slowing in unison with the Allied craft. The American captain licked his lips. Once this first part of the operation was completed and the commandos were off and the Nazis were on, then the real stickler would start.

Wingate quickly checked the bridge for the heaviest pockets of shadow. The darkness he sought was under the chart table as well as just behind it. He looked up toward the enemy ship again. He had to have his men get off before the Germans came astern. Before the Germans could see them through the bridge's broken windows. The *Varsø* was almost upon them. Wingate put the engine in idle, then swung his head to nod at the commandos.

The whole group crawled over the side and slipped into the sea. Wingate didn't hear a splash. So far, so good. He crawled over to the open door opposite the booby-trapped entrance and slid it shut. Then, before the enemy craft could pull alongside, he propelled himself back along the floor to his position against the wall.

He couldn't leave yet. The Germans would board and enter the cabin, probably by the way he hoped, but there was also a chance someone would enter by the door opposite. Then the whole plan would be meaningless. He didn't have the time or the equipment to set up another trip wire for the other door—he would need some nails to keep the second rope flat against the back wall, then taut on the bottom of the door. Somehow, he had to make sure the Germans came into the cabin only one way.

Waiting, as always, was excruciating. And as always, Wingate's body responded by flushing almost all the liquid it could find out of his pores. Even in the chill of the Arctic morning, Mac pressed himself against the wall swimming in sweat. To make things all the more suspenseful, he couldn't chance looking at the *Varsø* out of the windows above his head. At this angle they were sure to see him if he was anywhere but plastered against the right wall.

He heard no gunfire, so it seemed reasonable to assume that they had not discovered the men in the water yet. But he did hear muffled voices, a fact that elated and frightened him. It probably meant the Nazis had boarded. But how many? And where were they?

Mac looked out forward. He saw the top of a capped head moving toward the bow. Taking it as a cue, he crawled quickly to the chart table. He shrugged his Sten gun off his shoulder and into his hand. With his free arm, he rubbed his side to be sure his Browning was secure. He couldn't see any Germans through the top of the chart table, but that meant they couldn't see him either.

He looked to his right. The *Varsø*'s roof bounced in and out of sight. He looked to his left. Just empty sky. He listened carefully. Muffled voices, an occasional shout. No sign of alarm. Just caution and wonder. Mac had chosen his hiding place well. The bridge was the last place they'd check, and they would check it carefully.

Finally, Wingate could hear German voices clearly. They were near the broken windows of the bridge. One German wondered why there was no trapdoor to the hold in the deck. That was usual, as far as he knew. Another Nazi verbally shrugged. The eccentricities of Norwegian sea power were beyond him. Another voice wondered if the men were lying in ambush inside the bridge or belowdecks.

A voice, obviously used to command, answered. It ordered the men to surround the bridge on all sides. Then, when he gave the word, they would lob a grenade in a broken window. After that exploded, they would charge and hurl another grenade down the hold stairs.

Terrific plan, Wingate thought in a nearly manic state brought on by the sudden rush of adrenaline throughout his body. But he wasn't going to wait around to congratulate them. He waited just long enough to hear the Nazi's boots walking around both sides of the cabin before roaring into action.

Wingate was on his feet and out of his hiding place in a split second, bringing the Sten up in the same motion. What he had going for him was surprise, and he used it to the fullest degree.

He faced the rear of the bridge, but his torso and arms were twisted to the left. He tore open the nearest Nazi's head with two 9 mm bullets from the silenced barrel. The effect was impressive. To his fellows it must have looked as if the sailer's head had erupted of its own volition. Wingate didn't pause to admire his handiwork. He pivoted and raked the whole opposite wall with a line of lead. The three Germans who were taking up positions on that side were mowed down in a messy row.

Wingate turned again, to face the way he had shot originally. He saw the German commander hop back to the deck of the *Varsø* while pushing a few more underlings toward the bridge. The first underling ran forward. Wingate shot him full in the face as he slammed against the opposite door. The second man ran off to the side as Mac hurled the door open. A third man slipped around to the other side of the bridge.

The third man crouched and took aim just as Wingate's bullets ploughed into the second man's side. He fell forward across the deck as Mac turned and emptied the last of his magazine over the head of the third man. He kept his finger tight on the trigger until the click of the firing pin in the empty chamber was audible to all.

It worked. If not perfectly, then effectively. Rather than trying to shoot him immediately, the third man turned to call to his commander. In that moment, Wingate swung the Sten onto his back again, slammed both feet onto the deck, and dove right over the side, headfirst.

The Nazi commander screamed for the third man to prevent Wingate's escape, while starting to jump back onto the Allied trawler. The third man, not wanting to take up any more of his superior's precious time, slammed open the door nearest him rather than running around the bridge to get to the other side. He hurled himself forward, hardly feeling the rope that pressed into the ankle of his boot.

He didn't hear anything. The ring-pin clicked out of the detonator belowdecks. Then the C-2 exploded. Then the engine exploded. The double detonation tore the boat in half, then into many other pieces.

First the hold blew out and down, spreading kindling across the waves. Then the cabins and bridge blew up in a fiery tornado of yellow, red, and orange. The yellow and orange was the flame. The red was the blood.

All the Nazis on board were torn apart and spun out in all directions. The German commander, in the air halfway between his ship and the other, was shot backward onto the *Varsø*, slamming headfirst onto the deck, bouncing the rest of the way, and spinning into the ocean from the other side.

Wingate didn't see any of it. He let the weight of the Sten and the Browning pull him down, while he was diving as straight and kicking as hard as he could. Even so, the shock wave was enough to nearly knock him out. Since he was expecting it, however, he held on enough to kick his way back to the surface. Rubble and little patches of still burning fuel surrounded him. He looked around for any sign of the others. He saw them a football field or so away—six bobbing heads on a rolling sea.

He looked in the other direction. Through the smoking wreckage of what was once a fishing trawler, Wingate saw the Norwegian captain standing on the deck of his ship, a P-38 automatic pistol clutched in one hand.

As Mac watched, the Norwegian stuck the weapon in his waistband, cupped his hands around his mouth, and shouted in Riksmaal, "Are you all right?"

"*Ja, ja!*" Wingate shouted back, waving him on.

The *Varsø*, still seaworthy despite the explosion, trudged through the remains of the trawler toward Mac. The Norwegian captain helped him to board.

"SOE?" the Norwegian asked.

Wingate shook off a little of the water, pulled his Sten off his back, and made a motion with his hand that said "sort of."

"MILORG?" Mac asked back.

The Norwegian led Wingate back to the ship's control room, making the same "sort of" motion. Mac smiled and nodded. At least they both knew where they now stood.

"*Takk,*" Mac said, meaning "thanks."

"*S'goo!*" the Norse captain replied, meaning "you're welcome, here you are, may I help you, and make yourself at home." Wingate could identify with all four meanings.

Making himself at home inside the *Varsø*'s bridge was made a little difficult by the two German corpses that lay there, bleeding on the wooden floor. The Norwegian motioned at them, asking, "*Voer sa god . . .?*" He was wondering if Mac would "be so good" as to rid the cabin of the bodies. Mac nodded again as the Norse captain headed the ship in the survivors' direction. As Wingate dragged the pair out and dumped them overboard, he understood why the Norwegian had been holding the gun after the explosion. The man had taken the opportunity to rid himself of all his unwanted sailors.

Mac returned to the bloody bridge, introducing himself as he entered.

"Ah, Captain Wingate," said the Norwegian. "I am Lars Harald. I was forced to pilot this group from North Cape to Trondheim. I am sorry we crossed paths, but . . ." He shrugged as if saying, "What can you do?"

Mac commiserated with him. Norway had been hard hit by the Nazis when the war started. They had attacked early in April 1940. In twenty-five days, southern Norway gave in. A month later the whole country was in Hitler's hands. The Norwegians did what they could, but their government was woefully unprepared and there just weren't enough soldiers. Even so, it seemed as if the Nazis were willing to pay any price for the conquest. As it was, the Norse lost only 1,335 men as compared to the 5,636 Germans who died and the thirteen battleships they lost.

Harald kept an eye on the treading commandos. But a small shape coming from offshore caught Wingate's attention. As he watched, it crept out of the mist and took shape as another fishing vessel. As the *Varsø* neared the commandos, Mac tapped Lars on the shoulder and pointed.

"Ah," said the Norwegian, "MILORG." He nodded optimistically at Wingate, then want back to the delicate task of approaching the swimming men.

As the last man was dragged out of the water, the approaching ship was gaining ground. Mac could see the word "*Varfeinal*" on the front of its bridge. Then he felt a heavy hand on his shoulder, made all the more heavy by the sodden coat sleeve that surrounded it. He turned, expecting to see exactly who he did. Colonel David Walters, back from Davy Jones's locker.

"Congratulations," the Englishman said flatly. Wingate couldn't be sure whether he was being blusteringly honest or craftily sarcastic. "You nailed the Jerries, but now we're without a ship. Do you have any idea about how we might get back to Shetland?"

Wingate shrugged the hand off his shoulder. "I don't even know what the mission is yet," he said pointedly. "How should I know how to return from it, let alone complete it?"

Walters looked down at the rapidly growing puddle that was collecting around his feet. "In the future," he said precisely, "you may wish that you had gone down with my ship."

Wingate's attitude took a 180-degree turn. They were no longer on Walters's turf. They were out in the field, where the colonel was more dependent on Wingate to stay alive than vice versa. Wingate just had to make sure Walters's stupidity didn't seal their fate. He wasn't a man to be hated. He was a man to be pitied. Wingate decided to treat him accordingly.

"Let's just be glad we survived that confrontation, sir," he said calmly. "Now you'd better get inside. You'll catch your death out here."

Walters stared at him, then nodded and walked away. Donald Neill sidled over to Mac as the rest of the men went below to warm up.

"Great going, Captain," he complimented Wingate effusively. "Even now I'm not sure how you pulled it off."

"I'm sure how," Wingate replied, concentrating on the second trawler. "I'm just not sure how well."

Neill looked in the direction that Wingate was gazing. "More trouble?" he wondered.

"Maybe," Wingate admitted. "But according to the Norwegian seaman, it's our underground contact."

"Talk about timing," the Canadian marveled. "They show up right after all the trouble. Just like the cops in a 'Captain Marvel' serial."

"Yeah," Mac drawled. "I was thinking about that myself."

Still musing, Mac went below to see if there were any dry clothes, Neill trailing behind. Thankfully for all, there were items for a full fishing crew of six, as well as some extra Nazi materials. Between the two sources, everyone was able to change and dry off. Mac sat in the hold with the other commandos tending to their wet weapons. He had just dried the Browning and put it back together when Colonel Walters and Tyler entered in the company of another man.

"Captain Wingate," the Englishman called. Mac looked up, but Walters said no more until the American had risen and approached the trio. "Captain," he repeated, "this is Captain Einar Sørum of the Militoer Organisajonen."

"Captain," Einar said, putting his hand out. Wingate took it and they shook. Sørum was pretty much what one might expect a normal Norwegian male to look like. He was blond, ruddy-faced, of medium height and of a solid musculature that hard work and a harsh environment combined to create.

"It seems," Walters continued dryly, "that your Colonel Erikson warned MILORG of your coming." The Englishman hit the word "warned" a little too strongly for Wingate's taste, but he refused to be baited at this point in the game. "In effect," Walters went on, "he told them that since you knew the lingo, it wouldn't be necessary for us to be met by a MILORG who knew English."

Well, bless Erikson's hard little heart, Wingate thought. Even from across the ocean, the Norwegian colonel had been able to pull a plum from the humble pie. Mac positively beamed at the MILORG agent, his handshake increasing in strength. Einar responded, smiling wider as well. The Norwegian looked at Walters, then rattled off an old saying for Wingate to translate.

"He says he knows a little English," Mac informed the other colonels, "but nothing in depth. But he wants you to know an old saying from the *Havamal,* their book of truths. Namely, 'Everyone in this country speaks four languages and three of them are Norwegian.' "

Tyler looked at Walters. Walters looked at Tyler, then back at Wingate. "I don't understand," he said. "What does that mean?"

Wingate didn't feel like explaining the various dialects. "It doesn't have to mean anything," he answered. "It's just from the book of truths."

Walters nodded as if he understood. Wingate was hard-pressed not to roll his eyes. Instead he turned back to Sørum.

"Let's get to work," he said. The Norwegian nodded and motioned that Wingate should follow him. "Hold tight,"

Mac called back to the commandos as he left. "We'll be back as soon as we know what's what." The men nodded listlessly. The last thing Mac saw before going on deck was Neill gingerly taking a pack of cigars out of his wet jacket and laying them separately on the floor to dry.

Back on the bridge, Harald was in the company of at least eight other resistance fighters. They were of varying heights, but Mac couldn't make out their features because of the cowls they wore over their clothes. Mac felt like he had stumbled onto a monks' vacation cruise.

"We cannot take any chances," Sørum explained in Norse. "It is important that you recognize me, but the fewer the men you know, the fewer you can identify under torture."

Wingate looked at the other captain. Einar spoke as if torture were a foregone conclusion. "If I'm captured," Wingate reminded him.

"*Ja*, of course," Sørum agreed. "If you are captured."

"Where do we go from here?" Wingate wanted to know.

"We must get you ashore and to safety," Sørum informed him. "Then we must wait."

"Wait? Wait for what?"

"For word," Sørum said cryptically.

"Word of what?" Wingate pressed on.

"Word that we can proceed," Sørum answered, as if his reply were perfectly obvious.

Wingate was reluctant, but still he decided to press the conversation to its natural conclusion. "Proceed to what?" he said, steeling himself for the answer.

"Proceed to do the job you were sent to do," Sørum concluded simply.

The circle was complete. Mac was right back where he started. He turned to look at Colonel Walters who stood among the cowled MILORGS like a Pope among underlings. Even without knowing what the two captains had been talking about, the Englishman smiled cannily. That sort of smug expression was primary in the Britisher's character.

Wingate turned back to Captain Sørum, the effort of the 'Shetland Bus' trip finally reaching the reaction centers of his brain. He was suddenly very, very tired.

"All right," he said. "Let's get going, then."

"Very good," Sørum answered. "You and your men will

come with us on the *Varfeinal*. Lars!'' he suddenly called. The captain of the *Varsø* quickly approached.

"*Ja*?"

"It is too dangerous for you to return home," Sørum decreed. "Whether you can make a valid excuse or not, the Nazis will blame you for the disaster out here today. Better that you should disappear along with the Germans. Maybe they will think it was a sea accident, *ikkesant*?"

The Norwegian captain had ended his statement with the Norse phrase meaning, "Is it not so?" It was obvious to Wingate that Harald did not think it was so. The reluctance on his face was evident.

"Do not worry," Sørum assured him. "It is more important that you do as I bid. We will destroy the boat and you will accompany some men over the mountains. You will be safe once you arrive. Understand?"

"*Ja*," Harald muttered, "but . . ."

"Do not worry," Sørum soothed. "Go now. Onto the other boat."

His face creased into lines of worry, Lars Harald joined a few cowled resistance fighters and left the *Varsø* bridge. Captain Sørum turned back to Wingate. Before he could continue, the American spoke up.

"I'll go get the others."

"Very good," the Norwegian commander said.

Wingate made his way across the cabin, keeping a careful watch on the adjoining vessel. Looking through the various windows, he saw Lars Harald make the transition, followed by the disguised MILORG agents.

The American had not liked the uncomfortable strangeness of the conversation between Sørum and Harald. There was something unspoken there. Something both were aware of, but didn't want Mac to know about. Harald's actions on the deck of the *Varfeinal* bore out Wingate's curiosity. Just as he was about to disappear into the bridge house, one of the cowled men handed Lars something. Something small, but tangible nevertheless. It could have been a message. It could have been some microfilm. It could have a cigarette.

Wingate wasn't sure, but he didn't like it. He liked it even less when he glanced around and saw Colonel Walters staring right at him. Wingate wasn't sure if the Englishman had seen

63

the handoff or was just staring at him. Either way, it made him uneasy. The uneasiness turned to a certain dread when, once more, the Britisher flashed him that empty, insidious death's-head smile.

CHAPTER 4

Trondheim was in the Twilight Zone for more reasons than one. First of all, it was September. Summer, with its riot of colorful flora and its "midnight sun," had ended. The horribly dark, depressing winter of November had not yet come. So Norway hung in the pale purgatory between seasons, when the fjord mist filled the streets and the pine trees dripped white, misty shrouds. Night came early in September, but unlike the Norwegian winter, it did not stay all day.

Secondly, it was 1943. It was the third year of German occupation. And it wasn't a pleasant one for either side. The manic-depressive seasons, the almost continual cold, and the lack of any battle action brought out the worst in the Nazis. The Norwegians trudged down the slush-filled streets as quietly as the mist itself, trying not to attract the attention of the Germans, who swarmed the streets like flies in the summer and held sway like termites inside for the winter.

Although the Nazi presence did much to diminish the country's beauty, the "Land of the Generous Sea" had much to be admired. And Mac had plenty of time to admire it. The *Varfeinal* coursed north, into the Arctic Circle region, for two days. In that time, no Norwegian talked to him. Instead, he studied his surroundings. The coast was beautiful in a rugged sort of way. And all around, everything was enveloped by the mist made from the water of the ocean and the density of the cloud-wrapped sky.

The trawler finally stopped just west of North Cape, in a tiny inlet seemingly made up of millions of sea-smoothed rocks. Almost as soon as they had set foot on somewhat solid ground, the cowled MILORGs led them into a thick of pine trees and close to straight up. Each of the Allied commandos had to navigate painfully from one tree trunk to the next, using the wood as the rungs of a ladder. The Norwegians, naturally, were a lot better at climbing, and often had to slow so Wingate and company could catch up.

They stopped several hours later on a ledge in a clearing overlooking the expanse they had just traveled. The view was magnificent. Down below them was Alten in miniature, complete with a quaint little town made up of cottagelike structures, lovely green fields, patches of darker green forest, and beyond all of it, the bay—just a small section of the Barents Sea. It was rich, marble blue with streaks of foamy white cut into it. And rising around it were more mountains, made up of the same rocky olive as the one they were standing on.

"Very good," said Einar Sørum, hardly breathing heavily. "I must leave you here for the moment. I have pressing matters elsewhere. The others will be known to you with code names."

Mac was not winded enough so he was unable to talk. But he was winded enough not to want to try. He accepted Sørum's declaration by nodding. There was very little he could do about it even if he thought it was a bad idea. And he had no evidence that it was.

"Follow Snow Queen," the Norwegian captain said, pointing at a cowled figure to Wingate's right. Mac turned to see just another shapeless resistance fighter in monk's clothing. "We will meet again soon," Sørum promised, turning toward Harald and several others. They marched off into another section of the woods.

"*Goddag*," Wingate said after him, saying the simple Norwegian "good day." The new MILORG leader motioned for everyone to follow. Wingate nodded at the commandos and moved after the already striding figure, walking off in the direction opposite Sørum's.

They continued walking for many minutes more, everyone putting one foot in front of the other in perfect silence. The sudden dunking Wingate had given the commandos and his superiors a couple days earlier was at odds with the expectations of everybody but Wingate. It threw off their equilibrium, so now they were anxious to get to their destination. They wanted to relax and do what Sørum had said. Wait. Just wait.

Wingate's battle sense was alert the moment anything unusual happened. So when the cowled leader leaned over to whisper in another's ear, Mac concentrated on it. He wasn't taken by surprise when the MILORG who had been whispered to stopped short and silently motioned for everyone else to do the same.

The MILORG who had halted quickly approached Mac. "Snow Queen says you should be on guard. This is the most dangerous section of our trek."

Mac looked around. The area looked no different from the wood they had been marching through for quite some time. But on second glance, he noted a sparseness of foliage in front of them to the left, where the ground made a notable dip. In between the evergreens there, he saw something dark, something brown and deep blue. Studying it further, he waved the other English-speaking soldiers to him.

"Why have we stopped?" Walters demanded, some of his bluster returning to him.

"Be on guard," Wingate suggested. "We may run into trouble." The group responded by unslinging their weapons. Tyler moved a little closer to Walters, holding up his M3 as protection.

Wingate nodded at the Norwegian who had spoken to him. That agent went to the one called Snow Queen. Snow Queen waved the small group forward. In a few seconds and with just a few more steps, Wingate could see fully what he had just glimpsed before. On the crest of a hill on the other side of a dip in the ground was a strikingly angular Nordic pagoda.

The six-tiered structure, made up of sharp gables that rose, ever smaller, off the center of each preceeding it, lay atop a square stone fence that reached all the way around it. At the very tips of the gables were sculptures of angry dragons, mythical heads that resembled Viking figureheads.

At the bottom of the dip that led to the structure was the remnant of a path. Although overgrown and broken, it was still a walkway. It was little wonder Snow Queen had sent out a warning. During their entire trip after landing, the pagoda and the path were the first signs of humanity.

Mac quickened his step toward Snow Queen's motionless figure. He was intercepted by the agent who had spoken to him before.

67

"Snow Queen is thinking," he explained. "There should be no disturbance."

"Can't we go around it?" Wingate suggested. Snow Queen must have heard him, for the agent's head shook "no."

"We would lose too much time and put ourselves in certain danger," Snow Queen's seeming assistant said. "We must pass by, but we must take care."

"What's the delay?" an English-accented voice said behind Wingate. The captain spun toward Walters, his right hand up in a casual "stop" signal.

"Just take it easy, Colonel," he said. "There's a possibility of an ambush inside that place."

"Nonsense!" retorted the Britisher. "Who is going to use an ancient, out-of-the-way church as an ambush? Why, it is obvious that no one has traversed this path in weeks! We have nothing to fear and no reason to pause."

"Don't you think . . . ." Wingate began.

"Come on, Tyler," Walters interrupted, brushing by the captain and walking between Snow Queen and the other MILORG member. The two Norwegians reacted with surprise as they saw the Allied colonels go by. Wingate made no move to prevent the pair from going out in the open. Breaker moved forward, but Wingate put out his arm to stop the Australian.

"Forget the heroics," he said quietly. "If you're not right, they'll court-martial you for manhandling them. If you are right, well, then they're doing us all a favor. If somebody shoots them, they will have been asking for it and then we'll know for sure there's an ambush."

The MILORGs must have been thinking the same way, for once the colonels had passed, none of the cowled figures made a move. Quickly, Wingate scanned the area around the pagoda. Below the stone wall was a large rock covered with ferns. Nearby were some thin trees and heavy, moss-covered tree roots.

Walters and Tyler strode right out in front of this, stopped, looked around, and turned back toward the waiting MILORGs. The possibility of Walters doing what he did entered Wingate's mind a second before the colonel did it. As soon as Walters's arm started to rise, Wingate was moving. Out of the corner of his eye, he saw Snow Queen doing the same.

Only, while he was racing toward the bottom of the rock, the MILORG agent was running directly at Walters.

The English colonel was going to wave the others ahead. Essentially, he was going to silently announce to whomever might be around that there were others where he came from. Neither Wingate nor Snow Queen wanted to chance somebody strafing the wood with high-powered machine gun bullets, grenades, or mortar fire. If something like that happened and they were caught on the other side of the path, the crew would either have to retreat or risk being pinned down and killed.

Wingate moved because he trusted the Norwegians to know their own country and what they were up against. If it turned out that no one was lying in wait in the pagoda, then all Wingate would have done was run across the road. No shame in that.

The American sped past Walters a split second before Snow Queen was able to reach him. Just before the MILORG agent bowled him over, the shooting started.

The forest was suddenly filled with the thudding crackle of 7.92 mm shells pumped out of the pagoda's third level. Wingate saw the telltale crackle of fire just before he threw himself forward, rolled, and wound up against the rock hill below the stone wall. He turned his head to see Snow Queen and Tyler dragging Walters toward him, the American colonel using one hand to lay down a protecting fire with his M3.

Mac couldn't do any good with his Sten from this angle, but the men among the trees were helping as well as they could, given the distance and the protection the pagoda afforded the snipers.

Walters was dropped by Snow Queen a few feet away from Mac. Then the Norwegian resistance fighter tumbled over to Wingate, coming up in a crouch after a perfectly executed somersault. For some reason the MILORG agent couldn't crouch completely. After Snow Queen pulled aside one side of the monkish garment, Mac could see why. In a special harness across the front, the agent had a Suomi submachine gun, model 1931.

Snow Queen wrenched out the weapon, cocking it behind the rear cap of the receiver. Wingate was pleased by its appearance. It gave them a better chance of getting to the snipers with no bodily parts missing. As he watched, Snow

Queen reached down along one leg and pulled out a 71-round drum from another special holster. The agent slammed it home, then rose to a sitting position.

"Cover me," the agent said in Norwegian. Wingate was initially surprised by the light timbre of the voice, but he had no time to ruminate on it. Snow Queen was up and scrambling over the rocks toward the stone wall.

Wingate unconsciously reached inside his jacket for one of his four grenades until he realized that they had gone down with the Allied ship. Or up with the C-2 explosion, as the case may be. Instead, he rolled out from cover, shouting for his men to do the same. He came up on one knee facing the pagoda, his Sten aimed at the third level.

He emptied his rounds, hearing the forest behind him erupt with sound. As the Sten clicked on an empty chamber, he threw the weapon down and pulled out his Browning. He was up and running, glancing at both the third level and the cover fire behind him.

The sight was inspiring. Each commando had broken cover and was blasting away with his gun as the other MILORGs had each magically produced another Suomi, all with 50-round boxes or 71-round drums. And that weapon smashed out a stunning 900 rounds per minute. The swarm of lead it produced was phenomenal. Actual holes the size of cannonballs appeared in the wall of the pagoda. The flashing of the snipers' machine gun stopped.

Wingate jumped up the rock hill and vaulted over the stone wall in time to see Snow Queen kick open the two front doors. The American sped after the agent, holding his automatic at the ready.

Snow Queen ran in, dotting the ceiling with bullets by simply holding the Suomi up and pulling the trigger without looking. Instead the agent was seeking out a vantage point to plug the snipers without getting plugged back. Wingate slowed just inside the pagoda doors to search out the ambushers. He spied them almost immediately, dragging a heavy machine gun on a tripod across a wooden catwalk with banisters that stretched across to balconies on both the front and back walls.

Wingate picked up speed, changed direction, and ran until he could see one of the two men trying to pull the weapon to a safe place. They were not Nazis. At least they were not in Nazi uniforms.

He brought his Browning up and blasted away at the retreating pair. His 9 mm bullets chipped away at the wood all around them, but didn't touch the snipers. It was enough, however, to panic the man behind the gun. Without thinking, he pivoted the barrel in Wingate's direction and pulled the trigger.

The sharp, thick bullets ripped through the floorboards at Wingate's feet, and as he threw himself aside, the lead blasted out the side wall. Most of the action happened behind the gun. Since the tripod wasn't secure on a flat surface, the machine gun bucked like an enraged bull, catching the sniper in the chest, then pushing up under his chin. His shirt was ripped open by the force, a quarter-inch gouge was ripped into the flesh of his chest, and his jaw was broken by the concussion.

The wounded sniper was vaulted over the side of the catwalk's banister to fall almost two stories to the pagoda floor. He spun lazily, fell on his side, bounced, and landed heavily on his back, spread-eagled. Wingate wasn't taking any chances. He quickly shot the body in the head.

He returned his attention to the second man just as the surviving sniper dropped the machine gun and ran as fast as he could toward the back wall. Snow Queen waited until the sniper was almost parallel to the barrel of the Suomi, then opened fire. The protecting banister was cut away by the lead, which then punched into the second sniper's body. They made him dance for a moment, then threw him off the catwalk to follow his partner down to the wooden floor.

Snow Queen didn't need to make sure of the second man's demise. Lowering the smoking Suomi, the agent silently walked past Wingate and back outside. The American put his gun back in its holster and followed.

No one was lazing around outside either. The entire group of Allies and MILORG agents were collected in front of the pagoda's double doors. Wingate saw Walters's sleeve and right pant leg ripped open. A makeshift bandage had been wrapped around his upper arm, but his now revealed leg showed only a thick scrape and a thin scratch. The machine gun bullets must have just missed him as Snow Queen had knocked him over. Wingate held little doubt that had the agent not intervened, the bullets would have ripped Walters open like so much newspaper.

71

Walters didn't say anything, just stared at Wingate, not smiling this time. Wingate remained silent as well, just imperceptibly shaking his head as he followed the MILORGs, who were already marching behind the pagoda and into the forest beyond. The commandos followed the captain, with the two colonels bringing up the rear.

Silence reigned for a while longer while Wingate found himself walking abreast of Snow Queen's aide. The cowled agent looked at Mac, revealing a young-looking mouth and chin with a few days' stubble.

"Snow Queen wants to thank you for your help," he said in Norwegian. "You are a good shot."

"Can't Snow Queen speak for himself?" Mac replied irritably.

The aide ignored what Mac had said. "Snow Queen knew snipers used the Nordic pagoda. Snow Queen had seen countrymen die there before."

"Those weren't Germans" Wingate said, taking another tack.

"No," the MILORG said gravely. "They were Nasjonal Samling members. Quislings." The aide said the word with disgust. "Norwegians, but traitors still. They deserve to die."

Wingate reacted to the MILORG's passion with indifference. Anyone who shot at him deserved to die. Outside of the basic concept of defeating Hitler, Wingate didn't think of war as a cause to die for. He thought of it as a cause to kill for. And the plain practicality of killing is that one had to be alive to do it.

He agreed with Patton. The object, the great general had said, is not to die for your country, but to make the other poor, dumb bastard die for his. As long as Allied Command kept shoving bombs and guns into his hands, it was a point of view Wingate would subscribe to.

The group moved on through forest that was denser than before. Just as Wingate was beginning to feel that he would never see civilization again, a small hillside village appeared. It was made up of what the Norse called *goattes*, small teepeelike tents and a long *stabbur*, or barrackslike barn. Wingate noted a gray shale mountain rising above the tiny town and a winding narrow road that ran down into a cloud-covered valley below. The serenity of the place was complete. There were small fields of grain dotting the outskirts, and various animals, like goats and sheep, wandering around. But the American saw no other people but the hooded MILORGs as they entered the barn building.

Inside the wooden structure were several plain, two-wheeled carts made to be pulled by one man each. On top of these devices were plain, peasant garments. Snow Queen seemingly ignored and moved past these things, disappearing out the other side of the *stabbur*. Wingate was about to follow, when the aide stopped him.

"You must stay," he said. "Snow Queen will prepare the way." He explained that they couldn't chance walking into the town of Alten as they were. They couldn't risk a Nazi spying them. So several MILORG agents would accompany them disguised as simple merchants.

"You." The aide pointed at Neill. "And you," he said to Wingate, "will also help. Please change now."

Walters and Sumner were put atop one cart, Tyler and Baker were on another. Biggins had one all to himself. Green tarps were put over them and secured with boxes placed strategically so the cart top had the proper look. Mac and Neill changed for the third time, into the common street garb of gray pants and rubber boots, light blue shirt, drab blue raincoats, and a simple gray cap.

The aide took off his monk habit to reveal a young, dark-haired Norwegian. Another MILORG threw back his cowl to reveal an older, plainer-looking man.

"He will act as my father," the aide explained, kicking off the garment. Beneath the garments, both wore generally what the Allies had changed into. "You will be my brother," he told Wingate, "and he, the white-haired man, my . . . uncle."

Wingate translated for Neill, adding, "His deaf and, if you know what's good for you, dumb uncle." The Canadian got the message.

"Do not stop for anything," the aide said, shrugging on his own thin, knee-length coat. "We will take care of everything." Without another word, the MILORG "father" took the Walters and Sumner cart and moved out of the barn. Wingate grabbed the Tyler and Baker one, leaving Neill to haul Biggins. He trusted Sumner to quell any complaints about a rough ride Walters might make and he trusted Neill to be powerful enough to handle Breaker's girth.

The cart convoy moved down an unsurprisingly steep, inordinately curved road. It seemed as if they were making a U-turn every two hundred yards. They would walk southwest, then southeast, then southwest again, southeast, then straight down south, then, strangely, moving down still but in the opposite direction they had been traveling before. Wingate felt like a marble bouncing off outcroppings along a bottomless pit.

Even more surprising was that the road was smooth and seemingly unaffected by the generally inclement weather and the sharp, twisting turns. "How is a road like this possible?" Neill asked in honest amazement.

The aide took a moment to look back at the Canadian. When Wingate translated, the man smiled. "No one is sure," he answered whimsically. "We attribute the engineering feat to the mountain trolls."

Wingate translated back. "Mountain trolls," Neill repeated. "Right."

"No more talk!" the MILORG father said sharply. Neill needed no translation.

The road with its snaking curves was one thing, but the eeriest part of the trip was dropping down into the solid, puffy white blanket of mist that hung over the valley. All the men could do was look at their feet to be sure they were still on the path, and listen carefully to the creeking wheels of the other carts nearby.

For a few minutes, that creaking was drowned out by the sounds of rushing water, but then they dipped under the mist and saw a few cottages on one side of the road. Although solid and well maintained in the more mountainous regions, the road changed from stone to dirt as soon as it reached the first dwelling's foundation. It may act as a boundary line, Wingate thought.

The group of cart pullers never touched the dirt way, however. As soon as the simple yellow house with the two chimneys grew near, the aide pulled his cart off the road and trotted to a cellar entrance at the side of the place. Wingate came up as the MILORG men pulled the doors open. There was a board laid across the steps downward to facilitate the carts. The MILORG son and father lowered theirs quickly, then came back to help both Wingate and Neill with theirs.

74

As they closed the doors and locked them from the inside, Wingate took in the new surroundings. The small size of the house above them was misleading. The cellar was cavernous and lit by candles positioned in various places on the floor. The only interruption between the stones of the walls were rugged wooden support beams secured in the hard, cold dirt of the floor and the heavy beams of the ceiling.

The MILORG aide threw off the tarps and waved everyone up. He then picked up a candle and walked quickly away. Mac followed, expecting to see another door appear from the gloom. Instead the Norwegian disappeared into a tunnel opening in the opposite wall. He turned a corner and the light seemed to go out. The American hastily made the turn himself to see the dim, flickering light appear before him again. He heard the footsteps of the others behind him. He hoped no one was claustrophobic. If any of them were, at least he didn't hear about it.

They continued down the now straight tunnel until Mac could feel moisture around his shoes. The sloshing was just momentary, then the way inclined upward. Finally the way ended in front of a dirt-lined door. The aide unlatched it and pulled it back. He motioned for Wingate to follow in silence. The American turned and made the same movement, which was repeated down the line. The MILORG father brought up the rear, closing the door behind him with nary a whisper.

The nine men then traversed an even narrower passage, made bearable only by the golden light that streamed in on one side of the slatted, wooden walls. As he went, Wingate glanced through these narrow cracks, seeing glimpses of carpentry and furniture. He realized that they were inside the walls of a house, following a secret passage that lay between the walls of the inside room and the outside wall.

The passage ended at a bedroom. The aide slid open a simple panel, moved some hanging curtains aside, and waved the men past him.

It was a pretty grim place, cheered only by a comfortable-looking bed and some antique furniture. Otherwise the walls were dank stone and drab wood, the ceiling was low, and the floor uneven. A fireplace flickered to one side.

The men spread out, trying to find a little space in the wide room, which seemed smaller than it actually was. The low ceiling and the thick curtains and carpets that hung on the walls created that effect. The floor, too, was strewn with thick rugs, overlapping to muffle the hardest of footfalls. Walters moved unerringly over to the bed, holding his arm, groaning, and lying down before anyone else could lay claim to it.

"This is below ground," the aide said, trying to explain the situation. "There is more than one room. Enough for you all. You will be safe here. Snow Queen has seen to it."

"Where is Snow Queen?" Wingate wondered.

As before, the aide ignored any attempts to find out more about the resistance fighter. "You will wait here."

"I would like to thank Snow Queen personally," Wingate pressed.

"You will wait," the aide repeated, turning.

Before anything else could happen, a hooded MILORG swept into the room from the other side. The agent swept aside some of the curtains, revealing an entrance to another room.

"All went well?" the agent asked in a soft voice Wingate recognized as that of Snow Queen. The aide nodded. "*God*," Snow Queen said, the Norse word for "good." The aide nodded again and left the room by the secret passageway.

"*S'goo!*" Snow Queen told everyone. "The man who speaks our language, come with me. We must talk."

Wingate moved forward, a strange thought taking shape in his mind. He watched Snow Queen's figure carefully as he translated for the others. "Check the layout. See if there are any other exits."

"Wingate," Walters said from the bed, "where are you going?"

"Snow Queen wants to talk with me."

"I should be included in this!"

"Sorry, sir, there's nothing I can do," Wingate said with satisfaction. "You told me yourself; I'm the head of the mission and am at the service of MILORG."

"Wingate! . . ."

"Just rest, sir," Wingate advised as he followed Snow Queen between the curtains. "Keep your strength up."

Wingate watched Snow Queen move ahead of him. The cowled agent was taller than Mac by an inch and moved with the fluid assurance of a dancer. The monks' garment still disguised the shape, but Wingate noticed the hands were encased in thick gloves. But not thick enough to prevent the forefinger from wrapping around the trigger of a Suomi.

They moved silently up another passage to another set of curtains. The room inside was the final clue to the theory Wingate had been working on. So he wasn't surprised when Snow Queen threw back the cowl.

Snow Queen was a woman.

The only thing that surprised Wingate was that she was a beautiful woman. A truly strong, stunning female who looked as if she had Amazonian blood mixed in her Nordic heritage. First, there was the height. If she wasn't six feet tall, she was mighty close. Her whitish-blond hair fell down to her neck, where it rolled atop both shoulders. Just like the aide, she was wearing drab, simple clothes beneath the burnous, but it couldn't completely hide her solid, attractive shape. She wore no makeup, but the cold weather gave her color. The well-circulating Norse blood reddened her high cheeks and thin lips. Her nose too was thin, but not sharp, and her eyes were blue beneath blond brows and lashes.

The brows narrowed a bit as she examined Wingate's placid expression. She was slightly disappointed she had not taken him aback. "I am Kirsten," she said, holding out her hand.

The fingers were long, the palm was solid, the nails were short, and the entire hand was somewhere between the description of shapely and strong. Mac shook her hand. She must have prided herself on her grip, because she squeezed hard and just once.

"I am Wingate," he answered. "And I love you."

Her laugh was short, but honest. It was he who took her by surprise and it broke the ice. Mac had long ago lost the illusion that war was not for women. Women made some of the best fighters. They were cunning, thorough, vindictive, and best of all, not readily suspected. Certainly very few of them were in uniform, and none of those were on the front line aiming a gun. But those battles managed to touch everyone, even innocent women. And Wingate had more respect for those who prepared themselves for it than those who let themselves be mowed down.

This girl, certainly, had proved herself to be a major mower, rather than a victim. She moved around the relatively sumptuous bedroom, getting rid of the monk trappings as she went. Mac stood in place, taking in the view. The bed took up the center portion of the room. It was canopied, and decked out in colors of crimson. Beyond that was a rich-looking bureau, with scattered cosmetics and a large, circular mirror, gilt around the designed edges. On the side of the bed where Mac was standing was a plush easy chair in blue with deep purple arm covers. Next to that was a working fireplace.

There was really only one logical explanation for such opulence in such a cold, small, unassuming town. Adding that opulence to the fact that Kirsten could come and go as she pleased, there was no doubt in Wingate's mind as to where they were hiding.

"You acted well at the pagoda," she said, not looking at him as she pulled off the peasant pants. She was wearing dark, warm, wooly tights underneath. They covered her lower body, but sharply delineated her muscular, shapely legs. "You moved quickly and shot straight. I can trust you."

She seemed to be testing his trustworthiness again, because as he watched, she unselfconsciously took off her shirt, exposing the top half of the wooly underwear. Her breasts were covered, but easily discernable. She seemed totally unconcerned by it. Wingate watched, but at no time did she even so much as glance at him for a reaction.

It was too bad in a way, he thought. He'd be happy to give her one. The only things that were bare were her head, hands, feet, and just a thin sliver of flesh that appeared between the bottom of the shirt and the top of the tights. In the light and warmth of the fire, the effect was enormously sexy.

"Thank you," he said, acknowledging her compliment. "Where are the other girls?"

She stood up straight, holding a multicolored wool skirt in her hands. She decided to answer directly, without any digressing banter. "They are not here yet," she said, stepping into the skirt. "They come this evening. After their farm work."

Mac raised his eyebrows. This time he was surprised. "Do their parents know they come here?"

"They have no parents," Kirsten said, pulling on a white shirt with puffy sleeves. "They are war orphans like me.

Some were killed in the first attack, some . . ." She paused, paying close attention to the tiny, delicate buttons she was attaching. "Some later," she finished. "By others."

She turned back to the American as she pulled on a green vest which she tied over the white shirt. "I came here after my parents were murdered by the Germans. It was the only way I could avoid going to the breeding camps. The ranking officers promised to keep me safe if I gave them personal pleasure. They said it was a shame to waste me on strangers."

Wingate was a trifle incredulous. "And still they trust you?"

She walked right up to him, looking directly in his eyes. "Once they come in here, they forget about trust. They are so blinded by lust, they really don't care what I do. As long as I am here for them at night." She looked down at herself, knowing, but not really understanding, why. She had lived inside her body all her life. She found it incredible that her skin, her shape, her features, could make such fools of them, but she took full advantage of it.

"Traditional Valkyrie dress," she commented on her outfit. "It excites my captors even more."

"Captors?" Wingate responded. "Is there someone keeping you here? A madame?"

"There used to be," Kirsten said, moving over to the fireplace. "No more. She was reluctant to join the underground forces."

"Where did she go?"

"She finally did go underground," Kirsten explained, looking into the fire. "I killed her."

She waited for another reaction. Wingate gave her one. He sighed.

"You seem intent on shocking me," he said.

Kirsten looked at him, smiled suddenly, and shrugged. "Force of habit. I feel I must always prove that I am not just a woman."

"Not just a woman." Wingate was hit not by the oddness of the phrase, but by the aptness of the sentiment. When did he ever have to prove he was "not just a man"? He supposed that if he were locked in a room and used like meat night after night, he'd have the same inferiority complex no matter how good a fighter he was.

"You've proved it," he assured her, not feeling right about

79

his reply, but finding nothing else to say. "Now let's see if we can aid each other's cause. Why the cowls? Why the code names? Why all the mystery? We're allies."

"It is as Captain Sørum says. He is an officer of the Militoer. If he were seen by the enemy, he would be shot. Such a man needs no secret identity. I am an important double agent. My identity must be a closely guarded secret. Hence the 'Snow Queen.' Many of the other men don't even know my identity."

"What do you know of my mission?"

"Just what Einar says. That you must wait for word from him."

For the third time, Mac was back where he started from. All his attempts to discover his reason for arriving in Norway had been for naught. Either they didn't know or weren't talking. The mystery was made deeper by the various petty intrigues and the sudden violent dangers. He couldn't understand why such a blithering fool as Walters and such a well-meaning but inexperienced officer as Tyler were included on such a supposedly vital operation.

He didn't know what was going on, and that disturbed him deeply. It also set his suspicion on a fine edge. Something had been passed between Harald and Sørum on the trawler. Something had passed between Sørum and Kirsten. Something was definitely happening above and beyond the confines of conventional warfare, but no one was willing to let Mac in on it.

He looked again at the beautiful woman in the dress straight out of Norse folklore. She appeared to be a combination of innocence and experience, attractiveness and guile. And so far it looked like she was plopped down right in front of him. The question was, did she want to or was she ordered to? He was sure it was all an act, but to what purpose? To occupy him? To keep him unaware? To, pardon the expression, keep him off his feet?

Wingate decided it made no difference in the long run. She had gained his sympathy and impressed him with her looks, but neither emotion blinded him to rationality. It didn't look like she was a triple agent—the *Varsø* and its Nazi crew were about to leave when Walters showed, so the Germans weren't sicced on them. And the pagoda snipers, the Nasjonal Samling officers, certainly weren't too particular who they shot at. The violent dangers came with the territory, Wingate concluded, just as the curtains behind Kirsten's bed flew apart and the MILORG aide stumbled in breathlessly.

"Reprisal!" he cried. "They are going to attack the Harald farm!"

CHAPTER 5

"It is as I feared," Kirsten said, striding quickly up the tree-covered hillside. "They will take every opportunity to kill us."

"You have brought this on our heads!" the aide said stridently to Wingate.

"Quiet, Karl," Kirsten instructed.

"No, it is true," the aide panted, his shorter legs having a harder time of the hill. "If he had not killed the Germans, this would not have happened. They should not have come."

"They had to come," Kirsten said purposefully, "and it was not their fault. Now, be quiet!"

Karl clamped his mouth shut and slowed. He drifted behind, to where Baker was bringing up the rear. Both colonels were back at the whorehouse. "For reasons of security," Walters had proclaimed.

"Karl is anxious," Kirsten explained quietly to Mac, neither of them lessening their pace up the mountain. "There is a girl at the farm . . ."

"I understand," Wingate told her. He looked back at the commandos. They were, as usual, handling themselves professionally. All were still wearing their peasant outfits, keeping their weapons close to their chests. Some had extra magazines in their waistbands. Others had them strapped to their thighs. All their faces looked ready and almost eager for action.

"Are we near the farm?" Wingate asked, wanting to give his men plenty of warning.

"We are not going to the farm," Kirsten informed him. She did not elaborate, so Wingate did not press further.

Wherever she was going, she was leading them with purpose and speed. He trusted her to be a good soldier, especially after the pagoda attack.

Soon Wingate recognized their destination. Essentially they were retracing their steps to the hillside village. The one where they had found the carts and the change of clothes. Although she was circumventing the winding road, the rest of the environment was the same. Mac heard the same rushing of water and saw the same majestic, almost empty countryside, devoid of anything but nature's bounty.

As they neared the town, he saw smoke. As they came upon the *stabbur,* he saw the smoke coming from its chimney. He let Kirsten run right up to the barn door and swing it open. It slammed against the wooden wall, surprising all the MILORG men collected inside.

"Kirs . . . Snow Queen!" Captain Sørum shouted. "What are you doing here?"

"No more!" she shouted back, striding right up to the Norse leader. "It is the time for action!"

"Go back to town," Sørum shouted in return. "Immediately!"

Breaker Biggins leaned over to whisper in Wingate's ear. "What are they talking about, Captain?"

"I'm not sure, Breaker," Wingate whispered back. "And I understand the language!"

"You can't let them all just die," Kirsten pleaded. "You can't!"

"If they do not die," Sørum said solemnly, "then many more will. You know what will happen. This reprisal will be followed by another, and then another, until no Norwegian is left standing. The Quislings and the Nazis will kill us on the slightest provocation, real or imagined."

Wingate listened closely. It was the second time he heard a MILORG refer to Quislings. Every occupied country had its secret police, its fascists, it traitors sucking up to the Germans. And everywhere they had their own names. In Norway, it seemed, it was the Quislings.

"We will not die if we fight!" Kirsten raged. "We know this country. They do not. There are more of us than them."

"But more of them can come," the Norse captain intoned. "And they will continue to come. More and more every day if we do not stop inciting them." The MILORG officer began

83

to move around the bonfire in the circular pit, talking to the other men and Wingate as much as answering Kirsten. "Do you not remember Grini? Forty thousand of our people languish there."

"We could save them!" Kirsten pleaded.

"Do you not remember Bodø?" Sørum retorted with renewed strength. He walked right past the woman to approach Wingate himself. "The Wehrmacht went into the town and left only scorched earth." The Norwegian whirled around to assail the others. "Namsos! Steinkjer! All the others! Bombed! Burned! Destroyed utterly! We cannot let it continue."

There were grumbles of agreement from all but the English-speaking commandos and the desperate woman.

"No, we cannot!" she agreed. "The entire Harald commune will be killed if we don't stop it."

"It is too late," Sørum said sadly. "They cannot escape their fate. The Occupation heads have decreed they die because of the loss of the *Varsø*. Their deaths were certain from the moment Captain Wingate destroyed his ship."

"Do they have any proof their men were killed?" Wingate asked in Norwegian. "Did any one on shore see the explosion? Their men could have been lost in an accident. You said so yourself."

"That was for your benefit," Sørum admitted. "They do not need evidence. They will use the least excuse for a reprisal." He walked over to face Wingate again. "We launched two raids in Lofoten, above the Arctic Circle, in 1941. Two days later, dozens of the local fishermen were slaughtered. Seven months ago we destroyed a heavy water plant in Rjukan, near Oslo, only because the SOE demanded it as an absolute necessity. The next day every captured patriot in the city's Møllergata 19 prison was tortured and executed."

Wingate felt good and bad. He wasn't happy about all the Norse corpses and he didn't like the thought of being responsible for Harald's family being killed. But he felt sure of one thing. His mission here *was* of vital importance. Contrary to what Walters told him, it was not a minor diversion. Sørum had just told him so. If the Norse were willing to risk reprisal to pick them up and hide them, their job had to be at least as important as blowing up a heavy water plant.

Although Mac was now assured of his importance, it only deepened the mystery as to why no one was telling him what he should be doing. He was certainly the man for the job. He spoke both German and Norwegian. He was a trustworthy, dedicated demolitions expert. To top it all off, he had led multinational groups before. What was there about him that kept everybody's lips sealed? Was it his breath?

"So if some kraut trips and hits his head, your farmers and fishermen are going to be killed?" Mac answered him. "And you're going to stand by and watch the slaughter because you don't want to make anyone angry?"

"Captain Wingate," Sørum said, unflustered. "There are ten thousand Quislings. There are twenty thousand of us. But there is one important difference. We are not sadists. We are not torturers. We are not rapists."

"And what are you," Mac said solemnly, "if you just watch it happen? What are you called then? Voyeurs? Witnesses? Or accomplices?"

That did the trick. Sørum's flat feathers definitely got ruffled. He reacted a bit like Walters might in the same situation. His mouth worked, his fists clenched, and then he turned abruptly away. "We are patriots!" he yelled at the ceiling. "How dare you . . . ! How dare you!"

"Yes, patriots!" Kirsten almost spat, her eyes almost as bright as the fire. "And while you declare your patriotism, innocent women and children are being murdered!"

"Captain Sørum," Wingate said steadily, "I don't doubt your honor. I just want to make up for any problem I've caused."

"All right!" Sørum exploded. "Very well! Go! Do what you can to save the Harald commune."

Kirsten turned in radiant triumph, almost hopping back to Wingate. She stopped, putting her hands on the American's chest when the Norwegian spoke again.

"But you shall see," Sørum warned. "I have warned you. There will be a terrible price for others because of your action."

The Norse man and woman locked gazes. Both their faces were expressionless. Wingate took the time to prepare his men. "Hit and run, boys," he said. "Move in fast, salvage what you can, and get out. No heroics." He gripped one of Kirsten's elbows. "Lead them out," he told her. She dropped her gaze from Sørum, looked at Wingate, nodded, and did as he said. Wingate approached the motionless Norse captain.

"It isn't meaningless," the American told him, "no matter how much it seems that way. It's war. Those who die do so for a purpose. Those who are captured have no meaning unless they are rescued. If you want to face yourself after this is all over, get used to that. You won't regret what you've done. Only what you did not do."

He turned to follow Kirsten and the commandos. Sørum interrupted his exit. "Captain Wingate." Mac turned. "Our national motto is 'Yes, we love our country with fond devotion.' Everyone in this country feels that. Even Quisling has said it. We do what we have to for our country."

Wingate nodded. "I'll do what I have to for yours, too."

"Take care of her," Sørum called after him.

Mac turned at the door. "She has an identity to protect," he reminded the Norwegian. "You don't. Would you care to join us?" Mac's meaning was clear. He wanted Sørum to take Kirsten's place at the Harald commune.

"No," the man said, looking at the dirt between his feet. "I cannot."

"Remember what I said about regret," Wingate said and left.

The others were halfway out of town. Kirsten had communicated enough to start the men on their way. Wingate ran to catch up and then slowed to match pace with the girl. "When are they coming?" Mac asked, getting the important information first.

"Soon, though I think not yet," Kirsten said. She motioned toward the young Karl, who trotted on the other side of her. "My information only said that a group of soldiers would attack the farm in retribution sometime today. The Quislings usually respond very quickly to a decree like that."

"Now just who the hell are the Quislings?"

"The head of the Nasjonal Samlings is a man named Vidkun Quisling. He made a deal with Hitler even before the war started. Then, when the Reich was set to attack, he and his men did much to weaken our resistance. Finally when our king, Haakon the Seventh, was forced to flee, the Nazis made Quisling premier. Quisling has come to mean traitor. And the Quislings are his band of traitors."

"Pretty story," Wingate commented. "Any idea how many will move on the town?"

"They move in packs," Karl answered. "Like dogs. Anywhere from twelve to twenty-five."

"Can we expect any Nazis with them?"

"One or two at the most," Karl said.

"It depends," Kirsten disagreed. "If enough Germans are bored and sadistic enough, they may come along if they hear there is sport to be had."

"Usually, they let the Quislings do their dirty work for them," Karl apologized.

In other words, Wingate thought, it was a toss-up. Their best chance, however, lay in the fact that the enemy was so sure the Norse wouldn't fight back that they'd be surprised to find a team of well-armed, well-trained commandos in their midst. Mac hoped it was enough.

"You cannot come with us," he suddenly told Kirsten. "Karl can show us the way. Go back to your house." He kept up his quick pace, so if she stopped, she'd be standing alone.

Kirsten didn't stop. She kept moving, acting as if it were a joke. "What do you mean? Of course I'm coming. You are doing this for me, are you not?"

"I'm doing it because I see some immediate good coming out of it," Wingate said with no trace of humor. "And that good would be countermanded if your cover was blown."

Kirsten realized he was serious and it made her angry. "You are doing this because I am a beautiful woman!" she flared with no modesty. "You think I am soft."

"If I thought you were some weak little girl, I wouldn't be sending you back to Alten alone. You can take care of yourself, Kirsten, I'm not doubting that. But if one Nazi or Quisling sees you and just one man gets away, your usefulness to me, MILORG, and your country will be nil."

If she wasn't smart enough to see that, Wingate reasoned, she didn't deserve the courtesy of an explanation. She saw the light, much to Wingate's relief.

"Very well. I will go back and await your return."

"Good," Wingate said without a pause. "If, for any reason, we don't come back, keep away from Walters. He is not to be trusted. Work from your own instincts."

"Do not worry," she said, breaking away from the group. "The mountain trolls will protect you."

87

"You'll have to tell me about these trolls, sometime," Wingate smiled.

"When you return," Kirsten promised. Then she was gone, disappearing among the heavy greenery.

"The least she could've done was lend me her Suomi," said a voice behind Mac. The captain turned to a disgruntled Donald Neill, dubiously cradling the Reising 50. "I'm not too sure about this."

"Oh, thank heaven," Wingate exclaimed. "An English-speaking voice!"

"You didn't look too upset when the Snow Queen spoke," Biggins kidded him.

"*None* of us looked upset when the Snow Queen spoke," Candy reminded them. "And only one of us could understand her!"

"Now that's what I call a perfect wife," Sumner said dreamily. "Looks to knock your socks off, her own cathouse, and you can't understand a bleeding word she says!"

Everyone laughed except Karl, who picked up on the general drift that they were talking about his MILORG superior. He reprimanded the captain.

"The Nazis have ears, too, you know," he chastised.

"All right, men," Wingate announced in a low voice. "You've lightened the mood, but we don't want the enemy chortling over our corpses."

The silence was total and immediate. Even the sound of their footsteps seemed to disappear.

"Hurry," Karl urged. "We must not be too late."

The group made the rest of the trip in double-time. As they grew nearer the Harald commune, the sound of the flowing water grew louder. Karl halted behind a row of bushes. The rushing liquid was so loud, he had to talk in a normal voice to be heard at a whisper level.

"It is just through here," he said, pointing to the other side of the foliage.

Wingate hazarded a glance. It was another awe-inspiring vista. In the foreground was a lush series of fields, all coming together in the center, like the petals of a flower. The eye of the flower consisted of many buildings. There were cottages, *goattes*, and *stabburs* stretched out in all directions.

In the background was the centerpiece of the scene and the reason the farming was so lush. Behind the commune was another mountain, but at the base of this mountain was a waterfall. A thundering, dramatic waterfall that crashed into a misty lake held in by natural rock formations, which led in turn to a bountiful river that flowed through the very center of the farm.

From his vantage point, Wingate could see some figures moving in the yards. They were causal, unconcerned figures. The reprisal had not yet started. A sudden thought flew into Wingate's mind. Instead of arguing about a rescue, why not stage an evacuation? If there was no one there, there would be no one to kill. Then he realized that Sørum and MILORG were so sure of reprisal that if the sadists didn't find anyone here, they'd be so frustrated, they'd go kill that many more innocents.

Still, since this rescue was going ahead, an evacuation might not be such a bad idea. Just as he was thinking about it, another roar joined that of the waterfall. It was the roar of a truck engine. Wingate saw the field figures begin to run when he turned to his men.

"They're coming," he said and just managed to catch Karl as the young man tried to leap right over the bushes. Mac pulled him back and threw the Norwegian boy on the ground. "You'd be throwing your life away. We've got to wait until they move in. If they know we're out here, they'll pick us off one by one."

The wait was blissfully short. The men watched and counted an even twenty men broiling out of the truck and racing in all directions at once. The ferocity with which they pounced on the commune satisfied Wingate that they would probably miss the commandos' entrance. The object was to shoot anything that moved.

"They're foaming at the mouths," Wingate told his men. "Put them out of their misery." Then he vaulted through the bushes and charged toward the buildings as fast as he could.

He had seen one Norwegian figure running through a field of tall grass get tackled by a pursuing enemy. He had seen neither rise. He pointed at the spot as he kept on a dead center course. He had seen the other innocent runner get grabbed around the waist and dragged under the truck. He pointed there with his other hand.

Candy got to the spot in the field, hearing choked cries and laughs as he got nearer. He leaped up in the air, seeing a swarthy Quisling ripping at a young girl's clothes with one hand and strangling her with the other just before he swung the butt of his Reising like a baseball bat. If the Quisling's head had been a ball, it would have gone for a home run. As it was, the traitor was driven off the girl and landed on his face, his body doubled over backward. Candy also landed, but on his feet, nimbly, shoving the muzzle of his gun as far as it would go into the Quisling's stomach before pulling the trigger. The Canadian didn't want the resulting *blat* to be heard by the rest of the enemy.

Sumner reached the truck first. The men inside had been so excited about attacking the farm that they had left the motor running. Since the Aussie couldn't see any way of getting to the man underneath without endangering the hostage, he leaped into the cab, slammed it into gear at the same time as he rammed the accelerator down, and drove forward. As soon as he had completed that move, he slammed down on the brake and let the engine die in gear. He slid out and around the front seat and still-open front door to see the Quisling straighten up on his knees over the form of another girl. As the screech of the breaking truck echoed off the barn wall, Sumner shot the man in the chest.

Wingate charged through the first barn he came to. He ran the whole traverse without spotting anyone, but he heard shots from behind the door in front of him. He kicked that open onto a sunlit passage that ended in another door, from which the noise was even louder. He kicked that door open onto a kitchen where a man and woman were being gunned down by two Quislings in another doorway. They eased up on the shooting, thinking Wingate was one of them come to join in the fun.

Wingate shot the nearest one without pausing and raced after the second, who had been safe behind his partner's body. Wingate heard him running up the front steps to the cottage's second floor even before he got out of the kitchen, so when he turned the corner he was already firing. The second Quisling had tried to time it so that if he didn't make it up the stairs before Wingate came in, he could at least turn and kill Wingate before Wingate killed him.

His timing was off. The Sten's lead gave him a second set of buttons up his shirt as his own German pistol poked a hole or two in the ceiling above Wingate's head. The second

Quisling fell forward down the steps as a third appeared, curious, at the top of the stairs. His curiosity came to an end as Wingate drove him back with another burst from the Sten. The American then charged up the stairs and ran down the hall, the submachine gun out in front of him. There were no more targets. In the last room, a young Norwegian boy lay dead, his chest a bloody sponge.

Out the window behind the corpse, Wingate could see Breaker and Neill on either side of the barn, flushing out the killers inside. The Canadian would shoot into one door, sending some Quislings out the other where Biggins would be waiting. Then the Australian would run to another opening to return the favor. Wingate saw them mow down five more Quislings that way before he smashed open the window, yelled, "Coming down!" and jumped.

He landed, rolled, and came up to join Biggins and Neill on their way to the second cottage. Sumner and Baker ran up from behind. "Where the hell is Karl?" Wingate grumbled. The rest of the men either didn't know or didn't care.

"Biggins, Sumner, move in from the back," Wingate went on. "Baker, Neill, the front." He didn't bother telling them what he'd be doing. They would just have to trust that it would be something useful. They didn't question his orders. All four moved off quickly, a couple switching magazines as they went.

Whatever they thought, there was method to Wingate's maneuver. The simplest part was pairing each man with his most familiar countryman. Splitting the Aussies and Canucks might have resulted in a better fighting team, but Wingate didn't have time to experiment. If the countrymen had gotten this far into the war together, Wingate wasn't going to split them up just to see what would happen.

Secondly, he didn't want everyone in the same house at the same time. Just in case a Quisling with a grenade was nearby, one well-placed throw and they'd all be done for. Wingate, and hopefully Karl, were the trump men. There would still be a chance of a mop-up if the second cottage became a slaughterhouse.

Wingate moved past the quaint structure to the last remaining shelters beyond—the teepeelike *goattes*. He found the first few empty just before he heard fighting behind him. As he turned, a body went hurtling headfirst out the front win-

91

dow, followed by a pattern of bullets. As it fell heavily in the front yard, Mac could see it was not one of his boys. More gunfire could be discerned from the second story. A terrified man scrambled out the front door. Wingate shot him just as a small window upstairs erupted and Sumner shot down at the escaping man.

Wingate's shot pushed the Quisling back against the door jamb. The Aussie's bullets slapped off the man's forehead. His brains started pouring out before he fell. Wingate turned back to the *goattes* just as one tried to stand up and run away. A man erupted from of the sticks that intersected at the top of the canvas wrapping, lifting up an automatic pistol as he came. Wingate crouched, secured the Sten's butt against his waist, and pulled the trigger, making a short, sharp swinging motion from left to right. The teepee cloth was perforated near the top, dark stains blossomed out from the holes like light rays from the sun, and the man fell back while his gun kept moving up. The hidden Quisling landed a few seconds before his flying gun fell between his stiff legs.

A bullet whipped by his right ear, followed by a report that slapped his eardrum a split second after. Wingate did not pause in his sweep from left to right. He let up on the trigger for a second, then depressed it again as soon as a target entered his peripheral vision. His shots went over the head of a Quisling who was lying in the mouth of a *goatte* he had passed. As Wingate saw the man take aim again, he let his legs go limp.

He fell as the Quisling's gun went off. He never knew by how much it missed him and it hardly mattered. On his side he poured the remainder of the Sten's magazine into the Quisling's face. It split open like a water balloon with cherry fizzies inside. He heard the ripping plopping sound right after he saw the man's face fall apart.

Right after that sound came the noise of movement behind his back. He rolled over to see a darkly dressed man running toward the waterfall. Wingate jumped to his feet and brought up his submachine gun. Just as he was about to pull the trigger, another form got in the way.

Wingate adjusted his focus. Karl had gotten between the Sten and its target. The Norwegian's hands were empty and his back was heaving. Wingate ran to the lad. He saw that Karl was crying and bleeding from a cut on his jaw.

"Where's your gun?" Wingate demanded.

"He's got my gun," the Norwegian sobbed.

What did he need or want Karl's gun for, Wingate wondered, even as he ran forward. He saw the back of the last tent ripped open and then he saw the figure inside. It was a young blond girl. Her blue eyes were wide open, but dull and lifeless. A man's handkerchief was stuffed in her mouth. Her long skirt was pushed up over her hips. Her tights had been pulled down. To his disgust, Wingate saw why the last Quisling needed Karl's gun. He had left his own pistol inside the girl.

Beside the girl was a hand-held ax which the traitor must have used on Karl when Karl interrupted the perversion. Sure enough, there was a stain on the blunt side of the instrument. Wingate put the scene together as he ran through the field after the Quisling.

The fifth columnist probably didn't hear the commandos attack at first. All he knew was that he had a pretty girl in his arms and didn't want to share her with any other sadist. She was probably chopping some kindling outside but her little ax didn't faze the fascist. He must have dragged her into the tent for some fun, either covering her with his gun or her own hatchet.

When he realized there was some serious fighting going on, he must've gotten really excited. He gagged the girl to keep her from attracting attention; then, holding the blade to her neck, he did the gun act. Whether she died from strangling on the cloth down her throat, or his pulling the trigger, or simply from the shock, was beside the point. Wingate was aghast at the viciousness of her death.

The last Quisling ran toward the waterfall. A few more yards and he would disappear in the mist. Wingate was still too far behind to get a sure shot, but he fired off a long burst just for chance. He saw the bullets dig up the ground behind the running man, split off some rock from the boulders in front of him, and cut down some grass tips around him. Everywhere but on his person. Wingate kept up his pursuit even after the traitor made it to the heavy drizzle.

Stalking was going to be a bloody problem, Wingate realized as he dove into the mist himself. The waterfall was so loud, it drowned out even his gunfire. The mist was so thick, he couldn't see the rocks he was climbing. The one good thing about the situation was that the Quisling couldn't go very fast under these conditions, either.

Wingate clenched his teeth and propelled himself up as rapidly as he could. As he got higher, the fog got thinner. He dug in, ignoring the slickness of the stone under his feet and hands. To facilitate matters, he slung the Sten on his back, knowing the Browning was within easy reach if he needed it in a hurry. He climbed faster, willing his limbs not to tire or slip. He couldn't let the final Quisling get away.

He could now see a few feet ahead of him. He could make out the hand- and toe holds he was utilizing. He pulled himself up a few more feet. Scraps of rock shards stung his face just before he heard the chatter of Karl's Suomi. Wingate threw himself down and didn't return the fire, his senses telling him the Quisling was firing blind.

Reality seemed to back him up, for the bullets whined past him and dug up several sections beyond him. It helped, though; he now had a better idea of where the fascist was. He crawled through the mist to his left. He remembered seeing an outcropping on the side of the mountain's base as he ran toward it earlier. If he could get under its umbrellalike protection, he might have a clearer view.

In a few seconds he felt a sudden rise to his left. It was no outcropping, it was the bottom of a cliff. No place to hide, but a guide with which to follow upward. Mac stood, pulling the Sten down. He held the weapon in his right hand and felt along the rock wall with his left. He kept trying to scan through the vapor.

After a few feet, the mist started to clear. A few more feet and it was no more than drizzle. Wingate was behind the Quisling. He was about to catch the man by surprise.

The Norwegian traitor stood near the edge of the rock incline. Immediately to his left was the waterfall basin, kicking up founts of liquid foam. To his right, about twenty feet away, was Wingate. The man must have thought his present position to be the most advantageous place. He was peering down, waiting for the first sign of his pursuer.

Mac moved up until he rested against a horizontal outcropping of stone. He steadied himself against it, rubbed the water out of his eyes, and waited until he was sure his gun barrel centered exactly in the middle of the Quisling's body. Then he pulled the trigger.

The firing pin clicked on an empty chamber. The waterfall was loud, but it was not loud enough. The combination of the proximity, the water's surface "carrying" the sound, and Wingate's movement combined to draw the Quisling's attention. Wingate knew he'd never get to his Browning in time. It was his last thought before he tried to fall and pull out his automatic at the same time.

The Quisling swung the Suomi around, firing. The bullets raced along the wall, making a straight line for the American. The bullets stopped three feet away from him. He wrenched his gun out and pointed it, but it was not necessary. He saw the dead girl's hatchet buried to the hilt in the facist's chest before the standing corpse toppled over backward into the raging water.

"I knew you would not let any escape," he heard a familiar voice shout from above him. He looked up.

Standing atop the outcropping he was resting on was Kirsten.

CHAPTER 6

At first, Kirsten was frisky. She didn't say much because of the waterfall's roar, and she couldn't move very fast because of the slope's wet treachery, but Wingate could feel her crackling energy every time he got near. He himself was keyed up after the nearly terminal showdown, while she was excited from saving his life and fighting the Quislings directly.

The scene at the commune settled things down. Karl was emotionally crushed. To find his girl friend dead, let alone that horribly, devastated him. He sat in the field, his legs crossed, his head in his hands, moaning. The body count was twenty Quislings and five Haralds. The only innocents to survive were the first two girls rescued and they only made it because their captors were more interested in sex than sadism. When the traitors went to work, they were fast and brutal.

Both girls were in stages of shock. The one Candy had rescued was simply hysterical—crying loudly. The one Sumner had saved was nearly catatonic. The Quisling's blood was flecked across her face and torso. Her own blood ran down her leg. These sights sobered Kirsten immediately. Fighting wasn't just an "I-kill-you, you-kill-me, then-it's-over" sort of action. There was always an aftermath and it was rarely very pretty.

Wingate rejoined his four-man unit as Kirsten attempted to bring Karl out of his grief.

"All set?" he asked the men.

"They didn't know what hit them," Biggins proclaimed. "Cleaned them out one, two, three." The Australian snapped his fingers.

"What happened to you?" Neill inquired.

"Getting rid of the last witness to our attack," Wingate answered honestly. "But he almost got rid of me. Snow Queen pulled my butt out of it before it was too late."

"So what now?" Candy inquired, looking at the victimized girls with concern.

"We've done our duty by MILORG," Wingate told him. "Now let's see if we can get this operation over with and go home."

Wingate turned to collect the Norwegian girls as Sumner commented, "Some vacation." Kirsten came up at that moment.

"Can the girls travel?" Wingate asked her.

"I think so," she replied. "Karl has finally recognized their need and I think his tragedy has lessened their own somewhat. They will be each other's crutches as they walk back to town."

Wingate glanced at the two girls, now standing with Karl in a huddled group. Then he saw Candy's concerned expression again. "Is there someplace for them there?" he asked Kirsten.

"They will come back to my house."

"Is it safe?"

Safe or not, that is all that's left them."

Wingate was in no position to disagree. He ordered Candy and Neill to stay by the three Norwegians. Kirsten would lead the way with Biggins and Sumner as protection, while he covered their asses. Slowly, at first, then with increasing speed, they made it back to the lone yellow house on the outskirts of Alten.

"Well, well, well!" blustered Walters as the group entered the whorehouse cellar. "What do we have here?" The British officer was still lying on the comfortable bed, only this time under the covers. Colonel Tyler sat off to the side of the overdone headboard, looking like a menial rather than an American officer of equal rank. And two girls Mac had not seen before were fussing with the bedclothes, making Walters as comfortable as could be. There were scraps of eaten food on a plate which rested on a tray on a nearby table.

"*Maudit sot*," Candy swore at the Englishman in a mumble as he led the young girls across the room and through the curtains opposite. As soon as Kirsten entered, she clapped her hands together to gain the other female pair's attention and waved them out of the room.

"Ah, my dear girl," Walters said before realizing she could not understand him. "Captain, please," he admonished Wingate, "tell her that I am most dreadfully sorry, but these two delightful creatures appeared and seemed intent on serving me . . . I should say, us. I certainly hope I have not unduly trampled on her hospitality."

Wingate turned to Kirsten and said in Norwegian, "This guy is a fucking idiot. If the whole operation didn't depend on him, I'd shoot him where he lays."

Kirsten answered, "He does look the fat oaf."

Wingate turned back to Walters. "She says forget it," he told his superior.

"Oh, that's grand," Walters replied, pleased.

Wingate pulled off his newly reloaded Sten and forcibly kept himself from slamming it down. Instead, he slowly laid it on a side table, turned, and started to undo his coat. "Been doing much planning while we were gone, sir?" he inquired pleasantly.

"Planning?" echoed Walters as the three other commandos found places around the room. "Planning? Whatever for, Captain?"

"For our operation here," Wingate answered, leaning his butt on the edge of the side table and folding his arms across his chest. "Operation . . ." Wingate looked up and crossed his ankles as he pondered a suitable name for the blind mission. "Operation Snow Queen," he decided aloud.

To his surprise, Walters stiffened and nearly shot out of bed. Halfway up, in a rigid sitting position, the Englishman suddenly returned to the blind, affable pig he had been when they had first returned from the Harald farm.

"Now where did you get a name like that?" Walters inquired lazily, drifting back down to his propped-up pillows. "Something Queen, you said?"

"Snow Queen," Wingate repeated. "You know, the MILORG code name."

"Of course, of course," Walters said easily. "You have been using your imagination, dear boy. There is no need to attach monikers to a minor diversionary mission. Especially since, I repeat, especially since we may not be called upon to perform it."

"Yes, sir," Wingate retorted. "You have said that before. But let's just say, for the sake of argument, that we are called upon for that 'minor' diversion. Wouldn't it help to know the target ahead of time?"

"Irrelevant, irrelevant." Walters dismissed it lightly. "You must understand, Captain, that this has all been worked out by powers greater than yourself. You will have plenty of warning. If and when the time comes."

Wingate maintained his nonchalant poise, but the others were leaning in, waiting for the main event to start. They didn't know what Mac's digressions were leading up to, but they could feel the tension in the air.

"I see," he said. "In that event, it may be necessary then to know what we are diverting the enemy from, so we'll know how large a diversion to mount and how thorough to be."

Walter's voice grew grim and authoritative. "I expect you all to be as thorough as possible, whatever the conditions. I have been assured by all your commanding officers that you are the finest men for this operation and I will expect you to live up to your orders at all times to the best of your abilities. Is that clear?"

Three listless, "Yes, sirs," drifted through the room.

"Sir," Wingate reminded the Britisher, "the diversionary source?"

"This has gone far enough, Captain," Walters said sternly. "I have told you before that everything you need to know or do has been worked out to the smallest detail. The target is known, the source is known, and all the ramifications and possibilities have been duly noted and worked out. If and when, I say, if and when the time comes, you will get your orders from me, and me alone, then pass them to your men. Is that clear enough for you?"

Wingate stood up straight. "Yes, sir," he said. Walters nodded, and rested more comfortably on his pillows, muttering. "I was just worried, that's all," Wingate said, seemingly to himself.

"What is it now, Captain?" Walters responded with infinite patience.

"Well, sir, headquarters can get accurate information on things like ammunition depots and U-boat pens from air-force reconnaissance." Wingate nodded at Tyler. The American

99

colonel smiled slightly and nodded back. "But they have no real way of knowing how large an ememy force there is and their state of readiness. Even spies with the best courier system can't keep us up on the day-to-day troop movements in a given area."

"So?" Walters complained. "Get to the point, man."

Wingate slowly but purposefully approached the end of the bed. "Sir. We have to know what we're dealing with. Not just the target and source but the opposition we can expect to face. We must know the size and makeup of the enemy. It is absolutely vital to the success of the mission." Wingate couldn't help himself but put the capper on his speech. "Whatever it is."

There followed a silence that would have been filled by applause from the commandos if Walters hadn't been in the room. Finally he said coldly, "What do you suggest?"

"Tell me about your system."

Kirsten looked up from her sewing. "What?" she asked.

"Your network," Wingate elaborated. "Your organization. Your informants. Tell me how you get your information."

He was sitting on her ornate bed, staring at the fireplace, while she knitted in the chair across from him.

"I'm not sure I know what you mean," she said demurely, eyes glued to the fabric in her hands.

"Come on, Kirsten," prodded Wingate. "Don't pull a 'Walters' on me. I can assume you get a lot of material late at night, but I'm talking about the news Karl came roaring in here with earlier today. How did he know there was going to be a reprisal?"

The girl sighed and put down her busywork. "Very well," she confessed. "Karl knows of two men who work with the Germans. One works at the Post Exchange. The other is a tailor. The Nazis like the Norwegian workmanship better than their own. These two men know several others. And so on, and so on. Why?"

"I need a target," Wingate mused, thinking over the new information she had given him. "It has to be small, strategic, and vulnerable." He hopped off the bed and started to walk aimlessly around the room, rubbing his lower lip between his thumb and forefinger. As an afterthought he asked, "How is Karl doing?"

"Better," Kirsten reported, returning to her knitting. "He knows the Harald girls need him to lean on. It is making him strong again. Giving him a reason to go on."

"Do you think I can talk with him?" Wingate asked.

Before she could answer, another voice entered the room. "What do you want?" Mac turned on his heel, still holding his lip. Kirsten looked up in slight surprise. Karl was standing amid some hanging curtains near the door.

Wingate dropped his arms and studied the young man for a moment. He looked sullen, but otherwise no worse for wear. Mac assumed that in the three years the Nazis had been occupying Norway, Karl had seen many tragedies and cruelties. It had toughened him.

"Are you all right?" Wingate asked anyway.

"Do not concern yourself," Karl answered flatly. "What do you want?"

Wingate explained the situation again, even though he was fairly sure Karl had heard it the first time. The young man pondered Mac's request for only a few seconds.

"Yes, I know of a site like the one you describe. I can take you there."

The American remembered the repeated evidence that time was the most valuable commodity in the mission. He looked at Karl's steady but haggard face with its darkening pockets under the eyes. "That won't be necessary. Just tell me where it is. We'll have to go tonight."

"Then we will go tonight," Karl maintained. "I said I will lead you and I will."

"Look," Wingate began understandingly, "it isn't necessary to prove anything to . . ."

"I'm not trying to prove anything!" Karl burst out, his calm demeanor breaking down. "Don't you understand? I want to do this! I need to . . . I need to get out of here. Just for a while. Either I lead you or you will not go!"

Without waiting for a reply, the young man strode out.

Both people remaining in the room stared at the empty doorway for a second. Then Mac rubbed his face with one hand, scratched his temple, and sighed. He felt like a father in one of those heart-tugging melodramatic movies.

Dutifully, Kirsten seemed to take on the understanding mother's role. "Is it that important?" she asked. The infamous hooker's heart of gold was beginning to appear.

Wingate shrugged. "It has to be done."

"What does?" Kirsten demanded with sudden anger. "What is so important?"

Wingate would not be drawn in or drawn out. He had enough problems on his mind to be sucked into the emotional turmoils of a grief-stricken youth and a hate-filled, idealistic resistance fighter.

All Wingate would say was, "Walters called this a minor diversionary mission, so a minor diversion is what he'll get. Just to see who comes running."

Mac stopped crawling when he reached the tree line at the edge of the clearing. He looked back just as Karl did the same beside him.

"You see?" the young Norwegian whispered, pointing.

Wingate peered out from behind a large pine into the predawn grayness. He saw a clearing that extended only about a hundred and fifty yards from the edge of the woods where they lay. Then it dropped off abruptly over a hill. The trees encircled the area, as if the location had been chosen by the Germans and then bulldozed in preparation for the camp.

"This is an ammo dump?" Breaker harshly, but quietly, inquired.

Wingate studied the scene carefully. Nothing more than twelve winter infantry tents sat squarely in the middle of the clearing.

"Could be," he replied softly. "Nothing short of a concrete roof would protect it from a bombing, so maybe they thought the tents would throw the air force off."

"Yeah," Neill added. "It hardly looks worthy of a full-scale raid."

The six men lay on the cold, hard ground and stared at the tents in silence. Karl began to fidget, feeling left out of the English-language conversation. "So," he whispered. "You see. What now?"

"What are the guard details like?" Wingate questioned him quickly.

"No guard detail."

"No guards?" The American didn't need to whisper the words. His face admirably expressed his disbelief.

"No guard details," Karl stressed. "One or two men pass by occasionally. As the mood hits them."

Terrific, Wingate thought. There was no way to judge the best time to move in. In addition, he could be moving into a disguised ammo dump, devoid of personnel; or he could be moving into exactly what the camp appeared to be—a full platoon of sleeping Nazi infantry men.

Wingate looked at Karl's young, set face. Then he looked through the trees at the still, quiet clearing. He made a decision.

"Fan out," he whispered to the four commandos, lying behind him. "Take up positions along this line of trees."

"What are you going to do?" Candy asked.

"Don't worry about it," Wingate shot back, then thought better of it. Unlike Walters, he didn't want to leave his men with too little information. "If it's what Karl says it is, I'm going to blow it up. If it isn't, I'll need all the cover you can give me."

"If it is," Sumner interjected, "we'll be lucky if we're not fried at this distance."

"If it's not," Neill told the Aussie, "we'll be lucky if we die that easily."

"Move," Wingate ordered them. Without another word, they complied.

"What are you going to do?" Karl inquired softly.

"Stay here," Wingate answered in Norwegian. "You'll know soon enough." The American captain looked around to make sure no Nazi was in sight and all his men were in position. Only Sumner caught his gaze. Mac pointed at the lithe Australian, then covered his right fist with his open left hand. It was the sign that he wanted cover if spotted by the enemy.

Sumner nodded and smiled. The joke was obvious. If the place was an ammo dump and everybody started shooting, the chances were that the whole team would make it back to Alten by air and in millions of little pieces.

Mac started out from the security of the trees and across the open area toward the tents. Just a few yards along, he found himself chewing on his lower lip. He felt hot sweat cool and chill on his back. He listened to his subconscious. It told him that if the tent formation was an ammo dump, there would be no protective mine field. But if it wasn't . . .

Wingate closed off that thought and concentrated on a possible plan of action, whatever happened. He crawled along the soggy ground for what seemed like hours, stopping every few yards to check for guards. The last time he did so, he noticed the sky beginning to lighten in the east. He crawled the last few yards faster than before.

He made it to the first tent and he wasn't dead. He was thankful, but still cautious. He lay outside for several minutes, listening for sounds of human activity inside. During his wait, he yearned for the solid, protecting feel of the Sten in his hands. But all he could do was wish. He had left it back at the tree line to afford him more mobility.

Finally, he was satisfied that no one was inside—that it was neither an infantry nor guard tent. He pushed himself into a squat, undid the flap ropes, and lifted the flap out. Looking in, he saw a demolition man's dream. Wooden ammunition crates were stacked on truck bed skids. Cardboard mortar shell containers peeked out from oil tarp covers. Packs of loose-grain TNT lay in front of his right foot. A single coil of German primacord lay in a wooden crate in front of his left foot.

It was everything he hoped for, except detonators. Even the Nazis weren't stupid enough to house explosives and detonators in the same place. They'd house them separately, so there would be less chance of an accident. An accident Wingate was quickly going to mount.

The American tried to mentally figure the primacord's length. But since there was only one coil in the box, Wingate had little choice but to use it. Hopefully it would reach back to the edge of the woods, and from there, everybody would just have to take their chances.

Again, by instinct, Wingate reached inside his coat for something that wasn't there. His detonators, like his grenades, wire cutters, and tape, lay at the bottom of the Norwegian Sea. Those that didn't sink with the ship were ruined by Wingate's little swim. Cursing his luck, Wingate duck-walked inside the tent, already formulating another demolition method.

Primacord, he remembered, was not set off by a flame, like a fuse. It was, essentially, an exploding wire that needed a booster on both ends to work. And without his lipstick-sized detonators, Wingate had no immediate boosters at hand.

One end at a time, he mentally told himself, calming. He lifted his pant leg and slid out his commando knife. At the same time, he pulled one of the packs of loose-grain TNT and set it on the ground between his bent knees. He cut a small hole near the top of the sack. He grabbed the primacord and allowed a meter of the stuff to fall free. With it, he tied a large double knot in its length.

Mac also remembered that primacord burned at a rate of 200 *miles* per second. With that kind of ferocity, any mass of the stuff would have the cumulative power of a bomb. It was conceivable that the cord could serve as its own booster if tied into a big enough bunch.

When he judged the size was right, he grabbed the primacord end, the long tip that looked like an exaggerated trunk of an elephant, opened the TNT bag, and stuck the tip in. He kept pushing and pulling until the knot behind the tip had also disappeared into the loose grain. Then he felt under the sack with his other hand waiting for the tip to protrude.

After another long minute, he felt the primacord tip through the canvas with his forefinger. He immediately pinched the bag, effectively securing it. Pulling his other hand out, he grabbed his knife and carefully cut another hole on the bag's bottom—just large enough for the tip to escape. He pulled it gingerly out while shifting the sack up and down. Satisfied that the primacord knot was now resting right in the middle of the pack, he wrapped the free end around it and tied it to itself. There was little chance now of it accidentally working free.

Suddenly he felt his body stiffen. He immediately emptied his mind and paid close attention to his senses. He was either shot or his subconscious was hitting him. Thankfully, it was the latter and Wingate became aware of a bird singing outside. It meant that dawn was rapidly approaching. A bad time to get caught in a tent of TNT.

He quickly put the bag in the middle of the floor. He moved for the flap, paying out the remaining coiled primacord as he went. He was thankful to the Germans only because they had the sense to color their primacord green. The Allied manufacturers, in their infinite wisdom, kept their stuff a natural, obvious, easily seen white. Wingate had spent many a long saboteur's night rolling the stuff in the dirt for camouflage.

Wingate looked carefully out the corner of the tent. He saw no one and heard no other human activity. He was coming to appreciate Norway more and more. It may have been a small country, but it was sparsely populated. Mac hazarded a more complete look, sticking his head halfway out. Dawn was rolling in quietly in the company of a bank of mist. The vapor had already obscured the bottom half of the trees beyond. He would just have to take the commandos' continued presence for granted.

With his feet facing the treeline, Wingate began the return crawl backward toward the rest of his party. He payed out the primacord as fast as he could without jerking it. He depended on the others to be his eyes now. He couldn't afford to look for guards every few seconds as he slithered across the rocky, sodden ground.

Suddenly the coil ended. He looked around, realizing that he had literally come to the end of his rope. What he saw around him nearly pushed him over the edge. He was lying only halfway between the dump and the woods. There was a full seventy-five yards left to go. It was not enough. There was no way they could detonate the ammo from where he was without going up with it.

Wingate lay in the rapidly diminishing darkness in a strange sort of calm panic. His brain worked furiously, but with a logical order. Mac looked over his shoulder. He saw glimpses of Karl as the patchy mist moved slowly over the wet earth. He signaled for the Norwegian to join him.

The young man gave his Suomi to Neill, then fell to his stomach and came at Wingate with speed borne of frenzy. While he waited, Wingate pulled the Browning out of its shoulder holster. He resigned himself to its sacrifice and went to work.

He released the clip from the butt and pulled out the first round. Then he pocketed the clip. No sense throwing everything away, he rationalized. Pressing all his arm and shoulder muscles into service, he extracted the bullet tip from the shell casing with his teeth. Then Karl was suddenly next to him out in the open.

The Norwegian could only watch in frustrated silence as Mac took the remaining tip of the primacord, inserted it into the mouth of the Browning barrel, then carefully pulled back the slide so it made no sound. Then he threaded the cord through the opening until a few inches protruded from the breech.

"I need some kind of extra line," he whispered to Karl.

He shut up when voices started filtering up from over the hill on the other side of the tents. Both men froze until it was clear that the voices were not increasing in volume. Finally Mac continued in his pained whisper. "I need enough to tie the gun down, then enough to reach from the trigger into the woods beyond."

As he spoke, his fingers kept working spasmodically. He emptied the powder out of the shell casing and then pushed the tip of the primacord inside the now empty metal hole. He kept pushing until he was sure that the tip of the cord was all the way inside, so that the end would be pushing snugly against the primer at the base of the casing. He now had a round with a length of primacord instead of a lead bullet running into the Browning's breech and out the barrel.

"I don't care where you get it," he continued to the Norwegian, "as long as it isn't any of the men's shoelaces. We may have to get out of here in a hurry and I don't want anyone hampered."

Very carefully, Mac slid the shell with the cord back into the breech and tenderly let the slide close. His makeshift detonator was now loaded, armed, and ready. All he had to do now was cock the hammer and fire the weapon. The primer in the shell casing would go off, igniting the primacord. The primacord would burst inside the TNT pack. The TNT would explode, setting off a series of detonations which would seem like one gigantic hell-on-earth.

But Wingate wanted to be alive to see it. He couldn't pull the trigger at this distance without getting fried in the ensuing fireball. He had to secure the gun upright and set it off from a distance.

He pulled the commando knife out again and stabbed the ground with it. It sank to its hilt guard, making a small pole with which he could secure the gun butt. Mac yearned for his all-purpose rolls of black tape that he had brought; but, like everything else, they were lost at sea. He'd have to use the string Karl brought him.

With a jolt, Wingate realized that Karl hadn't moved. The young man was still lying right beside him.

"What are you waiting for?" Mac hissed. "Get going! The sun'll be up any minute."

Karl did not move. He just stared at Wingate with a blank expression. Mac turned away from him. He heard the German voices on the other side of the camp grow louder and more numerous. He saw a slight shadow underneath him. It was his own. The sun was coming up. It was getting too light. Lying right out in the open, they could be spotted any second.

Mac couldn't understand Karl's sudden hesitation. It just didn't seem possible that the lad would lose his nerve and freeze under pressure. Suddenly, Mac remembered the boy's cringing, crying form at the Harald commune. He had grieved rather than taking action.

Their only chance now was for Wingate to race back to the tent, find some sort of string, and hope he could get the thing set before he was seen and an alarm was raised. He tensed to move forward. At his first action, he felt something hard in his side.

He looked back to see Karl sticking a pistol in his side—a German Steyr Model 12 automatic.

So, Wingate thought, they had been set up all the way down the line. Karl was a secret Quisling spy who had informed the Nazis of their coming, prepared the fascists for the pagoda ambush, and arranged for them to fight at Harald farm. And this was the final setup. A trap that he, himself, had asked for. Mac was sure Karl was going to hold him there until his friends could capture them all.

But then he wondered why the lad had waited so long. Why not have his associates move in while Mac was setting up? And why lay a trap in the most dangerous of surroundings, where one errant bullet might kill everyone? Then he realized that the Steyr was an obsolete Nazi weapon, rapidly replaced by the Luger, the Mauser, and the Beretta. It was a gun that was often taken and used by the underground.

And then Karl spoke. "Get back, Captain. No other materials will be necessary."

Wingate looked into the Norwegian's calm eyes. It didn't matter whether Karl would actually shoot him or not. Mac wasn't about to heroically wrest the weapon away to find out. He didn't have the time or inclination. If the Norwegian was willing to threaten Mac's life to throw his own away, Wingate wouldn't waste his breath in argument.

He got up and ran for the woods. He scooped up his Sten with one hand and waved frantically at the commandos to follow. The men reacted immediately, splitting off from their tree cover and speeding through the woods.

In the distance, Wingate heard the German voice first. "Hey, you! What are you doing there?"

Mac took no chances. He fell, rolled, and came up in a crouch behind a tree. He spun to face back toward the ammo dump. He saw a small crowd of Nazis standing amid the farthest tents. He saw Karl rise calmly to his feet, the Steyr pointing at the ground and the Browning pointing at the Germans. He cocked the 9 mm with his thumb. The Nazis brought up their own weapons.

At the last moment, Karl turned his head in Mac's direction.

"You will never regret what you have done," the Norwegian yelled. "Only what you did not . . ."

His epitaph was cut short by the cracks of the German weapons. The bullets punched all over Karl's body. In the manic strength of death, the young man managed not to fall back. His body seemed to ripple and jerk in place, his feet actually leaving the ground. But the arm holding the Browning remained straight out and level.

Karl's feet dropped back to the ground. His muscles contracted as he began to crumple. He was almost dead when he pulled the trigger.

It all seemed to happen at once. But, in actuality, it happened in a rapid succession. The first flash came from the sides of the Browning barrel. Then the first tent billowed outward. Then the tent all but disappeared in an awful eruption. Then the whole clearing blasted up.

It was as if Hades had boiled, bubbled over, and then erupted through the magma into the heart of Norway. Karl's corpse was rocketed back and upward into the air by the very first blast. The second explosion disintegrated him in midflight. The shooting Nazis were swallowed up, leaving nothing where they had stood.

The concussion bent the first line of trees, buffeted the second, and rolled through the rest of the wood. Wingate was picked up from behind his hiding tree and hurled backward into the trunk of another. The other commandos were thrown forward, each flying like Superman for a moment, before they fell or collided with an obstruction.

It wasn't the plan, Wingate's brain yelled as he tried to fight his way out of the shocked daze the explosion had dropped on him. They were going to detonate the camp from a distance. A safe distance. Then they were going to observe the number of troops who came running. The kind of rein-forcements that were called up. The size and sweep of the mopping-up operation. Now it looked like they were going to be part and parcel of the mopping up.

The thought helped snap Wingate out of it. His vision cleared and strength returned to his limbs. He leaped up, and ran to where his men lay, strewn about on the forest floor. Breaker was clearing his head while sitting against a tree trunk. Neill was clawing at another tree's bark, trying to regain his feet. Candy was huddled in the fetal position on the ground. Sumner was sitting up, blood drooling out of his nose.

Wingate saw to them as a wave of smoke swept through the woods. This acrid, acid-smelling smog had all but replaced the fjord's mist. The American felt they had to use it as a smoke screen if they were to avoid discovery.

"Come on," he urged. "We've got to get out of here. We have to keep moving."

Sluggishly, but surely, the men reacted. They pulled them-selves and drove themselves forward. All were unsteady on their feet initially, but then their strides gained momentum and assurance. Soon they were matching Wingate step for step through the dense explosive cloud. They stayed in a solid bunch for direction and protection, Breaker in the lead, Sum-ner and Baker to either side, Neill right behind the big Aussie, and Wingate taking up the tail position.

The five-man team sprinted out of the forest, through the smoke, and into the new Norway morning.

Breaker Biggins simply died. He didn't see or hear what killed him. He just ran out of the smog and right into three 9 mm bullets from a chattering Schmeisser. A normal man would have been driven backward by the terrible force of the driving metal, but Breaker kept going forward. Three foun-tains of blood poured out of his chest as he fell over.

The other men turned back into the smoke cover. As they did so, Wingate saw the source of their trouble. At the top of a hill, on a curve of the road they had traveled to get here, was a German transport filled with soldiers.

The stunned survivors charged to their left as the other Nazis in the truck fired indiscriminately into the artificial fogbank. Wingate heard more soldiers coming from the other side of the blast site. In a matter of seconds they had been sandwiched in.

Wingate didn't think about dying. A man he had worked with, trusted, and almost come to know had been voided in front of him, but he didn't think about it. It was too late to think about Biggins. He had to think about Sumner, Neill, and Baker now. There was still a mission to consider. They had to find a way out.

Going against the platoon of men in the truck was unthinkable. They were too rested, too well armed, too thoroughly trained, and too many to take on with four guns. Others from the camp over the hill were trying to cut them off at the head of the column of smoke. More men were probably circling around them to seal off a rear escape. Wingate realized there was only one chance left. They had to walk through the fire.

He whistled sharply to the others and raced back the way he had come—toward the devastated ammo dump. It would still be in flames, but hopefully not hot enough to melt them as they ran. Hopefully it was just hot enough to keep the Germans away from it. It might just give them the space they needed.

The smoke cleared in front of Wingate. A German infantryman appeared to his right. The Nazi stopped short in surprise just as Mac shot him down and kept going. It was a good sign, Mac thought. He was doing what the enemy wasn't expecting. He was coming out of the place the Nazis were expecting him to stay in.

There was about a ten-yard space between the flaming dump and the edge of the smoke. Mac ran right into the inferno in between a few Germans who were running cautiously around the flames. Sumner and Candy turned with their backs toward each other and killed whatever was in front of their guns as they followed their leader. Neill dodged in between them and took up second position.

The clearing was a mass of charred rubble, huge burning branches which had fallen from surrounding trees, and twisted, red-hot wreckage. Bonfire pockets protected the commandos from the mass of Germans who were looking for them. The trio gathered around the captain.

"Fight your way out east," Wingate ordered. "The men from the camp have already moved into the forest. We have only a few minutes before the smoke clears and everybody doubles back this way. Stop for nothing. Let's go!"

They charged down a narrow, crooked path in between

piles of flame. Wingate felt the hair on his hands and his eyebrows crackle. He saw a clear way ahead of him and closed his eyes. The heat gave him a faster speed than he had ever attained before. He came out the side of the ex-ammo dump in one piece but minus most of his facial hair.

The cold morning air did much to relieve his seared skin. He plowed through the small stretch of forest on the east side, hustled up a steep incline, and raced over the top of the hill. Spreading out below him was Alten fjord. The entire town snuggled against the steeply inclined mountain wall Wingate stood atop. In the blue, misty morning he could see all the cottages, all the stone buildings, and the entire harbor with its large ships.

The mountaintop was a perfect place for the ammo dump and infantry camp. It was just high enough to give them a panoramic view of the entire area and just low enough to arrive at any trouble spot with a minimum of delay. And Wingate's team had waltzed right into it.

Wingate jumped off the edge of the precipice without thinking. He landed on his feet thirty feet below. The jolt felt like his legs were driven up into his torso, but the pain subsided as he fell over, only to be replaced by more pain as he rolled down a rocky, bush-laden incline of seventy degrees. Rocks slammed into his thighs, shoulders, and back before he braked himself to a skidding halt. He brought up his Sten scratched and battered, but in one piece, and steadied it.

He turned to find Neill tumbling down after him. He looked up to see Candy jump. Sumner was standing on the top, his back toward Mac, firing at an unseen target.

Wingate ran over to stop Neill's roll. He caught the hurtling Canadian, almost losing his own footing again. Then he hopped nimbly around the recovered man to cover Candy's leap. Candy landed heavily, his Reising flying out of his grip. Mac caught it on its second bounce. Baker slid the rest of the way down on his front. Neill served as his backstop while Wingate turned back toward Sumner. Wingate mowed down two Nazis as the last Australian traversed the space.

Candy got up with long cuts across his face and torso. Sumner, seemingly made up of coiled liquid steel, bounded up without a scratch. Bloodied or not, all the men backed down the rest of the mountain, shooting up at any German who tried to follow.

The land flattened and the vegetation grew thicker the farther north they went. Soon the top of the mound was obliterated from their sight by flora. Only then did Mac stop firing and turn heel. He tore through the plants, trying to get into town as quickly as possible. It was only a matter of time before the majority of the Germans learned about their escape route and drove down to cut them off.

There were other ways they could be trapped. If their communications were as fast as their reactions, the Nazis could have radioed down for the shore patrol to come forward and search. As soon as he considered that, Wingate burst out from the foliage into a fishing field.

It was a strange sight for the commandos. Row upon row of gigantic wooden racks, all at least thirty-five feet high, stretched across the entire length of the field. It was an escape route seemingly sent from above. The racks consisted of leaning poles, set across from each other and intersecting at the top. They were joined there to make an upside-down ''V'' in the ground. Each one was attached to the next by thinner horizontal poles. Fifteen of them rose up along the vertical structures like rungs of a ladder. They were drying racks, but not for clothes.

Along each of these horizontal lengths were codfish. Thousands of codfish. Not satisfied with one fish per position, their tails had been tied together and a pair of cod hung within inches of the next pair. They made a huge bamboolike curtain for the commandos to hide in.

Wingate immediately raced toward the rack nearest him, fell to his stomach, and rolled inside the A-framed rack. Neill, Baker, and Sumner followed in after him. They stood for a few moments, trying to catch their breath. The mood inside the rack was unearthly and tragic. Sumner hadn't had time to adjust to his friend's death before. It started to affect him now.

The smell inside was incredible. Wingate looked around to see every fish's beady little blind eyes staring at him. He looked in front of him, past the commandos' shoulders. The rack ended in an open A. He looked behind him. The rack went on for many yards, ending with another rack intersecting it lengthwise.

''Come on,'' said Wingate, nodding his head in that direction.

The men walked slowly, their bodies bent, their weapons held limply in their hands. Only Wingate held his Sten in a defensive position. The others acted as if it were all over. They had made it out alive and they needed some time to gear up for the next fight. Only Wingate acknowledged that they weren't out of the woods yet.

The danger, when it came, came from behind them. The eerie silence inside the rack was dispelled by an echoing burst of gunfire. The ground was torn up and fish ripped apart around them. Wingate heard Candy grunt as he fell, twisted, and threw himself behind a vertical pole. Wingate was just able to see two Quislings move in opposite directions out of the nearest end of the rack.

The escape route had suddenly become a cage. The commandos were inside, with at least a pair of Quislings outside, one on either side. Each man tried to peer out between the heavy curtain of fish. But no one made a move from the ground where they had thrown themselves. They waited for another move, the stink of the seafood filling their lungs and the stench of death still in their minds.

"Any damage?" Wingate whispered.

"I think I twisted my ankle," Candy answered. The Canadian looked terrible. The cuts on his face had dried, but left bars of blood trapping his face. His shirt was soaked with red. He was breathing too fast and blinking too much. The leg injury was the last straw.

"Neill," Wingate quietly called.

Before the other man could answer, one Quisling came roaring through a line of cod behind Baker. The Quisling had come in blind, screaming, hoping to catch the commandos by surprise. He succeeded with Sumner and Neill. Candy and Wingate were prepared. Baker whirled as Wingate was on his feet and running.

Mac had hit upon an immediate plan. He was sure one of the other men could handle the attacking Quisling, so he second-guessed the traitor's reasoning and went after the other one. He figured that while one Quisling would charge in yelling from one side, gaining the targets' attention, the other would come in right after from the other side, catching the Allies in a cross fire.

Wingate's part of the plan worked perfectly. He raced the length of the rack, threw himself sideways between two horizontal racks of hanging fish, and landed on his stomach with the crouching second Quisling lined right up in his Sten sights. He pulled the trigger. The Quisling dropped dead.

The rest of the plan would have worked perfectly if Candy's Reising had not jammed. The drop down the mountainside had damaged it and got its mechanism dirty. Candy, although wounded, had the attacking Quisling dead to rights. He pulled his trigger and nothing happened. The Nordic traitor fired point-blank at the same moment Neill swung Karl's Suomi to bear.

The Quisling fell amid hundreds of torn codfish. The seafood's silvery flesh drifted down after all the noise of gunfire had stopped. Wingate bent over and came back in as Neill and Sumner got up. Eugene Baker, Candy, remained totally motionless. He would never move again.

Mac Wingate approached the body slowly. Silently he reached down and took the useless Reising from Candy's dead fingers.

"What are you going to do with that?" he heard Neill say behind him with infinite loathing.

Wingate turned, strapping his Sten on his back and holding the Reising out in front of him like a particularly offensive slug. He started moving down the length of the cod-drying rack, going faster as he went.

"I'm going to take it," he said with growing anger, "and ram it down Walters's throat!"

CHAPTER 7

Colonel David Walters was not to be found.

Wingate and his two remaining men came pounding into the whorehouse cellar ready to pull the Englishman's heart out through his mouth.

They went right for the plush bed just inside the curtained entrance, but it was empty. They stamped through the rest of the cellar, but there was no one there.

Wingate suddenly got the feeling that more things were going wrong than he had imagined. His rage dissipated, to be replaced by battle-borne cunning.

"Stay put," he told the confused, depressed, exhausted commandos. "I'm going upstairs."

Mac moved up the steps silently. He cautiously parted the entry curtains to Kirsten's room. Through the crack, he saw Colonel Tyler sitting with the Norwegian girl on the bed. Before acting, he checked out the rest of the room. It was midmorning. The patrons had all gone.

Wingate threw the curtain aside. Both people on the bed looked up in surprise. Mac held the dramatic pose for a second, then slowly approached his fellow American. Tyler looked at him with confusion clouding his features. Unlike Walters, the Yank colonel was seemingly guileless.

Now here, Mac thought, is a man I can intimidate!

As Mac neared, Tyler opened his mouth to speak. He closed it again as Wingate wrapped one hand around his lapel and the other around his neck. The captain pulled his superior officer up and off the mattress.

"Where is he?" Wingate quietly, seethingly demanded, holding Tyler's face above his own.

The American colonel may have been less forceful than Walters, but he was an officer still. Rather than answering the question, he marched out his indignation.

"What are you doing, Captain?" he cried. "Take your hands off me! Put me down!"

His large, long hands slapped at Wingate's fists ineffectively. Wingate shook him once, hard, for good measure.

"We're not at the goddamn officer's club now, Tyler," Mac said in the same low, threatening tone of voice. "Or that fucking château in Datchet. Men are dying here, Colonel, and I want to know why."

Kirsten was up, holding on to Mac's shoulder. She was going to try to calm him down, until she saw his bruises. "Mac, what happened?" she interjected.

"They were waiting for us," Wingate told her. Then he told the man he had dangling off the floor, "We crawled right into the better part of the German Army."

"All right," Tyler declared, upset. "All right! I'll tell you what you need to know. But not this way! You gain nothing this way!"

Without another thought, Wingate casually dropped Tyler back onto the thickly padded bed with a simple shove. The American colonel bounced, settled, then delicately loosened his shirt collar and felt his neck.

Kirsten kept her attention on the captain. She didn't speak until after Tyler had calmed somewhat. "Karl . . . ?" she asked hesitantly.

"No," Wingate told her with more anger than gentleness. Then he turned on Tyler once more. "And Biggins. And Baker. All killed without knowing the reason why."

Tyler shook his head, staring at the bed covers. "It wasn't supposed to happen like this . . ." he muttered.

"It never is!" Wingate flared. "Famous last words, Colonel. Famous last words. You keep smug and superior, telling your men next to nothing until they throw themselves on the enemy's guns and then you cry, 'Isn't it a shame' back at headquarters. Now where is he?"

Tyler looked up into Wingate's tight face. "You mean Colonel Walters?"

"Of course I mean Colonel Walters. Who do you think I'm looking for, Eddie Cantor?"

Tyler looked down again. "I don't know." Wingate went

for him again. Kirsten grabbed the captain's shoulders while Tyler scrambled back across the bed.

"I swear!" the colonel cried. "I swear I don't know. I went into the kitchen for something to eat and when I returned, he was gone."

Wingate said nothing. Just stood over the bed, his elbows bent, his hands clawed.

"It's true," Kirsten agreed. "We looked everywhere for him."

They had slipped. Wingate nearly did a double take until he regained control and spat back at Tyler. "Too easy, Colonel, too facile. The Third Reich comes down on me and Walters just happens to waltz out at the same minute. It doesn't wash."

"I swear it's true, Captain," Tyler declared. "I don't know what went wrong or why."

"I'll tell you what went wrong, Colonel," Wingate announced, moving around the room. "They were waiting for us."

"It was a trap?" Tyler asked incredulously. "A spy informed on you?"

"Not specifically us," Wingate explained. "Just anybody like us. This was no accident. Those truckloads of men didn't just magically appear on the roadside. They were ready and waiting for trouble. They were *expecting* sabotage. They had been trained for it. They were stationed to prevent it. There was no informer or else they would've killed us before we destroyed our target. They just reacted instinctively afterward. They were waiting for something just like this to happen."

"Then they must know the mission's target . . ." Tyler said in shock.

"Of course they know the target!" Wingate said, annoyed. "They knew the target before we even set sail for Norway. They knew the target before this mission was even planned!"

"How can you say that?" Tyler demanded.

"Don't you get it yet?" Wingate threw up his hands in amazement, then lectured very slowly. "I said there was no spy. I said they were not informed about us. That means that the mass of men who attacked us were stationed there before we ever arrived. That means that whatever this woebegone mission's primary target is, the Germans think it is important

118

enough to station a veritable army at this godforsaken point to protect it!''

Tyler looked at Wingate with no surprise in his expression. Only understanding. Mac had told him nothing that was new. He had known it all along. He just wanted to see if Wingate had realized it. ''I suppose you'll want to know what that primary target is,'' Tyler sighed.

What Wingate said next did surprise him. ''I *know* what the target is,'' the captain said. ''I just want to see if you're smart enough to tell me yourself.''

The two Americans stared at each other. Kirsten watched the sitting colonel and the standing captain face off for several seconds before she interrupted. ''What is the matter?'' she asked in Norwegian. ''What has just happened.''

Mac quickly translated the situation for her, then left the ball in Tyler's court. ''Well?''

When Tyler didn't respond, Kirsten tried to fill up the dead space. ''How do you know what the target is, Mac?''

''I jumped off a cliff today,'' he told her. ''I saw something on the way down.'' He quickly translated her question and his answer for Tyler. The colonel nodded solemnly. Mac was right in his guess. All Tyler had to do was fill in the details.

''It was not my mission,'' he said, starting with an excuse for not speaking up earlier. ''I was an adjunct to Colonel Walters. It was not my place to countermand his orders.''

''Save me the conscience-absolving,'' Wingate groaned, moving to the chair next to the fireplace. ''Let's have the facts.''

Tyler restarted with a question. ''Do you know of the supply convoys the British call the Murmansk Run?''

''Sure,'' Wingate replied with no expression. ''Two convoys move out at the same time. One bound for Murmansk, one coming from it.''

''In order to accomplish their missions, they must pass by Norway, round North Cape, and pass through the Barents Sea to the Russian coast.''

''Yeah,'' Wingate drawled. ''So?''

''So these convoys are attacked by destroyers, submarines, and torpedo planes. Anything to cripple them. Still, they fought back and some got through.''

''I love happy endings,'' Wingate cracked sarcastically.

"Captain, please," Tyler pleaded. "This is hard enough as it is."

"Don't look for sympathy here, Colonel," Wingate said flatly. "Go on."

"On July 5th, another convoy set out. Up until then the Germans had only threatened to use their 'heavy ships.' That day they finally did. The hunt became a massacre. Twenty-two of the thirty-three Allied ships were sunk. We lost 210 aircraft, 430 tanks, 3,000 vehicles and over 100,000 tons of other material."

"I don't need an itemized list," Wingate said. "What's the point?"

"Captain, have you heard of the *Tirpitz*?"

The name. Finally the name. It was a name Wingate had been expecting and dreading at the same time. As he had stepped over the edge of the cliff next to the ruined ammo dump, he had glimpsed it, all alone, in the harbor. Even with other merchantmen and cruisers around it, it would still have looked alone, for it was that big. The *Tirpitz* was one of the two biggest battleships in the world. The other was the *Bismark*. And both were Nazi vessels.

If anything, the *Tirpitz* was larger than her more famous sister ship. It was so big, the Germans were even moved to lie about its size, saying it was over fifteen thousand tons less than it actually was.

It actually was 822 feet long, 118 feet wide, weighing in at over 52,000 tons when full, with an armament that included eight 15-inch guns, twelve 5.9-inch guns, and over forty rapid-fire antiaircraft guns. It had excellent compartmentation, very heavy armor, the best Zeiss optical range finders, precision controls, a speed of thirty-one knots and a range of eight thousand miles.

Wingate closed his eyes. He thought about being sick. No wonder Alten fjord was armed to the teeth. Just having that thing in the harbor was enough to scare away anything that floated.

Which, as it turned out, was exactly what was happening.

"I see that you have," Tyler went on, recognizing Wingate's expression. "While the rest of the German fleet has been all but eradicated, the *Tirpitz*'s presence simply grows stronger. It was refitted the first of the year. It has been

120

anchored here throughout the spring and summer. No one dared go against her."

"Except for two other missions," Wingate said, his eyes still closed. He didn't have to see Tyler get taken aback again. The subsequent silence was evidence enough.

"Uh, yes," the colonel said, trying to decide whether to be honest about that as well. He remembered Wingate's strength and then decided to come clean. "In her more southernly anchorage we tried to long-range bomb her."

"Didn't work," Wingate said for him.

"Right. Then she moved up here . . ."

"Which is out of range."

"Uh. Correct. We then tried to use a manned-torpedo attack . . ."

Wingate opened his eyes. This was more Walters's speed. The manned torpedoes were like hitching a ride to suicide. If that was the failed mission before Wingate, Allied Command must have expected Mac and his men to go after the warship with kamikaze gliders. "What screwed up there?"

Tyler was embarrassed to say. "They were being towed to within striking distance by a Norwegian trawler. The towlines broke and they sank."

"No second tries?" Wingate asked incredulously. "Just send Wingate and his blind mice instead?"

"Captain, really," the colonel chastised. "This attitude doesn't become you."

Wingate was on his feet and stalking toward the bed again. Tyler held his seat, secure in the knowledge that he was psychologically in the right. Wingate kept his hands to himself, all right, but his words were like verbal fists.

"Listen, I don't mind getting my head hammered into sheet metal, but I do like to know what I'm in for. If you guys had only opened your big traps before, I could've worked something out. I could've planned an effective attack with all the proper equipment! What are we going to do now? Attack the *Tirpitz* with war paint and tomahawks?"

"I can assure you of this," Tyler said definitely. "I really have no idea."

The sentence stopped Wingate in his tracks. His circuits felt overloaded. "Repeat," he said.

"I told you before, Captain," Tyler responded. "This is not my mission. Colonel Walters has the details. I have no choice but to assume that what he told you was true, the mission has already been planned and will commence on his word.''

"So where is he?"

"I told you that before too. I don't know."

"So what the hell are you here for?"

"I told you that as well. I am here in an advisory . . ."

"Not that jack shit!" Wingate snarled, sweeping his right hand in front of Tyler's startled face. "How the hell did you get included in this operation? What the hell are you doing here?"

Tyler swallowed, unconsciously looking for a way out of the room. "Well. That. It was . . . well . . . professional courtesy."

"I beg your pardon?"

"We first heard of the mission from the Admiralty's Operational Intelligence Center," Tyler admitted abashedly. "My superiors felt it was an important enough mission for United States participation. They wanted to be represented. So it was arranged for me to go along . . . in a consultative capacity."

The insanity of Allied HQ never ceased to amaze Wingate. They had sent an inexperienced, ignorant Yankee colonel behind enemy lines simply because the Americans threatened to hold their breaths until they turned blue.

"Does this operation have a name?" Wingate asked tiredly.

"Why, yes," Tyler answered, seemingly surprised that Mac did not know it. "We heard about it as 'Operation Source.' "

"Operation Source," Mac repeated. "Thank you." He closed his eyes, running his hands down over his face. He made an elaborate show of stretching. "So, Colonel," he said sullenly, "what do you suggest we do now?"

"We have no choice," Tyler said indifferently. "We have to wait until Walters comes back."

"If he comes back," Wingate said miserably, dragging himself over to the chair. He sat heavily, the very picture of a resigned, unhappy, subservient underling. "I'm sorry, Colonel," he told Tyler. "I apologize. It was just the shock of losing two of my men . . . the battle . . ."

"Of course, I understand," Tyler said soothingly, rising from the bed and straightening his shirt. "Must have been a hell of a blow." The colonel swept aside the curtains behind the bed. "I'll rejoin the men. Believe me, Captain, I'll let you know as soon as I get any word from Walters."

Tyler left the room shaking his head sadly. Kirsten watched him go, reacting to his sensitivity. She turned a warm, understanding face toward Wingate, who was still sunk miserably in the well-padded armchair.

"I did not understand the words," she told him in her native tongue, "but I could feel your pain."

Wingate's voice rose from his slumped figure softly, but harshly clear. "I want to see this tailor of yours."

"W-what?"

"I can't wait for Walters. Who knows what that idiot is doing. Something is very wrong and it's getting worse by the second. We've got to get to the bottom of Operation Source right now before the whole thing comes apart on our heads."

"But the colonel . . ." Kirsten stammered.

"We don't have time to argue," Wingate said, quietly but intensely. "We're going out. We're going out or I'm going to break your fucking neck."

"It was something Candy said," Wingate explained as the couple walked slowly down the street. "His immediate superior told him that the mission would be cutting it close. So then we sail for three days and jack around with Sørum for another. Doesn't seem to have the makings of haste, does it?"

"But your colonel and Sørum have said that it was a matter of waiting," Kirsten reminded him from under her shawl and drab ankle-length coat.

"No, that's what the Englishman and Norwegian said," Wingate continued to whisper while trudging down the way. *"My* colonel said it was a mission of great urgency and importance. And I trust my colonel."

"Then why would anyone lie to you?"

"That's what we have to find out. And fast."

Midafternoon gloom had descended on the Alten fjord. The sun hardly shone this far north as the second half of the year arrived. Being so close to the polar axis, northern Norway missed much of the sun's orbit. At times it seemed to hang in a perpetual gray purgatory. In town, no one seemed to look at the sky. Almost all attention was directed at the feet.

It was all to Wingate's benefit. That way no one paid

123

attention to just another Norwegian peasant couple and it gave Mac time to study his new environment. It was the first time he had been outside the whorehouse and in the middle of town. Putting on drab, disguising garb, Wingate and Kirsten had come out a side entrance into an alley. There, Mac had seen that the building was partly held up by ''Y''-shaped beams that attached to the edge of the wall. Between the buildings was a wood-paved alleyway. Out in front was a gravel-covered street.

The wooden buildings that lined the street were architecturally complex but aesthetically mundane. Although obviously well crafted, the shapes were eccentric, and the only colors were the olive, brown, red, and dark green of the wood planks.

It got so cold in the long winters that the town's founding fathers made it a point to build everything nearby, so it was only a matter of moments before the pair arrived at the door of Henrik Erling, town tailor. Kirsten took Wingate's hand and led him into an alley between the shop and the building next door.

"Did you see someone?" Mac asked.

"No," Kirsten answered, knocking on a side door beneath an awning. "He could never let me in the front door. Remember, I am a tainted woman."

The side door suddenly opened and a little man with gray hair poked his head and one arm out. *"Ach*, evil woman!" he said. "Go away! *Shah! Shah!"*

"Henrik," she whispered, "Karl is dead."

The man dropped his pretense immediately. "Come inside. Quickly."

The inside was utilitarian. The three stepped into a short, rectangular room with one sewing machine in the corner. The space was kept warm by the racks and racks of clothes that filled every inch of three walls.

"What happened?" said the tailor. "The Quislings?"

"The Germans," Wingate said.

"And who is this?" Erling asked of Kirsten.

"Captain Wingate of Allied Command."

The tailor looked at Wingate with great joy, taking his hand and smiling widely. "Captain Wingate! At last you've come. I, Kirsten, all of us have been waiting for your arrival!

124

Now, at last, we can throw off the yoke of oppression and rid ourselves of the occupying forces.''

Wingate thought he was overstating just a bit, before Kirsten uncomfortably corrected the old man. "No, Henrik. He is not the one. He is just one lone soldier who needs help.''

The tailor's face collapsed from great happiness to vast disappointment, then reconstructed itself into a hopeful tenacity. "Oh, I am sorry for the misunderstanding, Captain Wingate. What can I do to help you?''

Ignoring the psychic drama that had just occurred, Mac filled him in. "I need a uniform. A German officer's. High enough not to be stopped and questioned, but not high enough to attract attention.''

The tailor smiled again. He crooked a finger at Wingate and led him over to a rack on the side wall. He pushed the hanging clothes aside to reveal another rack. Behind that was another clothes-filled rack. Finally, behind that was a wall with two hooks nailed in. Henrik pulled on one of the hooks, swinging out a secret door. Inside was a narrow closet filled with Nazi uniforms.

"While I repair the originals,'' he bubbled happily, "I duplicate them!''

Wingate chose the outfit of a lieutenant. Erling merrily did some fast measuring and went to work on the necessary alterations. The American hovered nearby until Kirsten sidled over and took his hand. He turned and she motioned for him to follow. He didn't like the looks of it. The girl's face was infused with a strange look of desire. It was at odds with the MILORG fighter he had dealt with thus far.

"This will take a while,'' she said of Erling's sewing, walking over to yet another clothes rack. When she pushed some garments aside there was a door on the other side. As the two went through and up a flight of steps, Wingate inquired, "What was that all about? That thing about the 'yoke of oppression'?''

"Oh,'' Kirsten said lightly, waving it away. "He thought you were a representative of a large Allied expeditionary force that Sørum has been promising would land and aid us in our quest for freedom. I know it is just a lie, but it gives the others hope.''

They came out in a single, simple room, mostly taken up by a bed. There was one window in the small wall between the sloped ceilings. It looked out onto the water of the fjord. Wingate shook his hand free from Kirsten's grip and moved over to the glass for a closer look, being careful not to hit his head on the low ceilings.

Next to the water was a dock. Next to the dock was a low building. Next to that was a slightly higher building. Next to that was another, higher establishment, and next to that was the window Wingate was looking out of. The roofs made a makeshift stairway to the tailor's bedroom.

When Wingate turned, Kirsten was half-sitting, half-lying across the bed. She had taken off much of her drab peasant disguise and was wearing just the skirt and tight, crew-necked wool undershirt. "You wanted to know about the trolls," she said. Wingate did not reply. "I told you I'd tell you about them when you got back from the Harald commune." The words drifted up into the little white room. Kirsten continued talking quietly, soothingly—almost for her own sake. She did not look at him.

"I remember the stories my mother used to tell. She said they were very large and very ugly, except to other trolls." Kirsten laughed at the memory of it. "She said they liked to capture princesses and carry them off to their castles inside the mountains."

Wingate saw the tears. They were big and clear and rolled down her smooth cheeks without interruption. They did not affect Wingate. There was a lot to cry about. The Norwegians needed little encouragement for that. The bleak day outlined her profile through the window. Her attractiveness had not fled her. But that did not affect Wingate either.

Deliberately, and almost with resignation, Wingate stepped over and joined her on the bed. They made love without passion. They had sex without hate. As such, it was something completely different for Kirsten. She began professionally, making the right moves, making the right sounds at the right time. Mac would not let her lie to him. He changed his approach every time he felt she wasn't responding naturally.

He didn't ravage her, he appreciated her. He didn't bang her, or rape her, or fuck her. He worshiped her. With acknowledged consideration, almost forced sensitivity, he loved her body until he felt the spell broken. Then he rose from her warmth and sat on the edge of the bed, feeling nothing. He looked at the empty wall in front of him, seeing nothing.

Kirsten lay behind him, savoring the moment. She had never felt appreciated. She had never felt valued. She had never felt sexual affection. Her mind demanded that she say some sort of false compliment, something to bolster the male ego, but she found she couldn't. She didn't want to. For the first time, the actual sexual act had not been the primary force, the one and only consideration. Because of it, it was the most glorious moment she had ever had.

Wingate exhaled deeply to prepare himself for what he had to do afterward. "Tell me your part in it," he said.

She couldn't bring herself to talk. She knew if she opened her mouth, it would be to lie. Wingate knew it too.

"Don't make me play the scene," he warned. "It's the one where Bogie says, 'You're going to take the fall.' I've seen it too many times."

Kirsten didn't know what he was talking about. She had never heard of Humphrey Bogart and she had never seen *The Maltese Falcon.*

"The lies are getting dangerous," Wingate went on, still not turning around. She saw his back while she heard his voice. "I'm not going to die like Baker and Biggins. Like Karl." Her tears were real this time as she listened. "Tell me where you fit in," he demanded with no emotion.

There was a terrible pain in her chest. She wanted to tell him, but the words *"Ja, vi elsker,* Yes, we love with fond devotion"—the Norwegian motto—were loud in her mind. And in her mind they were being said by Einar Sørum. But she couldn't lie. So she destroyed the moment by trying to avoid it.

"What is the matter, Mac?"

She saw Wingate's head lower and his hand come up to rub his forehead. She heard his sigh. "Very well," he said. "You were talking to Tyler. Either you know English or he knows Norwegian. Either way, someone isn't telling me something."

"That?" she said with relief. "That? On the bed, when you came back from the ammunitions camp? But Mac, we weren't talking. He was trying to make me understand that Walters had disappeared."

This time Wingate did turn around. His expression was one of whimsical disappointment. He had caught her hand in the

127

cookie jar. He would never trust her again. She felt as if her insides were being torn out.

"I quote," Mac said, " 'I went into the kitchen for something to eat and when I returned, he was gone.' Then you said, 'It's true. We looked everywhere for him.' Only Tyler spoke in English. *You backed him up in Norwegian.*"

Kirsten remembered. She had been swept away in the emotional intensity of Wingate's survival. She was drawn into the battle of words between him and Colonel Tyler. She had spoken without thinking. Her clothes were off, but she hadn't felt naked until now.

"Understand," Wingate told her, "I don't know anything about your part in this. As far as I know, you could be a Quisling. Don't lie and don't try to move. If you do, I'll kill you." He did not emotionally threaten her. That would have been acting. Instead, he told her in the plainest of tones. She had no doubt that he could and would do it.

"I am a loyal member of the Militoer Organisajonen," she said to the ceiling. "Einar had told me that two Allied colonels needed my help desperately if their plan was to work. He said I had to be your shadow. I had to keep you from interfering in the colonels' work. He said it was the most important part of the operation. He said you were a well-meaning, but overeager gunman who might jeopardize the entire mission."

Wingate tried to be objective. He tried to see any truth in Kirsten's statements. He had to discover whether he felt any part of him was an "overeager" hothead who would jump the gun. It didn't hold up under his scrutiny. It was the colonels' way of maintaining their own fragile egos, he decided.

"Did Sørum say who told him this?"

"No."

"What is the mission?" As soon as she paused before answering, Wingate knew what the answer would be. She didn't know how he would react. She was afraid he would get mad at her ignorance. He was nodding when she finally did speak.

"I do not know."

He surprised her by moving right on to the next subject. "You're going to have to choose now. You've seen me in action and you've seen Walters and Tyler. You will have to judge for yourself who you would trust more with your life."

"But Sørum . . ."

"Sørum is up in the mountains. He only knows what he is told. He will do nothing to help us on this mission. You heard him say so yourself. Your only choice is between helping me or helping Walters. Choose. Now."

It had begun to snow as Mac Wingate moved toward the dockside tavern. His new uniform felt wonderful. It fit perfectly—the tailor had done a great job. He felt warm and at ease inside it. It was the inside of his mind that needed the work. He had to switch his mental system from Norse to German. The words had to be different, the dialect had to be changed, and his whole attitude had to be altered.

He was now a lieutenant of the Wehrmacht, stationed in Alten fjord, near North Cape, the northernmost tip of Norway. And a freezing, godforsaken hole it was, too. The gently falling snowflakes did nothing to improve his artificially dark mood. It wouldn't be snowing in Germany this time of year. Germany had lovely autumn months. He made himself look forward to getting inside the warm hostelry with his many friends and associates.

He was eager to talk to one in particular: a Norwegian who worked at the Post Exchange at the Nazi infantry camp on the mountain. A man named Arne Larsen.

The close-knit village didn't give Wingate much time to prepare his mental defenses. The tavern was practically right around the corner from the tailor's—just a few doors down from the first squat building Mac had seen out the seamster's bedroom window.

He navigated the wooden steps off the road down onto a moored wooden path set over the quietly lapping water of an inlet. Which was more than he could say for the two German seamen who staggered toward him, arms around each other's shoulders. Middle of the afternoon, Wingate made himself think, and already stinking drunk.

His Nazi-based attitude worked true. Instead of moving to the side to let them pass, he stopped right in front of them, blocking their way. His appearance sobered them up quickly. Their dopey smiles shrank and their bandy legs suddenly grew steel. Each gave him a slightly wobbly salute, which he returned crisply. Then he let them move around him.

Their footsteps disappeared rapidly up the steps to the

Alten main street. He heard one say to the other, "Quick, John, let us see the prostitutes. They can warm a man's bones on such a frigid night." "Not like my wife," said the other. "She could break a man's bone being frigid all night!" They both laughed into the distance.

Wingate stopped in front of the tavern. It lay in the center of the docklike walkway, marked by a glowing, swinging lantern on either side of the entrance. Mac looked down the path. All he saw were serene snowflakes drifting down on a quaint, quiet seaside town. He looked out to sea, deeper into the fjord. He saw the shadow of the battleship *Tirpitz* on the water. It was effectively camouflaged even at this distance. It lay peacefully, silently, motionless on the calm surface of the ocean. It seemed majestic, proud, noble, and more than anything else, alone.

Mac turned away from the ship and went inside the small tavern. Even though the sky was darkening in preparation for North Cape's early night, the inn was at its midafternoon lull. Only a few men sat around its many round tables, which were squeezed together under the low-beamed ceiling. Two fireplaces warmed the fairly empty space, one at the back and one on the right side, near the carved wooden bar.

More hanging kerosene lamps lit the interior, casting a golden yellow pall on the clammy interior. No one looked up from his drink or food as Lieutenant Wingate of the Third Reich walked in. Only a general or admiral could pull them out of their seats and that high-ranking an officer would always have an underling with him to scream, "*Achtung!*"

The only other thing noticeable about the place was that there were no pure Norwegians in it. There were some men Wingate identified as Quislings, but not one hard-working, Thor-fearing, salt-of-the-earth Norseman. The meeting place had been taken over by the Nazis and transformed from a rustic watering hole to a place to drown your miseries.

Wingate sauntered in. He passed a table of sailors near the door. They hardly glanced at him as he passed. He noticed a particularly Aryan group carousing by the side fireplace. They were all dressed casually in the exact same thing. Dark turtlenecks, thick slacks, and slick boots. They were a team of some kind. They were all good looking, muscular, and blond. Hitler's chosen children. Unlike their tavern compatriots, they were having a good time. One even tossed a cocky salute at Wingate as he passed.

Wingate smiled back and returned the haphazard acknowledgement. Moving on, he spied the man he was looking for. The man fitting Kirsten's description of Arne Larsen stood at the table that stood for the makeshift bar, nursing a tankard of ale. His shoulders were hunched and he stared into the brew's foam as if he were trying to see his future there.

Mac moved up to the bar beside him. It was a hastily put together, fairly tacky affair. From the door the bar looked permanent, but up close Wingate could see that it had been nailed to the floor quickly and a variety of liquor had been randomly placed behind it. Several kegs sat behind the thick legs of the German barkeep as well.

"What do you have to eat today?" Wingate asked the man in German. "I'm starving."

"Same as every day, lieutenant," the bartender said with boredom in his voice. He rattled off the choices with the memorized abandon of a man who has said the same thing thousands of times over. "Cereal, goat cheese, herring, and codfish."

"Herring," Wingate decided. He left off the please. "And a tankard of ale."

"Very good, sir," said the proprietor, leaning down to stick a flagon under the wooden faucet of a tapped keg. He rose with the foam slopping over the cup's sides and slapped it on the counter. Wingate waited to see if his minor strategy paid off. Cereal and even cheese could be left at room temperature much longer than the likes of fish. Herring would have to be cooled somehow. And Wingate was guessing that the tavern kept its seafood outside.

Sure enough, the barkeep wiped his hands on the cloth tucked into the front of his pants, rounded the bar, and walked toward the front door. "I'll be right back with your herring, sir," he said as he left.

"Very good," Wingate replied. He wasted no time. As soon as the bartender was out of earshot, he turned his back toward the door, blocking his face from the view of everyone except Larsen. "Snow Queen sends a message," he muttered in the Riksmaal dialect. "Karl is dead."

The man started, his ale splashing on the tabletop.

"Don't panic," Wingate continued through clenched teeth.

131

"Meet me outside. Ten minutes." He took a long swig of the brew. It was delicious. The herring, when brought, was just as good. Fresh, unadulterated, and homemade. Mac never had a taste for herring before, but anything beat the hell out of K rations.

Before Wingate finished eating, Larsen drained his tankard. He waved at the barkeep, who nodded and said, "Next time, Arne." Then Larsen moved out the door, on none too steady feet.

Wingate watched him go and turned to the bartender with a grin. "Likes the liquid, doesn't he?" he commented in German.

The man snorted. "Loves it, more like. He's in here the same time every week. Regular as clockwork. Puts the stuff away like it is going to run dry tomorrow. Don't know how he holds the stuff. They say he does that sort of thing along his whole route. Delivers the mail, you know. I do not care what happens to him elsewhere, but he always gets me my mail on time. I cannot understand it." The bartender shook his head at the all-encompassing wonder of the world he lived in.

While he was rattling on, Wingate had finished his fish and pushed the metal dish forward. He did not worry about payment. At wartime establishments like these, the camp always picked up the tab. "Some men work better with a little warmth in their veins," Wingate commented about the mailman's drinking habit.

"Or a little warmth in their loins?" the bartender suggested conspiratorially as he leaned in and raised his eyebrows. "Have you seen the two new girls at the whorehouse? Lovely flowers of Norwegian womanhood, I should say!"

Wingate's heritage and all his past teachings almost took over. His muscles bunched to leap on the barkeep's head, before he managed to relax through an effort of will. His brain ordered the muscles in his face to lift up the corners of his mouth. Reluctantly, they complied. He then showed his teeth in a wolf's grin.

"No, I haven't," he said. "But I'll go over and take a look. Maybe I'll see you there?"

"Positively!" the bartender promised, winking.

"Good," Wingate said.

The air was clearer outside. The sky had gotten much darker in the past quarter of an hour. Angry-looking clouds soared between Norway and the sun, casting deep shadows where there had only been shade before. He looked both ways. No one appeared to be on the walkway with him. He moved back the way he had come, toward the nearby steps that wound up and around their rock base and onto the main street.

"Voersyk," he heard next to his ear in the Riksmaal dialect. It was a comment upon Mother Nature, meaning roughly, "Weather sick."

He turned to look at Arne Larsen. The man did not look drunk anymore. His eyes were clear and suspicious. He stood under a low roof in a crook between two buildings, underneath the tailor's bedroom window. Squeezed in there, he could not be seen by anyone coming out of the bar nor anyone coming down the stairs.

"Ja," said Wingate, agreeing. *"Ikkesant?"*

"Who are you?" Larsen whispered harshly. "What do you want?"

"Information," Wingate answered immediately. "On Operation Source."

The American had to hand it to the postman. Even after emptying a couple of tankards, he still moved incredibly fast. Wingate didn't even see the blade. He just grabbed the arm driving up under his chest by instinct when he heard the sudden exhalation of air instead of a reply.

The Norwegian hadn't counted on Wingate's brawny strength. His arm was locked by Mac's burgeoning muscles. The American felt his fingers sinking through the cloth of Larsen's shirt at the wrist and forearm, while the Norwegian's whole limb vibrated with the effort to break free.

Both men had clamped their mouths shut at the first violent move. Neither wanted anyone running to their aid. For a moment they struggled in one frozen position. Then they seemed to move at the same time. Arne tried to chop at Mac's neck with his free hand. Wingate let go of Larsen's forearm to nimbly block the blow, then kicked the man above his left knee.

Larsen had to grit his teeth to choke back the cry of pain. Then Mac jerked himself backward, forcing the Norwegian to move with him. Arne took one step with his left leg, and it collapsed under him. He found himself on his knees before

Mac, his face staring at Wingate's stomach. Out of the corner of his eye, he saw the right fist coming.

The American slammed Larsen in the jaw, not retracting his blow until he felt the bone give under his knuckles. He heard the slap of flesh hitting flesh, then the tearing click that meant the end of the bone had cut off the blood going to the man's brain. Larsen snapped back against the wall, unconscious.

Wingate did not stand around to admire his work. He pulled the long, razor-thin blade out of Arne's hand, where it was still gripped, and slipped it into his greatcoat pocket. Then he hauled the postman on his back and threw him onto the low roof above them. He quickly looked both ways, then climbed onto the roof himself. Utilizing a fireman's carry, Wingate brought Larsen to the tailor's window. Kirsten opened it from the inside.

"What happened?" she asked as Wingate squeezed through the opening.

"Hadn't you heard?" the American said grimly, dropping the limp body on the bed. "Larsen always kills on the first date."

"What?" asked a confused Kirsten.

"Never mind," snapped Mac. He leaned over the groggy Norwegian and helped him back to the real world with a few sharp slaps.

Larsen's eyes opened, his head stopped shaking, and his vision cleared. "You are a dead man," he told Mac.

"Not yet," the American replied.

Larsen hurriedly took in the details of the room. He recognized where he was. Wingate could tell from his expression. At first, Arne thought the tailor had been captured as well, until he saw the now fully clothed Kirsten over Mac's shoulder. He put two and two together. "Who are you?" he repeated.

"Peter Magnussen Wingate. Captain of the United States Armed Forces. Special demolitions expert. Here trying to find out what I'm supposed to blow up."

Larsen considered the information. "You *are* a dead man," he finally concluded. The Norwegian snaked out from under Mac's leaning form and sat up on the edge of the bed, fingering his jaw. Wingate didn't let the subject rest.

"Kirsten tells me you can fill me in on Operation Source,"

he cued. Larsen whirled at the mention of the name, stared at Wingate, then looked accusingly at the girl.

"I had no choice," she told him honestly.

"That says something for you, Captain," Larsen informed him mirthlessly. He went back to testing his jaw, then rubbed his knee.

Wingate pulled out the knife Larsen had tried to stick him with. "I've run out of patience, Larsen," Mac warned, holding the blade in an offensive position. "I've run out of men, I've run out of equipment, and I've run out of room. Give me the information!"

Larsen turned to face Mac's anger and the knife fearlessly. "You've also run out of time," he sneered. "Operation Source is dead."

CHAPTER 8

Captain Einar Sørum moved through the night forest like a gazelle. He ran fast, silently, and unflaggingly, slowing for neither tree nor bush. He held the Suomi against his chest, the wind and snow blowing in his face as he went swiftly down the incline.

Even the slick wet snow that had already collected an inch high on the ground did not give him pause. As a boy, he had run on just such surfaces. He had long since stopped slipping and falling down. In fact, he had a much harder time on dry land.

He moved through the cold, feeling an elation and freedom that no Nazi or Quisling could quell. Up here in the mountains he was safe. Up here, among his natural habitat of wood and wildlife, he was liberated. There was no need to fight for independence. There was no need to spill the blood of the oppressor, the occupier. As long as he had the mountains of North Cape and Alten fjord to hide in, he would never give in.

Suddenly he felt his ears lay back against the side of his head—a canine trait he had never told anyone about and one that no one had ever noticed. It indicated a foreign noise entering into his sphere of consciousness. He realized that it was a strange nightbird calling. He stopped, unable to prevent his skidding a few feet. He listened closely again, but the birdsong had ended. Curious, he moved off in the direction it came from.

He started by walking, then he began trotting, finally he was running full speed toward the strange sound. He stopped again when a twig broke underfoot. But it was not his foot that did the breaking. He spun in the direction of the noise. All he could see was the empty blue horizon and all he could hear were the natural sounds of the forest.

Sørum moved cautiously to the spot where he had heard the twig snap. But there were dozens of broken branches all over the snow-covered ground. There was no way he could tell if one was freshly cracked.

His neck nearly cracked when he heard the birdcall again. This time it was right above him. He looked up only to see and then feel a massive shape fall on him.

The two forms crashed to the ground and rolled across the frozen hillside. Snow was thrown in all directions as the MILORG agent struggled to get free. He kicked out and tried to bring his submachine gun to bear, but the assailant was too close and was gripping him too hard.

Almost immediately after his vain attempts to extricate himself, Sørum felt himself lifted off the ground. A boot was shoved into his stomach, fingers gripped his sleeves, and he was vaulted over backward through the air.

He soared down the hillside upside down, the moonlit countryside jerking across his vision. He felt his arms and legs out, touching nothing in a spread-eagled position.

He was just beginning to enjoy the sensation, when his back met the trunk of a tree.

All the air was knocked out of him as his arms and legs tried to keep moving forward, stretching his cartilage like rubber bands. Then he fell to the ground and rolled to his knees.

Before Sørum could clear his buzzing brain and breathe again, a sudden savage pain erupted in his elbow and wrist. His Suomi was wrenched out of his grasp. Before he could react, another freezing gun barrel was jammed against the back of his head.

"*Stehen sie,*" a raw, guttural voice said the words for "stand up" in German.

Sørum cautiously raised his hands and got to his feet.

"Turn around," the same nasty voice instructed.

The Norwegian slowly twisted 180 degrees to face his captor. A captor who was grinning without a trace of humor.

"If I could find you," Mac Wingate told him, "think how easy it would be for the enemy."

• • •

"It's over," Wingate said, standing full length in the flickering light of the fire of the hillside *stabbur*. "No more lies, no more diversions, and no more running."

"Captain Wingate." Sørum pleaded with his voice and eyes. His hands were tied behind him with thin hemp. "What can you possibly hope to gain by these actions?"

"Just a chance, you apathetic son of a bitch," Wingate spat. He didn't like playing the sacrificial lamb. Especially when everybody had told him his part was that of the brave woodsman. "You'd sacrifice anybody to protect your precious hideout. You don't really care who dies, as long as no one finds you."

The two stood alone in the big, dark barn, empty save for the fireplace.

"You are acting insane," the MILORG chief maintained. "This is stupid, this is ludicrous . . . it is suicidal!"

"No," Wingate said. "It's the only way not to commit suicide. It's the only way to get everybody's ass out of the fire."

"I don't know what you mean," Sørum huffed.

"Let me make it clear," Wingate began. "On September 11th, six midget submarines—each manned by four sailors—left Scotland for Alten fjord. Each had a pair of two-ton charges armed with timing detonators." Wingate held up one finger. "One was assigned to sabotage the warship *Lutzow*." He put up another finger. "Two were sent to attack the battleship *Scharnhorst*." He put up his middle finger. "And the remaining three were sent to destroy the *Tirpitz*. *That* was Operation Source. Not this. Not what me and my men are doing."

The Norwegian looked patently confused. "Then why are you here? Why did we risk our lives for you?"

Before Wingate could answer, the barn door opened and the commandos Sumner and Neill marched in, each holding one arm of a third man whose hands were tied and whose head was covered by a bag. The Aussie and Canuck brought the bound man over to the American captain.

"Let's ask the dancing clown, shall we?" Wingate suggested to Sørum with bitterness. He ripped the bag off of Colonel Richard Tyler's head. "You want to tell him what we're here for?" Wingate inquired casually to his country-man. "You want to tell him about that little job you had

138

planned for us later tonight? You want to tell him about the 'word' you would finally get and the special instructions you would finally give?''

Tyler said nothing. He just glared at Wingate, his expression no longer innocent and confused. His face was set in a classic stonewall.

''What is he talking about?'' Sørum asked Tyler in Norwegian. ''What does he mean?''

''Don't listen,'' Tyler replied in rough Riksmaal. ''I told you he was dangerous.''

''Yeah,'' Wingate drawled. ''Only listen to the colonels. Everybody listen to what they have to say. Only don't notice they're saying something different to every person they talk to.''

''Wingate,'' Tyler raged, ''you're a certifiable psycho! You've just earned yourself a court-martial, mister!''

''Better a court-martial than a twenty-one gun salute,'' Wingate told himself, turning away from the colonel's beet-red face. As he pivoted, the barn door opened again and Kirsten came in from the night in the company of Arne Larsen.

''They coming?'' Wingate inquired.

''Yes,'' the woman assured him.

Wingate whirled back and paced to the fireplace, looking into the miniature inferno, trying to find a way out of the operational insanity. He put his back to the blaze, looking from Tyler to Sørum to Neill to Sumner.

''I'll tell you the whole story,'' he promised. ''Everybody needs to know.'' Wingate did not feel tired by all the intrigue, all the double crosses, and all the death. He was burning with a fierce light. Even as he filled in the others with what he had found out from Larsen, he was slapping together a plan in the back of his mind.

''We are not 'Source.' We never were. We were a diversionary team, but not a minor one. We were the only one, the major one that had to get the horde of Nazis away from the 'Source' goal . . . in this case, the *Tirpitz*. But there were so many of them and so few of us that Allied Command officially labeled our job a suicide mission. I'd imagine they weren't happy about it, but they had to find a minimum of men to do a dirty job in a minimum of time. By the time they decided they needed a diversion, the midget subs were already on their way.''

"I don't get it," Sumner interrupted indignantly. "If it was such a tough mission, why didn't they arm us to the teeth and let us try our damnedest, fully prepared?"

"Now there's a question," Wingate fully agreed. "Why not indeed? That's where the collected colonels' ego problems got in the way. They were part of the High Command, with a capitol HC. And once they decided through impressive research and planning that there was no way we could come out alive, they didn't need our lowly opinions. They had their own experts on everything." Wingate turned and faced Tyler again.

"Only one big difference, Colonel," he lectured. "Your pros knew they wouldn't be going anywhere near Alten fjord. They were safe in the knowledge that we were already pegged for execution. They didn't have the edge." Wingate hit the last word, twisting his fist as he said it.

"Now, that's not fair, Captain," Tyler spoke up. "We were planning to air-drop the necessary equipment. Once we got word of the setup and situation."

"That's the other thing," Wingate used the colonel's interjection as a taking-off point. "Information. Intelligence. Right or wrong, the colonels and their superiors figured we wouldn't be too happy if we knew about our lot, so they planned to have us do a minimum of on-site reconnaissance. They figured a better idea would be to collect intelligence the way they had all along! *Have their spies send the material over the mountains to the SOE!*"

"I've been collecting material for months now," Larsen cut in, explaining further. "It was a good system, but not foolproof. I'd get the latest movements of the warships, put them on microfilm, and send them with an escaping MILORG man to Murmansk, just over the Russian border."

"And it worked!" Tyler yelled. "It worked well!"

"When the agent wasn't killed by a Nazi or a Quisling, or in a climbing accident, or the information wasn't intercepted on the radio frequencies, or the microfilm wasn't sunk on the ship carrying it to England by the *Tirpitz*—which was the reason 'Source' was set up in the first place," Wingate managed to get out. "Like Larsen said, the system wasn't foolproof. Sometimes it took too long for the material to get from Norway to Russia to England. Sometimes, it never made the circuit at all.''

"Like now,'' acknowledged Larsen.

"Like now,'' repeated Wingate.

"What do you mean?'' Tyler shouted. "We have everything you need to know.''

"Wrong!'' said Wingate, with barely controlled rage. When he had manhandled the colonel back at the whorehouse, he had been faking the emotion. Now the feeling was real. He came at Tyler like a locomotive. "Wrong! You *think* you have all the info you need. You *pray* that you do. Since God is on your side, you assume everything will turn out fine. But it won't,'' Mac assured him. "It hasn't.''

"What do you mean?'' Tyler asked dangerously. "Explain yourself, soldier.''

Wingate nearly punched him. He stopped in mid-swing. He held his fist in the air, looking at Tyler's face. The American was smiling like the Englishman had. It was the superior death's-head look. Mac realized Tyler wanted him to do it. He'd love it, in fact. It would prove in his own mind, beyond a shadow of a doubt, that Wingate was the beast Tyler thought he was. The animal only good for throwing to the wolves.

Wingate thought about that, then slugged Tyler anyway. He didn't care what Tyler thought.

The colonel's head snapped back loudly in the cold, large barn. It moved so fast that it nodded twice before Tyler hit the ground. He lay on top of his tied arms with a bleeding lip and foggy eyes.

Wingate had punched him in the mouth on purpose. He wanted to sting and stun him, not knock him out or break his neck. He still had some things to tell him.

"You remember Walters's speech back on the boat?'' Wingate told the prone officer. "About how if I got in his way again, he'd hang my balls over Datchet Green? Well, you understand something, Tyler. *You* try to screw me one more time and we won't wait until we get back to England for a ball-hanging. I'll rip your balls out then and there and make you eat them.''

Kirsten had come over and put her hands on Mac's shoulders. He straightened at a normal speed and nodded appreciatively. "All right, Tyler,'' he continued, walking back to the warmth of the fire. "Let's talk strategy. We go waltzing off north somewhere, destroying things as we go, drawing off the infantry from the camp on the mountaintop, *ikkesant?* That leaves a few unorganized schleps to protect the ships from the submarine attack. Is that right?"

Tyler struggled to a sitting position, trying to lick the blood off his chin. "Yes, of course," he said with indignation.

"Wrong," Wingate corrected. "That leaves a highly trained group of undersea commandos that patrol the ship's hull *in shifts*. When one group is off gallivanting in town, the other is on shore or underwater. These boys couldn't miss the approach of a midget sub. They know what they look like."

Mac looked at Larsen. The Norwegian spy nodded in support. Wingate had seen one shift off duty in the tavern. Arne had seen their schedules and watched them work.

"Surely a small group of men couldn't stop three thirty-ton subs from reaching their quarry once the majority of troops were diverted elsewhere," Tyler complained.

"Maybe not," Wingate admitted. "But an antitorpedo net would succeed where they could fail."

"An A/T net?" Tyler echoed incredulously. "We received no reports of any A/T nets!"

"You should have," Larsen said solemnly. "I sent them to you. Lars Harald should have brought them."

"Your wonderful system strikes again," Wingate reminded the captured colonel. He rose placidly and stood over the sitting Tyler. "So it all would have failed," he said as kindly as he could. "We would have been killed, and all the subs would have been destroyed, either by the undersea commandos you didn't know about or by the nets you deal with because the news of their existence never arrived."

"I-I had no idea . . . ." Tyler stammered. "I didn't know!"

"That's the crime," Wingate told him sadly. "I'll see that it's chiseled on your tombstone."

The American colonel looked honestly aghast that his mission could have gone so wrong. He stared at the ground, his eyes wide, his mouth working. As he tried to comprehend it, a small group of MILORG agents began coming into the *stabbur* from outside. Wingate recognized the tailor and the man who had played Karl's father down the mountain. The last two to enter were the female survivors of the Harald commune.

"Wingate, I'm sorry!" Tyler had found his voice again. "Anything I can do. A-anything . . . !"

"You'll have your chance," Wingate assured him as he went to greet the new arrivals.

Once they were all comfortable around the fire, Wingate got down to cases. "It is time to take action," he said. "It is time to fight back." But while Tyler had seen the light, Sørum was far from repentant.

"No!" he yelled at the collected Norwegians. "Remember what happened at the Harald commune! Remember all the other atrocities! We must not attack the Germans. There will be terrible reprisals!"

"There will be reprisals whether you do anything or not," Wingate responded to the Norwegian's outburst. "The only question is whether you die on your knees or fight on your feet."

"No, it is not true!" Sørum babbled desperately. "Do not listen!"

Kirsten turned her head away. "Einar," she said into Larsen's shoulder. "Can you not see that it is over for us here? We cannot wish the Nazis away."

Wingate elaborated further. "The midget submarines are coming, Sørum, no matter what you say. And whether they get to the *Tirpitz* or not, they're going to deliver their pay-loads. And after those two-ton charges go off, there will be repercussions. The enemy will be crawling all over Alten and North Cape. Like it or not, there will be reprisals."

The Norwegian captain may have wanted to spare his country, but he was a realist. He bowed his head in defeat. "Very well, since it seems we have no choice, I will help if I can."

Wingate rubbed his hands together, both for warmth and in anticipation. "All right. Einar, are there captured German weapons and stores somewhere about? Somewhere I can get my hands on them?"

Head still down, Sørum nodded in the affirmative.

"W-what are you going to do?" quaked Tyler. "What *can* you do? The midget subs are scheduled to arrive tomorrow morning!"

"At 7:30 A.M." Wingate acknowledged. "Larsen informed me."

"But you'll never be able to pull anything off by then!" the

143

colonel went on incredulously. "You have to divert the bulk of the Alten infantry, fight the undersea commandos, and cut the A/T nets! All before tomorrow morning and with no equipment!" It was all too much for Tyler. He shook his head in disbelief, saying, "Face it, Captain. Operation Source is over. It's finished."

"Shut up and listen, Tyler," Wingate said irritably. He faced the MILORGs. "I'll need some things. I'll need to know whether you can get them to the whorehouse cellar in . . ." Wingate checked his watch. It was 9:30 P.M. Just ten hours before the midget submarines were set to arrive. "In three hours. Listen closely . . .

"Ten boxes of kitchen matches.

"Five hundred meters of cord.

"Four rolls of bandages.

"Two clothesline pulleys." Henrik the tailor raised his hand happily at that.

"Five winter knee socks." The Harald girls raised their hands.

"One large can of petrol.

"Three large tins.

"One faucet pipe.

"One roll of black tape.

"A pack of cigarette paper.

"Four large sheets of heavy-duty cardboard.

"Two large and heavy rubber bands and three small rubber bands.

"A pack of straight pins.

"And three rucksacks."

Not one item was left uncalled for. Among the group, everyone agreed they could get at least one item. Wingate sent them on their way, pulling out the blade Larsen had tried to stick him with. He talked to the postman while he hacked away at Sørum's bonds.

"What can I do?" Arne asked.

"You've got one of the most important jobs," Wingate said. "I need a thorough map of the Nazi infantry camp on the hilltop. I need all the buildings, all the cover, every detail. Can you get it?"

"In three hours?"

"Yes."

"Sure."

"Get going." Larsen took off immediately. Wingate cut through the last strand tying Sørum's hands together. "All right," said the American. "Let's see these captured stores."

The Norwegian led Mac and Kirsten to another *stabbur* within the confines of the village. Up a ladder and below a false floor section was an anarchist's dream: bits and pieces of what looked like an entire armament. Wingate picked out a Maschinengewehr 42 machine gun and a Madsen machine gun converted from top magazine feed to a bottom belt-feed weapon.

"Strange choice," Sørum commented.

"I need two, and they have to be different," Wingate explained, sifting through the rest of the equipment. "The MG-42 is perfect; belt feeding an unlimited supply of 7.92 mm shells and pumping them out at 1,200 rounds per minute. The Madsen only kicks out 450 rounds, but it's the best made, most dependable weapon of the lot. Besides, it is the only other belt-feed gun you have."

Wingate looked around. "You store your ammo elsewhere?"

"Of course," was the reply. Sørum was already moving across the barn to another fake floor section. Wingate followed and dipped in. He came out with several standard fifty-round belts of 7.92 caliber ammunition in a carrying rucksack. He then found a full cardboard grenade case.

"All right," he said. "Tools. I need tools."

"Mac," Kirsten advised. "I must get back to the house. I . . . we have . . . paying customers."

Wingate looked at her with understanding and gentleness. "This may be hard, Kirsten," he warned. "But there is something you must do for me as well . . ."

The prostitute part was easier than Mac had expected. He had planned to don the Nazi lieutenant's uniform and lure the off-duty undersea commandos to the den of hookers, but he discovered it wasn't necessary. On every cold winter night, the twelve men who comprised the unit took turns getting warm.

Each six-man group stood a twelve-hour watch. Unfortunately for his plan, the shift came at eight in the morning and eight at night. Wingate could only get to half the crew. He'd have to deal with the others underwater. But even to get that far, he'd have to make sure the half dozen commandos that visited the whorehouse never got out again.

Wingate looked at the ceiling of the cellar. He could imagine what was going on up there. That was all he could do: imagine. Kirsten had promised that she would signal him when the time was right. Until then, he had to keep working.

He had plenty of work to do. He took his eyes off the ceiling and put them on his watch. It was 2:00 A.M. Five and a half hours from blast-off. It was going to be close. Wingate would readily admit that. It would be close getting all the material collected. It would be close getting it prepared. It would be close getting it to the infantry camp. It would be damn close getting it set up to go off at the same time as the arrival of the subs. It was all ludicrously close, but the only chance they had.

Wingate looked around the room. It looked like Santa's workshop, only the elves were intent on taking over the North Pole by force. Everywhere and on every surface, the MILORGs were working on the raw materials to Mac's new specifications. Sumner and Neill wandered around occasionally to help out before they returned to their own preparations.

"Let's go over it again," Wingate suggested to Larsen, who was bending over a roughly drawn map on the side table next to him.

"Very well," Larsen concurred. "Around the outside is a chain-link fence topped with barbed wire. The fence is at the edge of the woods on the eastern perimeter. Twenty meters to the west lies an empty barracks. The men who used to be inside were transferred to a ski-troop course."

"Is the bottom of the fence buried in the ground?" Wingate suddenly interrupted.

"The bottom links are just barely submerged in a shallow trough. You can gain entry easily."

Wingate nodded. "Is the area mined?"

"There are signs to that effect, but they are more show than security. I have seen the guards walk everywhere with no big booms." Wingate opened his mouth. Larsen beat him to it. "The guard makes a full round every half hour. There is a single guard tower near the fence, forty meters from the empty barracks."

"Are there any more empty buildings?" Wingate got to ask.

"A small supply shack right in the middle of the camp," Larsen replied. "And the vacated tailor's cabin to the west of it. I assume that when you say empty, you mean empty of people."

"You assume correctly. Where are the inhabited buildings?"

"Not far from the empty barracks. There are two squads of crack riflemen headquartered there. Next to that is the officers' quarters. To the west is another barracks for visiting seamen, staff members, like myself, and office workers. The Quislings often have their meetings there."

Wingate studied the map. He saw a telephone pole adjacent to the officers' dwelling. He saw several trees inside the perimeter. It just might work, he thought. He tapped the map several times with his forefinger. He just might be able to pull it off.

"Why not give us the guns and let us attack the camp?" said Sørum, sitting in the corner and practically reading Mac's mind. "Why go through all this?"

"First," Wingate responded, still checking the map, "like you, I don't want to see anyone but the enemy die. Second and most important, I don't think it would work your way. No offense, but send the hookers, the old men, the tailor, and you against a crack troop of German infantry? They'd chew you up and go back to breakfast without missing a bite."

The American captain then left the side table and wandered around the basement to be sure everything was being done to his specifications. One group of three MILORGs was working on the can of petrol; another three were laboring over the MG-42; another trio was handling the deadly grenades and the smelly socks; and a final group was taking care of the Madsen.

The three working on the can were converting a harness usually used for carrying stretchers to a backrack for easier carrying. The large black can of petrol was strapped to the rack with strips of equally black cloth. The three empty tins had been wrapped in undershirts and strapped together with tape.

The trio slaving on the guns was knotting rubber bands around the triggers and securing them behind the hand grips. The rubber knot was then secured with a tight wind of cord. The cord continued to be wound until five feet of the stuff

147

was wrapped around the hand grip. Then everything was held in with tape.

Alongside the breech mechanisms, the rucksack had been affixed. They were braced in a perpendicular fashion to the side of the weapon, with the interior girded by the heavy cardboard sheets. In them were a couple of fifty-round 7.92 mm ammunition belts—attached together and coiled in an overlay fashion so they would feed smoothly when the time came.

A long knife slit had been cut in the top of the pack and the first few bullets pulled through. The sack would be closed and the first few rounds taped over the breech. Wingate had demanded they not actually load the guns. One bad jolt during the trip up the mountain and one of his men might get his ass shot off. To facilitate his men's carrying the guns, a belt of the pants kind had been attached. Finally the clothesline-type pulleys were taped to the gun barrels, right where the bipods used to be, along with two rolls of bandages each.

The people preparing the socks had first filled them up with gravel, dirt, pebbles, and various garbage of that kind. They were tied at the top. Wingate tested the heft. They were about ten pounds apiece. Then a grenade was attached to the top by running the knotted cord to the fragmentation device. Wingate examined that handiwork closely as well.

The five-foot length of cord ran to the pineapple body of the hand grenade and was tied tightly around the grooves. Then the length was folded over and over on itself. The resulting bunch was wrapped with a rubber band. That way it looked like a rock-filled sock tied to a grenade by a very short cord with an overlaying bunch in the middle. But pull both the sock and grenade apart and that string in the middle would rapidly unravel, leaving a rock-filled sock tied to a grenade by a very long cord.

That's where the more experienced commandos took over. Sumner wound a piece of electrical tape around the spoon and the body of the grenade. He then folded back the end of the tape on itself, creating a little tab so later he could pull off the sticky strip quickly. Then, with a pair of pliers Mac had found at the hillside *stabbur,* he bent back the ends of the safety pin and clipped them off. It made the release extremely sensitive and it was the reason Mac had assigned his men to the chore. He wanted to kill the undersea commandos upstairs, all right, but not by blowing himself up along with them.

Sumner tied a length of cord to the ring of the pin, with a large slipknot at the other end. Then he wound the length, carefully laid it over the knot, and taped it to the side of the grenade for easy access. He repeated these steps with another device. Neill, in the meantime, had been preparing a third explosive in a slightly different manner.

The same "quick-release" cord ran from the sock to the grenade, but in this case the Canadian attached it directly to the altered pin. Then he took all three sock-bombs and laid them carefully in another rucksack side by side. After that, there were only two gravel-filled socks left. Sumner gave one each to the MILORGs handling the two machine guns. They attached them to the length of cord hanging off the butt, which was tied around the trigger.

Neill had just closed the sock-bomb sack and sighed with relief when Wingate clapped him on the shoulder. "Donald, give me one of your cigars, will you?"

Neill looked up unassumingly. "Uh. What cigars, Captain?"

"Come on, Sergeant," Wingate admonished, curling his fingers in a "let's go" gesture.

"But Captain!" the Canadian blurted. "They're the only things I salvaged off the sardine scow!" Then he remembered the Reising. "Of worth," he added.

Wingate shrugged. "It's for the war effort."

As they played out the scene, everyone in the room began to watch. By the time Neill miserably handed over a stogie, everyone was smiling. They didn't understand the exact words, but they were all cheered by the expressions and obvious humor.

At that moment, the room was filled by the thin, tiny tinkling of a bell.

Wingate slapped the cigar down and moved swiftly for the side table and his Sten. "I'll take care of that later," he told Neill. "Positions, everyone. This is it."

It was Kirsten's signal. Earlier she had rigged up an absurdly simple string and bell system as an alarm. It meant that, as far as she knew, the undersea commandos were in position.

She was in no position herself to know for sure. All six would not be in her room. As much as she might have suggested it, the Nazis weren't as perverted as the Quislings.

They might indulge in a threesome, but they thought of themselves as the world's future-man. They drew the line at male-dominated orgies.

It made their execution more difficult. Making it doubly difficult was the fact that Wingate didn't want to bring the whole town down on the place while he did it. In fact, he couldn't afford even to let the other patrons know that men were being slaughtered just a wall away from them. The Aryan men had to die silently.

Wingate moved to the entrance of the tunnel. Sumner moved to the stairs leading to Kirsten's bedroom. Larsen whipped on a pair of gloves and started to wrap a thin copper wire around his palms. Tyler suddenly rose and approached the American captain.

"Wingate, I . . ."

"Now is not the time, Colonel," Wingate hissed. Tyler raised his submachine gun before Mac's eyes in response. His M3 had suddenly sprouted a silencer. "Been holding out on us, eh, Tyler?" Wingate commented.

"I said anything I could do . . ."

"Come on, then," Wingate urged. The two men moved down the tunnel. They followed its twisting, rising paths until they came to the section with the light between the cracks. Only this time there was sound to go with the sight. As they approached, they heard moaning.

Wingate hoped Tyler knew what to do. He had been present when they had worked it out with Kirsten. A solid hall of rooms off to the side was reserved for the Nazi commandos. Each would be taken into a different room, three on each side of the hall. The doors were positioned in such a way that an assassin could pivot from one room to the next in a very short time. All he had to do was kick open one door and shoot, turn, kick open another, shoot, turn, and so on.

But that wasn't fast enough for Mac. He took into consideration that these Nazis weren't the only ones in the rooms. And that the sound of the first door being broken into would alert the last Nazis in line for massacre. Even the best shot with a silenced gun couldn't be sure of getting everyone dead-to-rights.

So everyone had to do their parts quickly and wait for Wingate to handle the rest. Kirsten would work it so she would get on top. When the man under her was the most vulnerable, she would slip a knife out of her mattress, clap her hand across his mouth, and bury the blade where it would do the most harm. Only after she had accomplished that would she hit the signal.

The rest was even trickier, but Mac had faith in his men. He pictured their roles in his mind. Sumner and Larsen would enter Kirsten's room by the secret passage and make their way quickly and quietly to the next two quarters. Sumner would go across the narrow hall to the room opposite Kirsten's, sneak into the darkened place, wrap one arm around the commando's neck, and grind the knife into his kidney.

Larsen would enter the darkened room next to Kirsten's. Wingate had tried to convince him to use a knife, but his earlier fight with Mac had spooked him. He resorted to a garrotte. It was nastier, but just as silent and deadly.

As Mac and Tyler positioned themselves a wall away from the last of the rooms, Wingate listened for any undue noise above the orgiastic groans of the people in front of him. When he heard nothing else after a few seconds, he silently placed the barrel of his gun flat along one of the wider cracks. His silenced Sten was pointing into the room, right at the bed.

He looked through the crack, the dim light of the moon reflecting off his pupil. The lovemakers were silhouetted in the window. He saw a man's shape rise and fall. It reminded him of a penny arcade shooting game where the target popped up and down, only this was far more difficult and far more dangerous. He couldn't afford to wait too long before acting.

The gods of pleasure were with him. The girl suddenly cried out in climax, and the man's shape rose slowly, ecstatically, to expose his entire torso. Mac pulled the trigger.

The click of the bolt, the cough of the escaping air, and the tear of little wall pieces all mingled minutely. The loudest noise was that of the commando falling over and hitting his head on the back of the bed. The girl did not react to the blood splashing on her. In the darkness, it was just another liquid.

But she did respond as soon as the man died. She got up, pulled the many heavy bedclothes out from under the corpse and off the bed, then brought them over to the wall. She held them against the thin slats as Wingate pressed all his weight on them from the other side. Seeing what he was trying to do, Tyler added his weight. The centers of the wood started to crack. The blankets muffled the sound.

Soon, Mac could slip into the room sideways from the long rip in the wall. The water-logged slats practically bounced back intact. Instead of a hole, there was only a thin tear in the wall that a man could push himself through. Tyler followed.

"There are only two more men," Wingate whispered to him. "You help back us up." The colonel nodded. Wingate went to the door. He was at the end of the special section, but not the end of the hall. Directly to his left as he looked out the door were the stairs to the lobby, where other horny men —the local Quislings—waited. Farther to his right were several more rooms, where the traitors were entertained. None of Wingate's men could afford to be in the hallway too long. There was no way to regulate everyone's timing.

Wingate looked to the right. He saw Larsen and Sumner looking at him from the two doorways they had first invaded. The American nodded. On the count of three, he and Sumner would both move into the remaining two rooms.

Sumner nodded "two." Wingate nodded "three."

When they moved, they did not do it quickly. They did it smoothly. They didn't want to break down doors and attack frenetically. They did not want anyone to cry out in surprise. Each man simply went to the door he was assigned, easily twisted the knob, opened it just enough to slip in, and closed it again.

Wingate refused to deal with complications. He had set his killing instinct on automatic. He didn't care what the two people were doing on the bed. He unerringly moved over, placed the barrel against the man's neck, and pulled the trigger at the same time. The whole move took less than two seconds.

The commando fell dead atop the prostitute. In the moonlight Mac could see the girl was quietly crying. She slid out from under the corpse and nodded through her tears.

"*Takk dem,*" she said very quietly and very honestly. "Thank you."

Wingate looked out the door again. Sumner and Larsen were both looking back. Everyone was finished. Mac turned around. Tyler was in the door by the stairs, still checking. Wingate tapped the doorjamb. Tyler turned. They all signaled success. Wingate nodded again. On another count of three, they would all slip back into Kirsten's room, except for Wingate. He would join Tyler and go through the wall.

Three was reached and the men moved again. At that second a Quisling came out of the last room down the hall, tucking in his pants. Tyler did not wait. And he was a very good shot. He hit the traitor right between the eyes with the first pull of the trigger. It was all that was necessary. The prostitute serving the fascist had been worried about this very thing happening, so she was right behind the man to catch him as he fell. With quality of forethought, she dragged him back into her room.

The men continued their action irregardless. Larsen and Sumner disappeared back into Kirsten's quarters and Mac rejoined Tyler.

"I'm sorry, Mac," Tyler apologized.

"What for?" Wingate said with respect. "You had no choice and you hit him perfectly." Mac expected to hear no more about it, when the hooker who had caught the corpse appeared again.

"He has friends downstairs," she said in Norse. "What shall I do? What can I tell them?"

"Ah, fuck," Wingate said in English. He told the girl to go back into her room and stay there. Then he translated for Tyler. "Sit tight," he finished. "I'll be right back." Checking the hall first, Mac moved silently to Kirsten's room.

"Trouble," he told the trio inside as he closed the door behind him. "How big is your waiting room, Kirsten?"

"Fairly small," she said. "Like all the rooms. Rectangular. Barely enough space for a dozen people to sit comfortably."

"Good. Any doors or rooms off the lobby they could wander into?"

"No. There is only the front door and the stairway up here."

"Larsen," Wingate immediately ordered without comment. "Climb out the window and lock the front door from the outside. Kirsten, give him the key." She quickly complied. The Norwegian acted without question.

"What are you going to do?" the girl asked, already guessing the answer.

"Tie up all the loose ends," Wingate said, moving toward the door.

"No!" Kirsten hissed. Mac turned at the urgency in her

153

voice. "No matter how fast you move, they will be alarmed the second they see you. They will scream and run as they die."

Wingate thought about it and nodded. "Come with me," he said. Both she and Sumner followed him down the hall to where Tyler waited. "Give her your weapon," Wingate instructed. "It's much easier to hide than a Sten."

The colonel picked up on the new plan right away. And he agreed with it. With the Sten's magazine sticking out the side, there was almost no way Kirsten could block it with her body short of being triple-jointed. He handed his gun over.

"Go back downstairs," Wingate told Sumner, "and get Neill and Sørum."

For a few seconds, Wingate, Tyler, Kirsten, and the prostitute waited in silence. Then three men came single-file through the wall. "Einar," Wingate said, "can I trust you?"

He replied with a simple "yes."

"Kirsten and I are going to take care of the lobby. As soon as we go down, I want you and the others to kill everybody in the other rooms who aren't female."

Again, Sørum replied "yes."

"The door should be locked by now," Wingate said. "Let's go, then."

Kirsten didn't even take a moment to collect herself or square her shoulders. She had slipped on a robe after killing the first man, and she now put the M3 behind her. Being only thirty inches long, there was no problem hiding it. Wingate just hoped the men downstairs would not be tipped off by the one hand behind her back.

As she began to move down the stairs, Wingate let go of his previous thought. She was so beautiful, and she held herself so well, that the one hand toward her back looked natural, even alluring. He heard the men in the foyer respond as she came fully into view. He saw her from the back, midway down the stairs. Only he saw the machine gun resting against the back of her leg.

Immediately after their initial laughs and bawdy comments, she brought both hands forward and up. Most of the men were looking at each other to make remarks when the first bullets slashed out. The first few who died didn't even see the gun. They were lucky. Their last memories were of a beauti-

154

ful woman on the stairs. They didn't see Wingate leap down next to her and start shooting himself.

From his point of view, the massacre was difficult to watch. It was strange and frightening because it was silent. There was hardly any decoration in the sitting room so nothing really broke. The walls, the wood, and the flesh accepted the whirling lead with little sound. The loudest thing was the hollow "click-click-click" of the guns' bolts sliding back and forth.

In moments, they were all dead. Kirsten lowered her gun at the same second Mac did. She looked proud of her work. Mac realized it had been her revenge, her ultimate dream of paying back all the real whores of the town, all the men who had come to use her. Wingate hoped she was satisfied, because it was all the revenge she was going to get.

Wingate looked behind him. Colonel Tyler stood behind the upstairs banister with a bloody knife in his hand. He gave Mac an "OK" sign with the other. Mac looked at his watch. 3:00 A.M. Four and a half hours to go.

He went down the last few steps to navigate among the corpses toward the door. He rapped twice between the bullet holes in the wood. The tumblers turned over and Larsen slipped inside.

The Norwegian spy surveyed the silent, ugly scene dispassionately. He then shook his head and said quietly, "It is over for us here."

Mac had to hand it to him. It was the understatement of the hour. It had been over the minute Kirsten killed the first commando. The Nazis' lust couldn't save her this time.

MILORG was finished in North Cape. Their cover was totally blown. Any one of the bodies could have brought them down, let alone all of them. The Germans would assume there had been a spy in their midst and it would be only a matter of time before suspicion would fall on Larsen. Perhaps they wouldn't bother to suspect anyone. Maybe they would just round up all their Norwegian employees and gun them down.

The Quislings would turn the town into a slaughterhouse. The streets would run red with the blood of their innocent prisoners. The tailor and the prostitutes would be swept away in the process.

Together, the Nazis and the traitors would declare a blitzkrieg on Alten fjord. The mountains would be turned into a shooting gallery. They would raze them to the ground to find Sørum and his compatriots.

They all had to leave. Tonight. Immediately. Larsen had to take Henrik Erling, the whores, and everybody else across the mountains to Murmansk. Right now. Their usefulness had run out.

Sørum and Kirsten could follow later. There were still some things they had to do.

CHAPTER 9

Mac Wingate dragged himself under the chain-link fence of the hilltop infantry camp at 6:10 A.M. He had removed the petrol can from his back outside the perimeter, so now he pulled it through after him. The bag with the empty tins hung from his left fist, the Sten around his neck. He hauled the petrol can over his right shoulder and ran for the empty barracks.

He was cutting it close. He had to. He couldn't afford anyone getting the chance to foul up the works. He had left himself and the two other commandos no more than a half hour to set the diversion. He had to rendezvous with Kirsten no later than 6:45, be in the water and cut the net by 7:30, and be the hell out by 8:00 when the two-ton bombs blew.

Wingate sped stealthily into the barracks. His mind threw a picture of him entering a room full of sleeping SS men by mistake, but he threw it back as soon as it had taken shape. In actuality, the structure was perfect. It was a large wooden building on short stilts measuring fifteen yards in length and three yards in height. Its windows were all intact and the solid slat walls were a tribute to German craftmanship.

He stopped admiring the building and looked outside for any sign of a guard. He saw none, so he waved Neill and Sumner on. The two commandos immediately burrowed under the fence and charged for their respective trees. While they went, Sumner held a ball of cord while Neill had the free end. As they separated, the line was payed out quickly between them.

Wingate saw Sumner jump up into the low branches of a tree right in front of him. He saw Neill run out of his view along the side of the empty barracks. He turned around to witness the Canadian climbing a tree outside the opposite window. In the purple-gray dawn, he could just make out the cord being lifted off the ground as the two commandos pulled it up over the empty barracks' roof.

Seeing that that went without a hitch, Mac set to work inside, pulling out the topless tins. As he set them on the floor and broke out the petrol, he thought about how his plan had taken shape.

As almost anyone with an explosives background knows, an open cup of gasoline in a small, sealed room would evaporate into fumes so volatile that after one hour an open flame would cause an explosion equivalent to a stick of dynamite. That's how and why a lot of inboard motorboats blew up.

But Mac was dealing with a big building, so one stick of dynamite wouldn't do. And since he didn't have any TNT and he had previously destroyed the only place he could get it, he hoped three tins of petrol would do the job in fifty minutes. He was hoping that by 7:00 A.M. the empty barracks would erupt like the world's biggest firecracker.

The only problem had been the detonator, the open flame. Then he had remembered his first briefing in the Datchet mansion. He remembered the one cigar aimlessly smoking away. No one had touched it during the time he had been grilled. When he had left the room, he remembered it was still smoking. That had started him on a chain of thoughts that led to the materials he started pulling out at that very moment in the barracks.

First, the quick-burning fuse. Wingate had glued two pieces of cigarette paper together and folded them lengthwise. That formed a trough in which he poured black powder taken from a few of his bullet casings. Onto each end he laid a match, the head of which faced out on both sides. He then rolled the paper and put it on a precisely measured piece of tape. He wound the tape loosely around the paper so the powder wouldn't suffocate while burning, but tight enough so none would fall out.

Next came the delay fuse. He had taken Neill's cigar, cut an opening in the mouth end of it, and pulled out some of the tobacco. Then he stabbed straight pins all along its eight-inch length. Since the stogie went in the faucet pipe, the pins were to keep it in midair, so even as the cigar burned and ashes fell, the remaining pins would keep it aloft and shrinking steadily.

Wingate placed both items down on the floor and got out a manual drill. He walked over to the side wall. He found a spot roughly in the middle, basically in between the two trees the other men were toiling in, and facing east, away from the rest of the camp. He quickly drilled a hole right through the wall.

Then he returned to the makeshift fuses. He placed one matchhead end of the quick fuse into the opening he had cut in the cigar. He then taped it in place. Pulling out the faucet pipe with the faucet still on one end, he placed that next to the two attached fuses for easy access. Finally he took out the cardboard grenade case.

Essentially, it looked just like the tins, only made of cardboard. It no longer had grenades in it, but it was far from empty. It was completely filled with the remaining matches of the ten boxes Mac had asked for. A hole had been cut into its side to the exact shape of the faucet pipe. Just to be sure, Mac had glued a piece of cigarette paper over the hole so not one match would fall out.

He sat staring at the eccentric materials on the floor in front of him and waited. He waited for Neill to finish his part of the job. To take the next step, Wingate required the services of another man.

The American never could meditate. Several people had told him it was wonderfully relaxing in times of stress, but those people never did it behind enemy lines. Wingate couldn't think serene, loving thoughts with dozens of Nazis not fifty yards away from him. He got up and went to the window to see how the other work was progressing.

He saw Neill in the top of a tree, making like a bird. An extremely dangerous, violent bird. The Canadian was straddling a branch that angled downward toward the occupied barracks fifty yards away from the empty building. He wrapped the stock of the MG-42 to the bottom of the branch with a roll of the darkened bandage. He used a second roll to secure the barrel so that it was pointing right at the door of the infantrymen's quarters.

Satisfied with his knot-tying ability, Neill pulled the clothesline pulley off the gun. He then swung around to the other side of the tree with it, spying a solid-looking branch that pointed in the general direction of the tree Sumner was working in.

With a piece of cord that was already attached to the pulley's frame, he tied it to the branch so that it hung free beneath it. He next reached over his head and pulled one gravel-filled sock out of one of the packs on his back. He took his end of the cord stretching between the two trees and put it through the pulley. He tied the same end onto the sock. He then lowered the sock so that it swayed just a few feet below the pulley.

Holding it there, he grabbed the rope a bit further toward the other tree and yanked. That was the signal for Sumner to take up the slack. On cue, the cord grew taut and Neill could let go of the sock without worrying that it would fall to the ground. He returned to the machine gun branch. He worked faster now. He knew that Wingate would be getting nervous. Pulling out a five-foot length of cord from his pocket, he tied one end around the trigger grip. The remaining end was put through the pulley along with the longer cord. And, just like the longer cord, the five-foot one was tied to the sock.

The final maneuver involved loading the gun. Compared to everything else, it was child's play. Neill secured the rucksack filled with rounds from his back to the MG-42. He opened the breech, lay the first round in, and closed the breech again. With much more caution, he pulled back the cocking handle. The action slid open, gleaming in the suffused light of morning.

Neill realized he had been holding his breath. He exhaled, realizing what a devilish invention he had set up. He had to hand it to Wingate, he thought. The outlandish device was insidious in its possibilities. If all went well, Sumner would have done the same thing to the Madsen, only aiming it at the guard tower. Then they would have a long rope stretching over the empty building, both ends attached to a hanging sock under a pulley.

But also attached to the sock was a looser cord running to the weapons' triggers. So when the long rope broke, the sock would fall, the short rope would be snapped tight, and down would come Hitler's babies, cradle and all.

Neill climbed down out of the tree, sharp on the lookout for guards. Early morning was the best time for saboteurs.

The night guard would be tired and his relief would be in no hurry to get up. Neill raced to the empty barracks. He was met at the door by Wingate, who wordlessly handed him the grenade casing and pointed at the hole in the wall.

The two men traded places. The Canadian hopped inside the building while Mac ran along the outside wall, holding the fuses and faucet pipe. Neill could smell the heavy cold fumes of the petrol in the air. They made him a little nervous. He increased his speed, but when he arrived at the hole, instead of seeing the faucet pipe, he saw Wingate's finger. As he watched, the digit motioned him to come closer. He lowered his ear to the hole.

"Wait," he heard Wingate's whisper.

Neill understood. Before they could chance lighting anything, they had to make sure Sumner finished the final, and most precarious, piece of the diversionary puzzle. He had to climb down his tree, attach another cord to the corner stilt of the empty barracks, and then attach it to the top of a telephone pole just outside the occupied building.

But just as in the trees, it wasn't a simple tying operation. For Sumner had the pack with the three grenades attached to the gravel-filled knee socks. He had to tie one grenade to the single telephone wire where it crossed the heavy wooden "T" bar at the top of the pole. He had to lower the other two grenades over the two ends of the crossbar. And then he had to tie the other end of the rope that stretched from the barracks' stilt to the handle of the sack.

In this way, the grenades were attached to the heavy socks only by their pins. The heavy socks were in the rucksack. The rucksack was held up only by a cord tied to the empty barracks' stilt. So when the barracks blew, the rope would break. Then the rucksack would have a great fall. And all Hitler's horses and all Hitler's men couldn't put Alten together again.

Neill saw Sumner go by the empty barracks' door. As he passed, he gave the "OK" sign. He went on to the corner of the building to signal Wingate. Wingate acknowledged the sign by carefully lighting the cigar. With cupped hands, he drew on it heavily until the tip glowed red. Taking no chances, he swallowed the acrid smoke. Better a lung disease than a smoke signal.

Mac had undone the quick fuse to light the delay fuse, so

he quickly retaped them together and stuck the whole thing in the pipe side of the faucet until only the lone matchhead of the quick fuse poked out the end. That done, he stuck the pipe into the hole. On the other side, Neill jammed the grenade casing filled with matches over the pipe end. While this was going on, Sumner was neatly laying row upon row of extra ammo belts between the evaporating tins of petrol.

Wingate didn't need to look at his watch to know their time was up. All he needed to do was listen to the footsteps which were approaching his way from the left. It had to happen, he groaned inwardly. Something had to come along and screw up the whole plan. Mac wasn't so worried about himself. He doubted the exhausted guard would notice him pinned to the wall in the gloom. But he was afraid the commandos would come tearing out of the barracks toward the fence, destroying all their chances.

Wingate fingered the matches in his hands. Well, he thought, if worse comes to worst, there was always Tyler, Kirsten, and Sørum. Maybe they could cut the net before the subs showed up. Whatever the case, he concluded, fingering a match, they'd have their diversion. It might be a little early, but they'd have it.

The long night and the commandos' savvy saved the situation. Neill and Sumner didn't appear, and the guard passed by without looking back. The three Allies were moving even before the German sentry was out of sight. They practically tore off their clothes and the first layer of skin getting back under the fence. Only when they had gone through the surrounding woods for fifty yards did Wingate check his watch. It was 6:42 A.M.

The men slowed to a sprint, moving unerringly toward a road that lay along the eastern slope of the cliffs overlooking Alten fjord. Breathing hard, their heels slapped the road just as a truck turned the corner. Mac saw the little red flag whipping in the wind from the side view mirror stem. It was Larsen's mail truck.

Sørum was sitting in the driver's seat, staring straight ahead as if he didn't see the commandos crouching at the tree line by the side of the road. But he downshifted anyway, the truck slowing as it passed. The trio ran after the tailgate, which magically dropped just as they approached it. Then the canvas flap swung back so Kirsten and Tyler could help the boys aboard.

"Welcome back to the land of the living," the colonel said, clapping Wingate on the back. "Everything went well, I trust?"

"You'll see," said Wingate. "In about an hour."

They had timed it. While Mac had been putting everything else together in the whorehouse cellar, a lone cigar had been smoking its ash out for its country. The eight-inch stogie had taken fifty minutes to extinguish itself. Hopefully, in about fifty minutes, its brother back at the camp would distinquish itself by working perfectly.

It was primitive, but if all went well, the cigar would burn down to the quick fuse, igniting the matchhead, which would in turn ignite the black powder, which would set off the second match inside the grenade casing, causing the hundreds of matches therein to flame, which would get the fumes going.

At the least, the barracks would blow sky-high. At best, it would be an inferno. It hardly made a difference. As long as it cut the rope stretched above it. For Mac knew it wasn't enough for the empty building just to burn. It wouldn't be long before the Germans ventured forth to extinguish the blaze. That sort of simple diversion would only last for a few minutes, while drawing off only a small contingent of the infantry.

What Mac wanted was for the weapons and the grenades to go off after the fire. He wanted to pin the contingent down and force them to call for reinforcements. He hoped he had hit on a successful way. He was only sorry that he would not be around to see it. But he would know if it worked. If he was alive an hour from now, it had worked. If he was dead, he wouldn't care.

A single hurricane lantern swayed from the framed roof of the truck, throwing a yellow glow over everything. Mac walked on all fours to the pile of diving equipment in the back. He started to quickly separate the pieces. There were rubber fins, masks, gloves, weight belts, diving dress with open-faced hoods, rubber shoes, and a Draeger lung.

"A rebreather?" Wingate said aloud.

"That's all they had," Kirsten explained, referring to the equipment the dead undersea commandos had left in her establishment.

"It's much like the British Lambersten lung," Tyler informed him knowingly. "A closed system. The exhalations enter a purifying chamber where whatever is still oxygen-rich will be sent back to the mouth. Its greatest advantage is that it leaves no stream of telltale bubbles to mark you."

"Its greatest disadvantage," Wingate said with resignation, "is that depth, overexertion, or cold could knock you out. You haven't learned yet, have you, Tyler?"

"It was all we could get," Kirsten defended him.

"And this time," the colonel promised, "I'm not going to take the wheat and leave you the chaff." He was making an allusion to ordering Reisings for everyone else but using a M3 himself. "I'm going with you."

Wingate nodded. Tyler was somewhat taken aback. He was expecting an argument at least. Instead, Wingate said, "Where's the other stuff?"

Kirsten produced a burlap sack from the corner. Wingate took it and pulled out some huge cutters with beaks the size of a man's hand. Wingate had found them on the hillside farm. Sure enough, there were four of the makeshift mesh cutters. One for each of the mission's men.

Wingate looked at those mission men. Tyler's face was expectant and assured at the same time. He wanted to prove himself to Wingate, while thinking the captain already knew his true worth. Neill and Sumner were on the razor's edge. They had been dragging along behind everyone on most of this mission, not understanding most of what was said. They had seen their partners killed. But now they were excited. They were actually doing something themselves. They saw a chance to pay back for Baker's and Biggins's deaths. They were working with the man they trusted most: themselves.

Wingate looked at himself. He was at his full strength, but he was tired. All the others were trying to prove something. That was their primary objective. Somehow, winning the war had become secondary. They were going to succeed because they had to prove themselves. To Wingate. To their fallen brothers. And to themselves.

Wingate didn't want to prove anything. He wanted to win the war. He wanted to complete his mission. And most of all, he wanted to face the ringmaster. The man who had been pulling everyone's strings for the whole operation. The man who had disappeared right when the trouble started. Wingate wanted to see Walters.

"All right," he said aloud, nothing in his voice betraying his thoughts. "We reach the pier in ten minutes. Get changed."

Everyone moved quickly to respond, ignoring the presence of the woman. But Kirsten wouldn't let Mac ignore her. As he tugged the heavy rubber up his legs while sitting in the back of the truck bed, she came to sit down next to him.

"We will wait for you at the MILORG *stabbur*," she said.

"No, Kirsten," he answered her, still changing into the suit. "You will not wait."

The Norwegian woman misunderstood. "No, you will not die! I know it. I feel it."

Wingate stopped tugging and looked at her. She meant it. She was feeling. She wasn't working on just a sensory level anymore. She wasn't just thinking in terms of "I-hit-you, you-hit-me." She was beginning to feel some worth. He put his hand to her cheek. He didn't care about the macho overtones. Putting it on her arm as if she were one of the boys would have been ridiculous.

"It's not that," he said so no one else could hear. "I have some unfinished business to do after Source is all over. Accounts have to be settled."

"I could wait," she assured him.

"Then you would die," he reminded her. "Alten fjord is no place for you any longer. Go over the mountains with Sørum. I will see you again." Wingate suddenly banged on the partition between the cab and the bed. "You hear me, Sørum?" he called. "Take care of this woman. She's worth more than you are."

"I hear you, Captain," came the Norwegian's muffled voice. "And I obey. She will be protected. You will see."

Great, Wingate thought. Somebody else with something to prove.

They looked like something from another planet. They stood in their rubber boots, holding the fins in one hand and the mesh cutters in the other. They weren't in wet suits, the kind that warms the body with a thin layer of water that adjusts to skin temperature. They were in winter dry suits, the kind that allows no water to touch the body. Of course, some liquid always managed to get in, usually at the very edges.

Wingate made a final check of the equipment as the truck slowly lumbered toward the deserted boathouse and the rotting pier. The miniature aqualung was in place—the reducing valve, demand valve, pressure gauge, and corrugated tubes with the mouthpiece all in working order. He had the compass strapped to his wrist. He tightened his grip on the big cutters. For a second, he considered how absurd it all was. Demolitions men playacting divers using pruning shears as wire cutters. Then Colonel Tyler encroached on his ruminations.

"Wingate," he said, obvious tension in his voice. "What about the others? The *Lutzow* and the *Scharnhorst*. What if they have antitorpedo nets too?"

"The *Lutzow* has returned home for repairs," Wingate informed him, remembering what Larsen had said. "The *Scharnhorst* has left her berth for the day. The most important target . . . the only one, is the *Tirpitz*. If we get that, our job is done."

There was a knock on the wall separating the cab from the truck bed. "Trouble," came Sørum's voice. "There's a guard at the boathouse."

Wingate swore. "We don't have time for this," he complained to himself. "Do you know German?" he asked Sørum through the partition.

"Not enough to be convincing," the Norwegian answered, his voice getting higher in pitch. "And he might recognize me!"

"Keep calm," Wingate ordered. "Drive right for it. At the last minute, take a quick turn so the guardhouse is facing the rear of the truck."

"I cannot . . ." Sørum stuttered. "It will not work . . . I . . ."

"Just do it!" Wingate demanded. "You want us all to die?"

The truck suddenly lurched to the left, throwing everybody against the wall. Then it skidded to a stop. The gears ground and the truck lurched backward. Wingate didn't wait for someone to start yelling and ruin his hastily conceived strategy.

"Don't worry," he shouted at the top of his lungs in German. "I'll take it from here!" The other commandos quickly brought Tyler and Kirsten to the back of the truck bed. They understood what Mac was trying to do.

"Guard!" Wingate called through the canvas cover near

166

the truck lip. "We have the supplies the officer ordered! Come give us a hand." Wingate's logic was simple. If the Germans had stationed a guard at a run-down, out of the way pier, it was for one of two things. They were either updating the facilities or they were worried about saboteurs. Either way, the lone guard probably didn't know or didn't care about the reasons for his duty and the word "supplies" could mean anything from radio equipment to breakfast.

Besides, if the guard did anything except immediately fan the truck canvas with Schmeisser fire, he had a chance.

Wingate waited, his Sten pointing at the truck flap. The corner of the flap moved outward. A helmeted German's head appeared. At the same moment, Wingate pulled the trigger. The bolt slammed back and forth for two seconds and the corpse fell back. The body arched over the wooden platform, rolled under the pier, and came to rest halfway in the icy water. The head with the surprised expression rolled back into the tiny guardhouse, its helmet still on.

After that, no good-byes were necessary. The men were off the truck and into the water, dragging the headless body under with them. Tyler hesitated, looking back at the sentry post and the bleeding head. With a shiver, he followed the commandos. Without a word, Wingate gave Kirsten his Sten, then kissed her. It was not romantic, but it was not without passion.

Wingate took in her expression as they parted. She had loved him, but more important, an emotional bond had grown between them. They cared for each other. Wingate was sure that they could meet anytime and anyplace and feel the same deep affection without strings.

He remembered her expression as he sank under the freezing water. Her honest smile was the only thing that made the whole screwed-up fiasco of a mission worthwhile.

His breath came in hollow gasps as he heard the truck drive away. In the slow-motion, silent blue world all around him, he saw the three other divers pulling the German's body toward the bottom. The Nazi's blood drifted lazily out from his neck in a dark crimson cloud.

When the headless body had filled with water, the men let the body sink on its own accord. By then Mac's limbs were numb and he felt light-headed. He wished he had found some long underwear for beneath the suit and he could understand why some divers liked the pure oxygen of the Draeger lung: it made them feel high.

He heard the patrol boat passing overhead before they had gone twenty yards toward the gigantic shadow that seemed to fill the entire fjord. Mac feared the inevitable. It was the patrol boat delivering the contingent of undersea commandos. It would be their last sweep before the others were supposed to relieve them. Only the others weren't coming, and in a few minutes they would all find out who would surface and who would not. Mac longed for some sort of underwater weapon.

Instead, he held the compass close to his eyes and followed its directions as well as he could. The sooner he got to the net and did the job, the sooner they could get out—maybe avoiding the German divers completely. Their object finally appeared out of the liquid gloom fifteen yards beyond. They all kicked toward it, stopping and looking at Mac once they had touched the cold metal links.

Wingate reexamined the compass. He didn't have time to do any in-depth directional work to arrive at the proper bearings or exact entry location for the midget submarines. With three of them coming, at least one was bound to see the opening. Mac led the men to just five meters below the water's surface. They set to work immediately.

Spacing themselves out, Mac and Tyler cut along the top while Sumner and Neill cut parallel slits down along the net for five more meters. And after five minutes of furious work with the bulky cutters, the quartet had sliced open a huge patch in the A/T net.

Motioning for the others to join him, Mac pushed hard against the top of the cut. Together they pressed until it folded down and away from the rest of the net. Essentially, they had made a giant flap that looked like the rear opening of a pair of Dr. Denton's long johns.

Wingate cut short a period of appraisal with a chop of his arm. He waved the others back toward shore. Just because one man had to remain to signal the midget subs and wave them through didn't mean everyone had to put their lives in continuous danger. The sooner the others were on their way toward Murmansk, the better Wingate would feel. They already had done more than their share on the operation.

With only a slight pause, the three others started drifting toward shore. Wingate watched them go until they seemed to blend in with the gray underwater glare. Steeling himself against the suspense of waiting, he pulled himself over the other side of the net.

Then he heard the bubbling. It was very distant and dim, but it was there. As soon as he became aware of it, Mac knew it wasn't the subs or his men. He looked back the way the commandos had gone. He didn't see the Nazi divers' shapes at first. He just saw their air bubbles rising. They were on a collision course with his men.

He hoped Tyler had the sense to dive as soon as he heard the bubbles. He hoped the gloomy, dark Norwegian fjord would camouflage the Allies. But then he saw the Axis men moving far faster and more frantically than they had before. The trio had been spotted. It was two against one.

Wingate dove toward the fray as fast as he dared. As soon as he had initially darted forward a balloon seemed to pump up inside his brain. It was the damn rebreather, he told himself. The pure oxygen was scrambling his mind. He tried to ignore it as he propelled himself forward. But the further he went, the worse it got. Soon he could not tell whether the murkiness was the water or his vision.

Suddenly all the fighters appeared. He saw one Nazi diver falling slowly down, the blades of a cutter in his neck. He saw another clawing frantically up, his air hose cut. The commandos had attacked with the only things they had. But the Germans had more. Besides the knives attached to their belts, they held a spring-powered arbalest of some kind. A spear gun that Wingate had never seen before.

As he watched, one of the four remaining Nazis took aim at Sumner, who was chopping away at another diver's gear with his cutters. Just as the Australian sank the points of the cutters in the German's belly, the other German pulled the trigger.

The flashing spring clanged dully and a thin, solid bolt bore threw the water and into Sumner's side. The Australian grabbed at the hilt, writhing wildly. Raging, Wingate slipped out Larsen's thin knife from inside his boot and propelled himself at the Nazi. He came up from behind, thrusting the blade through the rubber and into the man's kidney. As a final revenge, he ripped the weapon upward across the German's back.

His victim never knew what hit him. Mac had appeared out

of the dark blue in back of the fight. Wingate pushed the gurgling, dying man out of his way, swinging his arm toward the next Nazi in line. He stopped the diver before he was able to aim his spear gun at Neill. The American knocked the weapon into the links of the netting and buried his own weapon in the Nazi's neck.

Both dead Germans fell away from Wingate, a stream of ooze slucing out of their wounds. Wingate suddenly realized he could hardly see anymore. The strain had been too much for his underwater lung system. Somehow he wrapped his fingers among the metal net and hung on while his circulation slowed. The water turned from gray to purple, then almost to a deep brown. Wingate closed his eyes and breathed deeply. When he opened them again, the water had only an orange frame. He was coming out of it.

It was too late for Neill. The cold, the depth, and the overexertion had their effect on both the surviving Allies. Wingate saw the last remaining Nazi driving his knife repeatedly in the Canadian's limp body while Tyler weakly pulled at the German's back.

Wingate tried to move. His limbs felt like the gravel-filled socks back at the infantry camp. He couldn't bring himself to let go of the net. He looked achingly around him. He saw the spear gun he had knocked into the links still hanging there. He managed to get his free hand around it.

Pulling it down, he tried to tell himself that it was no different than shooting any other weapon. All he had to do was make it part of his hand, point it like a finger, and fire. But the target kept blurring in and out of focus. He saw part of that target fall away. It was Neill, spinning lazily for the bottom. The last Nazi commando turned toward the weakened Tyler.

Wingate lined him up and pulled the trigger without thinking. The metal shaft dove down and smacked through the back of the Nazi's head. The man dove right over Tyler's head and into the blackness below.

The exertion and high oxygen level in his bloodstream made Mac nearly helpless. All he could do was shake uncontrollably. He had a vague awareness that Tyler had drifted over to rest beside him. Forcing his head to move, he looked at the hole they had opened behind them. In front of it, barely visible, was a long, cigar-shaped mass.

As he watched, the thing moved unerringly toward the opening, its little engine whining. It seemed to hesitate for a moment before the gap, as if wondering how it got there. Then the lone midget submarine moved through.

The men inside never saw Wingate.

CHAPTER 10

Somehow Wingate made it back to the surface. He wasn't exactly sure how, but he remembered seeing his hands crawling across the net's metal links. He remembered fumbling over the buckle of his weight belt. He remembered floating up. Once he had spit out the regulator from his mouth and sucked in several minutes' worth of air, he was all right.

Floating next to him was Colonel Tyler. He just bobbed on the surface, unconscious. Wingate didn't know how he got there, but when Mac saw his belt missing also, he assumed either he or Tyler had undone it. Mac also noted that he had had the innate sense to pull himself out of sight range of the *Tirpitz*. He was near the shore of Alten.

Wingate grabbed Tyler by the collar and dragged him along as he paddled his way toward the dockside tavern. The American wasn't sure what time it was, but the sun was up. Judging from the shore's desolation, however, it could've been the middle of the night.

Wingate pulled himself out onto the low dock planking below the roofs leading to the tailor's shop. He hauled Tyler up after him. Quickly, so no Norwegian or Nazi discovered him, he recreated his trip with the unconscious Larsen almost one full day ago. Carrying Tyler in a fireman's grip, he went to the tailor's bedroom

The window was already open. Wingate slipped inside, dropping Tyler onto the bed. He was about to revive the colonel when he saw a pile of materials on the foot of the bed. Looking closely, he saw his Sten lying atop the perfectly folded German lieutenant's uniform. The Sten was encased in the body harness with which Snow Queen had first carried her Suomi at the Nordic pagoda.

Even though he was still dripping wet with freezing water and his fingers and toes felt as if they had fallen off, Wingate felt warm inside. Kirsten had been here.

His pleasure turned to bitterness when he returned his attention to Tyler. He pulled off the man's headdress and woke him up. The colonel opened his eyes. From the moment Tyler looked through him, Wingate realized what had happened.

The colonel's oxygen had run out. For the last few minutes he had been breathing his own carbon dioxide. And in a matter of only three minutes, he had suffered massive brain damage from a lack of air. Colonel Richard Tyler was completely and irrevocably retarded. Wingate didn't know how long he remained, exhausted, staring at the American with numb indifference.

But finally Wingate left the bedroom. Tyler would die of starvation. Or maybe an accident. Or he'd be killed by the enemy. Perhaps he would even be imprisoned. Or left to wander until he expired from exposure. Until then, he would breathe, drool, and defecate without knowing what he was doing. He would never remember his name or his past or his loves or anything else. His brain would remain as fouled and foggy as the fjord water.

Wingate walked out the side door of the tailor's shop in the lieutenant's uniform. The Sten hung in the body harness below the greatcoat. He walked to the whorehouse. He broke in the side door. He went to Kirsten's bedroom. He threw back the curtains behind her bed and moved down to the cellar.

There he found Walters.

The English colonel turned from the side table as Wingate entered. His face showed shock at first, when he saw the uniform. But he relaxed into the same smug superiority when he recognized the face.

"Let me be the first to congratulate you," he said easily. His tones were still upper-class British, but they were not as thick as before. He held up the map Larsen had drawn of the infantry camp. "The underground told me everything. Your diversion was a smashing success. The men didn't know what hit them. They were shot as they ran out their doors. They were blown up and electrocuted when the telephone pole fell, and several died trying to put out the subsequent blaze. In a matter of minutes, almost everyone was called up from the town to quell the 'major attack by Allied commandos.' ''

"And the *Tirpitz?*''

"I'm afraid we didn't do as well with the *Tirpitz,*'' Walters said sadly. "Not your fault, of course. Your part of the operation went swimmingly. If you'll pardon the pun.''

"I'm not amused, Colonel,'' Wingate said dangerously. "What happened?''

"It was a muck-up from the start,'' Walters continued breezily. "There were six submarines, numbered 'X-5' to 'X-10'. X-9 was lost with all hands during the crossing. X-8 had to be scuttled due to extensive damage. The rest were plagued by disaster. Their periscopes failed. Their electrical systems failed. There wasn't enough air circulation, so several men suffered hallucinations.

"Only two of the three aimed at the *Tirpitz* arrived. Then something went wrong with X-6's surfacing equipment. It rose, alerting the captain of the ship. He shifted the bow 150 feet to starboard. When the charges went off, only the engine room was hit. The *Tirpitz* still had enough strength to sink the X-5 when it surfaced.''

"Too bad,'' concluded Wingate.

"All is not lost. All her engines were damaged. A rudder twisted, two turrets jammed, and there was massive equipment failure. The 'Lonesome Queen' won't be bothering Allied convoys for many months to come.''

"The 'Lonesome Queen,' '' Wingate mused, the two men still standing across the room from each other. "No wonder you got so upset when I named the mission 'Snow Queen.' ''

"Yes, old boy,'' Walters admitted. "You startled me there. I thought only I knew our double mission was called 'Lonesome Queen' after the *Tirpitz's* Norwegian nickname.''

"Triple mission,'' Mac reminded him. "How did your end of it go?''

Walters paused for the first time, startled for the second time. Then the wide, easygoing smile returned. "How did you know about that?''

Wingate shrugged. "I had it all put together except for your place in it. I knew Tyler wasn't sent along simply as an errand boy. Headquarters might be stupid enough to do some-

174

thing like that, but Erikson wasn't. Erikson wouldn't send me on a jack-off mission to keep you two out of his hair.''

''You have an inordinate amount of trust in your Colonel Erikson.''

''Justified. Once you disappeared, I figured Tyler was the real head of the diversionary mission. You were here for a completely different purpose. And when Larsen told us that he sent Lars Harald with some secret information over the mountains, I finally figured out what that purpose was.''

Walters remained silent, just smiling and waiting for Wingate to say it all.

''The Norwegian intelligence wasn't arriving. That spooked Operational Intelligence. The Norse had been supplying them with the best Nazi naval information in the entire war. They wanted to know where things were going wrong. So they sent you to find out.''

Walters smiled even wider. He lowered his head and nodded. ''Right,'' he said. ''Absolutely on the nose.''

''So it was all an act,'' Wingate marveled. ''The upper-class twit stuff. The 'veddy proper' stuffy English Lord shit. All the gross mistakes. An act.''

''To a degree,'' Walters agreed. ''I came up on the deck of our trawler for the reason I told you. I honestly thought it was our contact ship. I had no idea it was a Nazi interceptor. I only wore the uniform to get you upset, thinking you'd yell or stew on it a little bit.''

''And your move at the pagoda?''

''What do you think? I was on a schedule. Sørum was taking Harald over the mountains. I had to catch up. I didn't want to be pinned down for any length of time, so I forced you to act.''

''So you risked all our lives so you could keep your schedule clean.''

''Captain Wingate,'' Walters chuckled, ''I had my orders. Everyone in Allied Command agreed . . . well, almost everyone. We were informed that you were on a suicide mission. My superiors felt it imperative for that fact to remain secret. Your Colonel Erikson didn't think so, but we were all sure you would run out if you knew your real purpose.''

''I didn't run out,'' said Wingate. ''And I'm not dead.''

''No. No, you are not.'' Walters said it seriously, almost

sadly. His whimsy had all but disappeared. "How did you find me?"

"Where else would you be? If you were going to come back at all, you wouldn't meet Tyler in the MILORG village. That was in the wrong direction of your escape route to Murmansk. If you hadn't set your rendezvous for here, I *wouldn't* have found you. But then I was supposed to be dead, and at the time, Tyler didn't have the A/T nets to worry about. You two could go skipping back to Murmansk hand-in-hand."

"I have to admit your reasoning is sound, even if your allusions are a bit childish," Walters stated, his head cocking to the side. "We certainly did not have the finest of communication systems. I followed Harald all across the wilderness without knowing the information he carried concerned the underwater . . . shall we say 'obstacles?' If I had, I might have saved us all a lot of trouble."

"And five men their lives," Wingate said coldly. So coldly it managed to scare the Englishman.

Walters did not let the fear show in his manner, but it came through in what he said next.

"Come, come, Captain," he soothed. "There's no right or wrong in war. Out here there are only commands followed and commands not followed. That is the difference between a good soldier and a bad one."

"No, there's more," Wingate said flatly. "But even on those standards, you stink. You didn't even think it important to give us all our orders. After all, we were only dead men. Larsen told me our full 'Lonesome Queen' orders. I quote, 'More important than the diversion is the possibility that Intelligence will discover underwater obstacles to the midget submarines. The operatives must be prepared to foil these obstacles.' "

For the first time, Walters got defensively angry. "I left that in Tyler's hands . . ." he started with venom.

"Don't pass the buck," Wingate retorted with disgust. "You were the ringmaster on this mission, Walters. You got all the information direct from HQ The fault lies with you. And that is just what I'm going to say at your court-martial. And that is what Larsen, Sørum, and Kirsten are going to corroborate. They are the only ones left."

Walters stared in openmouthed wonder at the American. It

was like a ghost passing judgment on him, like Jacob Marley returning to haunt Scrooge.

"By the time we're through," Wingate continued, "you'll be demoted so low you won't know what stripes look like. And someday, you'll be assigned to work under me. And then we'll just see how good a soldier you are. Then we'll see how long you last."

Wingate let the speech hang in the basement between them for a moment. Then he went on in a lighter tone. "You see, that's what's more than simple order-following, Walters. It's called justice."

Walters looked sick. He may not have been the blithering fool he pretended to be, but he was an egocentric, glory-seeking man nevertheless. He would have marched over the bodies of Wingate, Tyler, the Australians, the Canadians, and the Norwegians to get a pat on the head, a slap on the back, and a star on his shoulder. He saw it all blow up in his face.

"By the way," Wingate inquired, "what happened to Harald and the information?"

"Nothing," Walters said distantly. "The security leak must be back at the London office."

"So there was no double agent in our midst this time," Wingate murmured, remembering all his other missions. "That's fucking amazing."

At that second, there was an incredibly loud boom and the entire cellar shook. Walters clutched at the side table, but it couldn't hold his weight. He went crashing to the floor. Wingate had anchored his feet. He stayed upright, calm.

"What was that?" Walters cried.

"Another reprisal," Wingate told him casually. "The enemy must have found all the bodies we left behind and put it all together. They've come to string Kirsten up. And failing that, they're going to raze this place until they find somebody else."

"But . . . but that means they'll find us!" Walters babbled. "They'll find the secret passageways and come down here."

"You're probably right," Wingate mused.

"Oh, my God!" Walters breathed, looking at Wingate in horror. "You're just going to let them get us, aren't you? You're not going to do a damn thing to stop it. In the name of justice, you said. You're willing to die, as long as they get me!''

Walters stumbled to his feet and sped for the other passage to the house at the end of town. "But I won't let them get me!" Walters swore. "I'll escape the back way! Find your own justice, Wingate. You won't take me with you!"

With that, Walters ran as fast as he could through the underground passage. Wingate walked slowly over to its entrance, looking at the floor.

Then the American heard the gunfire. He heard Walters scream and fall. It only made sense. If the enemy were tearing apart the whorehouse, they would find the opening in the wall Wingate had made to kill the undersea commandos.

Wingate entered the passage then and went to Walters's body. The Englishman's eyes were open in horrified shock and some Quislings were standing in front of the corpse, their weapons still smoking. All they saw was a Nazi lieutenant looking at the dead form of an Allied spy.

Wingate stared at Walters with more hate than he had ever expended on anyone. He hated the enemy, but this man was supposed to be an ally. A comrade-in-arms. A fellow soldier whose duty it was to destroy the Axis forces. Instead he stared at a man whose only concern was for himself. A man who didn't care about the Nazis or the armed forces.

"Another Allied dog," Wingate commented to the Quislings in Norwegian. "Get him out of my sight."

Wingate waited until the Norwegian traitors had taken Walters's arms and were dragging him away before he finished his thoughts.

"And hang his balls over the town square."

SPECIAL PREVIEW

Here are the opening scenes
from

MISSION CODE: ACROPOLIS

Coming in March!

"Colonel Olaf Erikson to Colonel Stephanos Sara-
phis, commander in chief of ELAS, September 26,
1943. Earliest opportunity will respond to your
request. Total London agreement with your assess-
ment. Severe disruption of communications your
area would pull two Wehrmacht divisions out of
Italy. Our best man placed at your disposal. Alex-
ander suggests code name: Acropolis."

Chapter 1

The ground was damp beneath Wingate's belly. It was more than damp, Wingate thought, as he felt the chill of his wet tunic strike upward through his belly. Damp was the understatement of the year. It was sodden. The whole week he had spent in northern England had been sodden. The sooner this thing was over and Erikson posted him to some warmer theater of operations, the better.

The man lying next to him was a British colonel. He had a pair of binoculars to his eyes and he was focusing on a tank that loomed in the distance through the rolling mist. He muttered briskly, "This damned waiting! God Almighty, why don't they get on with it!"

"How long have they had this stuff?" Wingate asked.

"It's brand new," the man muttered. "Laboratory testing— that sort of thing, but never been tried in the field."

"Let's hope we're not wasting our time," said Wingate. He felt that the whole week had been wasted. Erikson had insisted on it, though probably to give himself more leverage with Ike than to enlighten Wingate. There had been times in the past few days when he'd sat in a Nissen hut watching the rain fall continuously and wondering whether Erikson hadn't forgotten him altogether.

A voice from somewhere behind Wingate called, "Countdown!"

Wingate checked his watch. The big sweep-second hand ticked off the countdown: 58, 57, 56 . . .

The head of some French officer lying behind a low sandbag emplacement came slowly into view, craning forward toward the distant tank. A British sergeant-major wearing

183

Royal Engineers insignia bellowed from way over on Wingate's right, "When I say down I mean down—sar!" The head disappeared at once and a little group of sheep that had been nibbling the thin grass of the moorland turned and fled in sudden alarm.

Wingate smiled to himself. He glanced first to one side of his position, then the other. All around him, men's faces wore the same expression of eager anticipation. He wondered what the hell they would have thought of him back home in Sawyer County, Wisconsin, if they would have seen him now. Here he was, lying face-down on some barren stretch of moorland miles from anywhere, surrounded by top brass in the same prone position, waiting for some fireworks display that would put all the July 4ths he'd ever seen to shame. And as he smiled, the mental clock in the back of his mind ticked away the seconds: 42, 41, 40 . . .

They were having trouble with the field telephone. As he kept his head down and his eyes fixed on the isolated tank a couple of hundred yards away, he could hear a raised voice cutting through the damp air. "There's been a short. I can't raise them, sir. They acknowledged countdown. Now they've gone dead . . ."

It didn't matter, Wingate was thinking. If the guys with the blasting box had started the countdown, you didn't need to get in touch with them again until it was all over.

An American voice, full of dry humor, observed, "Those goddamn sheep! They keep chewing up the insulation on the wires. We oughta kebab the lot of 'em!"

There was a little amused laughter, but most of the men watching were too absorbed with the tank to join in.

The mental clock in Wingate's head had reached 35, when something caught his attention at the edge of his field of vision, something moving toward the tank through the mist. For a second he dismissed it as a sheep or a dog, but the explanation didn't satisfy him so he shifted his focus.

It took him a fraction of a second to see what was happening, then he sprang to his feet, leaped over the sandbag emplacement, and raced toward the command post twenty yards away. As he ran, he yelled, "Stop it! Stop it! Abort!"

The sergeant-major barked at him to get down. Wingate ignored him. The clock in his head had reached 31. Already he'd checked his run and begun to change direction. He had to figure on the worst: the guys with the blasting box were hidden deep inside the concrete blister in the middle of the firing range and the only contact with them was over the field telephone. There was no way the explosion could be aborted, and if the explosive was half as effective as the back-room boys claimed . . .

Wingate was headed now for the tank. He cleared the last of the low sandbag walls protecting the observers and reached the open ground. As he did so, someone behind him called out, ''Good God! There's a kid out there! For Christ's sake, do something!''

Wingate cut out the scene behind him and concentrated all his attention on what lay ahead. The ground was flat but broken here and there with shallow pools of water, not deep enough to stop him but enough to add precious seconds to his time. Stunted silver birches rose up occasionally, but for the most part he could ignore them. He had his eyes fixed firmly on the distant figure. It was a boy, as best as Wingate could make out, wearing a jacket and short pants and a school cap pushed toward the back of his head. He looked maybe twelve and he was walking steadily toward the tank.

Wingate screamed, ''Get out of there! Hey kid, get away!''

The boy either didn't hear, or ignored Wingate. At the back of Wingate's mind, the clock had reached 25.

A double-red Very light soared into the air behind Wingate, rose over the top of him, and fell in two brilliantly glowing balls ahead of him and to his right. Maybe it was an abort signal, maybe it was intended to warn the kid. Wingate had no way of knowing and it was a risk he wasn't about to take. As his feet drove down into the soft peaty surface of the moorland and every muscle in his legs propelled him forward, his mind was trying to figure out the odds. He took a quick glance at his watch as his left arm swung forward again. Twenty seconds of the countdown left—twenty seconds exactly.

A rough guess put the tank around ninety yards ahead of Wingate. He would arrive there about the same time as the kid. He had covered one hundred yards once at college in ten seconds plus, but that was in running spikes on a top-class track with only six or seven ounces of clothing on his back. He was in boots now and wearing full battle dress and the ground was like damp blotting paper. On the other hand, the incentive was greater now than it had been back in Madison.

He was running against the clock there—now there was a kid's life at stake. There was also his own.

The boy noticed Wingate at last. He stopped and looked toward the charging figure racing toward him out of the mist. Something about Wingate's desperate determination, his pumping arms and pounding feet, scared the boy. He turned and ran.

"Stop!" screamed Wingate. There was a tearing sensation in his throat as he forced the sound out as loud as he could manage. "Kid—listen to me . . . !" His voice failed him. His body needed all the air he could gulp into it. There was nothing left for speech.

The mental clock now dominated Wingate's mind. 9, it yelled, 8, 7 . . . Wingate wanted to cry out in frustration. All that effort and he wasn't going to make it. If the device hadn't been aborted, he had less than six seconds left on earth. His heart was bursting in his chest, his legs were beginning to disobey him. He'd hardly gained a yard on the kid since the boy began to run.

A moment later, the boy slipped. His foot came down on the half-buried remains of a rotted tree stump and his ankle went over. He cried out and limped a few yards and finally came to a stop.

5, 4 . . . The passage of time totally dominated Wingate's mind. He caught the boy around the waist in the crook of his right arm without slowing his momentum. He had checked the scene ahead during the last few yards of his approach. The tank was twenty yards away to his left. Fifteen yards to his right, the ground dipped sharply into a sandy area riddled with rabbit holes. He had the place firmly in his mind as he swerved around a birch tree and put the last few dregs of effort into the final dying seconds. 2, 1 . . . In his mind's eye, he could see the engineer with the Hell Box, the grip firmly in his hand, watching the last few seconds tick away on the synchronized clock in the firing strongpoint. He'd been in that position often enough to know exactly what it felt like—the tendency to give that twist a fraction early out of pure nervous tension. A fraction early this time and the war would be over for Wingate—permanently.

The two of them were still three yards clear of the sandy depression when Wingate took off for it. It seemed to him a lifetime before he finally hit the ground. As he did so, sliding and twisting on the damp surface, he clawed ahead of him with his free hand and dragged himself over the lip of the depression. As he hit the bottom, he had the boy underneath him, shielding the kid with his body. He put his hands up to cover his ears and found that somewhere during that hectic sprint he'd lost his helmet.

"Zero! Zero! Zero!" the clock in his head screamed.

He curled into a tight, compact ball and waited for the roar of the explosion and the savage thump of the blast wave. Nothing happened. Still he waited. Time was deceptive under stress. What seemed an hour might be only a split second. Still he waited. The kid underneath him hadn't moved or made a sound since they had hit the rabbit warren, and Wingate began to wonder if he was all right. Finally he had to conclude that somehow they had managed to abort the thing. He had an uneasy feeling that he had been a bit precipitate; with all that brass around, they would have taken precautions against every eventuality. He gave a little grin to himself, imagining the kind of remarks they were going to make to him when he got back to the observation position.

He began to uncurl. He opened his eyes and looked at the boy. The kid looked OK—pale and a little scared, but OK.

"What's your name?" Wingate asked, a touch of exasperation in his voice.

"Kenny Fields," the boy said, after a moment's hesitation.

"What the hell were you doing out here?"

The boy struggled to get up but Wingate held him where he was. He wanted confirmation of the abort before either of them moved. He was being over-cautious, he knew, but he'd seen too many guys chopped down by not being cautious enough.

The boy said, "My dad's in the army. I saw the tank. It's a Panzer. I wanted to see it. I never seen . . ."

Kenny Fields didn't get to finish the sentence. Wingate felt the earth move before he heard the roaring crash of the explosion and felt the crushing pressure of the blast. His eardrums were being impacted and the air was being driven out of his body. He could hear chunks of the disintegrating Panzer whistling over his head and smell the acrid smoke of the explosive charge. A thousand images flashed across his mind. He hung on to one of them as being more important than all the others. It was the image of the kid who had

187

wanted to see a Panzer close-up. Kenny Fields who wanted to identify with his dad in the army. What was important for Wingate was to hang on to the kid, and shield him from the fragments of hot metal that would start to fall as soon as they lost momentum. It wasn't the kid's fault he'd gotten himself into this situation. Jesus Christ, what the hell did they bother to post guards for if the guys were too blind to spot a twelve-year-old? He was going to hang on whatever happened . . .

He was still concentrating on hanging on to Kenny Fields when there was a dull thump somewhere in back of him. It was more a sensation than a sound and he felt more a sense of surprise than anything else, surprise that it was suddenly so tough to hang on to the kid anymore, surprise that concentration had suddenly gotten to be so difficult. He felt himself slipping into unconsciousness, and what made him madder than hell was that there was nothing he could do about it. As the final veil of darkness fell across his mind, he felt Kenny Fields struggling to get out from under him.

The ground was moving very slowly under Wingate's body. When he opened his eyes he found he was lying on his back staring up at a leaden sky. The clouds scudded across his vision. The back of his head ached. He put his hand up to find out why and found blood on his fingers. A scrubby birch tree came into sight, moved slowly across his line of sight, and disappeared. He began to get things together. The ground wasn't moving under him, he was being dragged by the ankles very slowly over the ground and whoever was doing the dragging was making a lousy job of it.

"Hey, you!" yelled Wingate, bracing himself against the pain in his head. "Put me down! For Christ's sake, you're breaking my neck!"

His body stopped moving and his heels touched the ground. A moment later, a kid's face came into view. The sight of Kenny Fields leaning over him, concern etched into every line of his expression, brought everything back to Wingate—the explosion, the blow on the back of the head, the drift into unconsciousness. He sat up slowly, testing his reactions, then put a hand up to the back of his head. Blood was oozing into his hair and beginning to trickle down his neck, but the wound itself didn't seem to amount to much. He figured it was only superficial and that all he'd have were a couple of hours of aching head.

He got to his feet. He wasn't all that steady, but he could walk. He beckoned to the kid to come closer, and when Kenny did so, Wingate put a hand on his shoulder to steady himself. In the distance he could already hear the wail of an ambulance and see the first of the observation party running toward him across the open ground. He figured he'd been unconscious no more than ten or fifteen seconds. What was ten or fifteen seconds in a whole lifetime?

"You all right, Captain Wingate?" called the sergeant-major, leading the half-dozen figures who were running toward Wingate.

"I'm OK," said Wingate, his left hand still gripping the back of his head. "Someone take care of this kid."

"I'm all right," said Kenny Fields. "I can take care of myself."

Wingate raised a smile and ruffled the kid's hair. "You could have gotten us both killed, you know that?" said Wingate. "I hope your dad takes more care of himself."

"He's with the 8th Army," said Kenny. "He's a sergeant." There was pride in his voice.

"Maybe I'll get to meet him," said Wingate.

The sergeant-major reached him and took a look at his head. "Flesh wound, sir," he pronounced. "Glancing blow. Couple of stitches . . ."

"Thanks," said Wingate, moving forward again. "I figure I'll live."

A British staff major came up to Wingate and said, confidentially, "One of your chaps wants to see you. Over at Elvington. He's laid on an aircraft for you. Chap called Erikson. Signal just came through."

"You'll find he's one of your chaps," said Wingate, unable to resist a little jab at the accent. The British weather the last couple of weeks had bitten pretty deeply into him. "We don't have many chaps in our army—mostly guys."

The major looked at him for a moment, then his face melted into a little amused grin. He wasn't offended. He said with mock surprise, "Is that so? Well, damn me—never tell you a damn thing these days, do they?"

Wingate managed a grin in response. "Where is this place?" he asked. "How do I get there?"

"It's a bomber drome. Ten—twelve miles away. I'll lay on transport after we've had the doc look at your head."

Four or five officers were now accompanying Wingate, escorting him to the ambulance that was rolling toward them over the marshy ground. One of them asked, "Who's the boy? Anyone find out?"

Wingate glanced to his right. Kenny was still with them, striding along between a Polish lieutenant colonel and an Australian flight lieutenant.

Wingate turned to the sergeant-major. "Take care of the kid, will you, Sergeant-Major?" he said.

The sergeant-major took a couple of quick strides forward and grabbed Kenny Fields by the back of the neck. "Come along, young feller," he said, voice friendly but very firm.

As Wingate got into the waiting ambulance, he saw Kenny being marched briskly toward one of the pickup trucks that had brought the party out to the range.

The trip to the bomber field at Elvington took half an hour. Wingate gazed out of the window of the big Humber staff car at the flat countryside, without much interest. Black-and-white cows grazed in some of the fields. In others, machinery was lifting the first of the sugar beet crop. The low clouds and mist hung a veil over everything. He found the scene infinitely depressing. The call from Erikson couldn't have come at a better time. He wanted a change of climate. Above all, he wanted action. The war wasn't going to be won by guys sitting around on their asses. Other guys were fighting, why wasn't he? Sure, the Allies had gotten Italy to surrender and they'd established beachheads in the south, but there were three divisions of Mark Clark's guys bogged down at Salerno. If they were ever to reach Naples, they could do with some help. It was near the end of September already. The weather wouldn't hold up forever.

The medication the doc had given him had left him woozy. There was a chunk shaved out of his hair around the wound and the wound itself had been stitched. It was giving him no pain. Even the headache that he had expected to develop into something savage was no more than a dull ache. But he felt drowsy. He needed to snatch a couple of hours' sleep until the drug wore off, once he had seen Erikson.

The security at the airfield was some of the hottest Wingate had ever seen. The car stopped at the barrier and an MP talked to the driver, glancing now and then at Wingate seated in the back. Then he turned to Wingate and asked to see his papers. He let nothing slip, checking every single entry with methodical precision. The man had acquired an ability to read official documents while at the same time examining the bearer. Wingate wondered how, with security like this, even the station commander managed to get to his office.

Wingate finally got his documents back. But it wasn't over then. The military policeman called his sergeant, and they stood outside the car, necks craned toward Wingate's open window.

"Captain Wingate, sir?" croaked the sergeant at last.

"Wingate," said Wingate. "Captain—that's right. Something wrong?"

"To see Colonel Erikson, sir?" There wasn't the flicker of a smile on the sergeant's face as he leaned forward into the vehicle, eyes locked on Wingate's, waiting for some hint in Wingate's expression that he wasn't everything he claimed to be.

"To see Colonel Erikson, Sergeant," said Wingate, resignedly. There might be some point in fighting the top brass, but there sure as hell was no point in fighting security. Experience had taught him that when an MP took it into his head to be difficult, he was willing to devote the whole of his life to it—twenty-four hours a day.

The sergeant seemed satisfied at last. He stepped back, threw up a salute, and waved the barrier up. A moment later they were inside the camp.

Erikson had aged in the short time since Wingate had last seen him. There were streaks of white in his fair hair, and the wrinkles around his eyes and across his forehead had deepened. The war was getting to him.

His preoccupation with the tales of horror coming out of his native Norway was leaving its mark. Wingate could understand that. He had returned from Norway himself just a week ago.

Erikson looked up from the table he was standing at, the moment Wingate came into the room. "You're late," he snapped.

"I—ran into trouble," said Wingate. "I needed to check with a doctor . . . ."

"I heard about it," Erikson cut in, irritably. "You're supposed to create trouble for the Hun, not for your allies."

"There was a kid, sir," Wingate protested. "A boy around twelve. He was walking into a death trap. I couldn't . . ."

Erikson cut him short with a brief wave of the hand. "OK," he said. It seemed that the mention of the kid annoyed him. He tapped the map in front of him. Even upside down, Wingate could see what it was. It covered the whole of Europe from Norway's North Cape to the Mediterranean, and from the Atlantic to the Urals. Erikson's finger was on northeastern Germany. "They're putting on a big show tonight. The marshaling yards at Hamm. This time they want to take them out completely."

"Any particular reason?" Wingate asked.

"Pressure from the Russians, mostly," said Erikson, as if the reason didn't particularly interest him. "Anything that disrupts internal east-west lines of communication can't do anything but good. Not that it concerns you. You're not going to Germany. But when they put up the bombers, we can sneak you out along with them. Once you're lost in the rest of the gaggle, you can drop under the Hun radar and head south."

"South?" asked Wingate.

"South," said Erikson, emphatically. He looked up from the table at Wingate and finally stood up. They had worked together now ever since that first meeting in Casablanca, almost a year ago. Since then, they had planned and executed between them half a dozen missions that had brought them to the attention of the Western leaders. Not that either Erikson or Wingate was particularly impressed by that. Recognition wasn't why either of them was in the war. They were in it out of principle. Erikson knew firsthand what German occupation meant. He had seen the Nazi invasion fleet sail unopposed up Oslo fjord and his own family taken away by the SS. Revenge had driven him into hiding and finally got him out of the country to join British Intelligence—and revenge was what still propelled him.

Wingate's experience had been different. His first contact with fascism had been as a student at the University of Wisconsin. There were some students on the campus who let their German background shape their thinking. Everything he heard from those ranting fanatics made him want to throw up. He was an American. There was also his Ojibway blood, inherited through his mother. On both counts, the streak of independence in his temperament was fundamental. The fascist view of subservience to the state was something he could never stomach.

"Take a look, Wingate," said Colonel Erikson, indicating that Wingate should go around the table and join him. As he did so, he reached forward and picked up a piece of paper lying there and stuffed it quickly into his pocket.

The two men stood side by side, looking at the map. They were oddly alike, despite obvious differences of detail. Wingate was an inch taller than Erikson, though both were under six feet. Erikson's fair hair, now whitening perceptibly, contrasted dramatically with Wingate's straight black hair and dark skin. Erikson's eyes were blue, while Wingate's were dark as sloes. But they took the same square stance, standing with feet set firmly apart and shoulders held a little forward, as if ready for immediate action. They were broad, firmly built and strong, with the mark of outdoor living and physical activity clearly on them.

Erikson put the tip of a ruler on southern Italy. "Things are going badly," he said. "What a crazy way for God to build a country. Look at it—it's like a herring: a central spine with coastal plains on either side and no way of communicating between. We have a beachhead at Taranto and another in Calabria. From one, we drive up the east coast, from the other, up the west. But there's no room. Look at this . . ." He tapped the map south of the Sorrento peninsula. "What do we have there—five, maybe ten kilometers in which to maneuver. It doesn't matter how many men we pour in from Sicily, they could be stopped by a troop of Boy Scouts! We have to get the hell out of there as soon as possible. We need Naples if we're ever to ship in the kind of supplies we need. Above all, we've got to get those men off the beach at Salerno. Two weeks of shit those poor bastards have faced already!"

Wingate waited. Erikson was preoccupied with some personal consideration. In the end, Wingate felt he had to bring Erikson back to the point and break the tension. He asked, innocently, "And you'd like me to take Naples, Colonel?" He asked without a trace of humor in his voice or in his expression.

193

Erikson wasn't amused, but it brought him out of himself. He said, acidly, "Well it would help, Wingate, if you think it's that easy."

"I'm sorry, sir," said Wingate. He had to admit that when you thought of those guys lying in foxholes 24 hours a day with mortar shells dropping on them from the hillsides, his remark hadn't been all that amusing. But he could see something was troubling Erikson. He felt a rapport with the man. He would have liked to help him if he could. But Erikson's manner made it clear that he didn't want any help. He could handle whatever was troubling him by himself. Wingate didn't press him.

"While you were playing with this boy on the test range, did you notice the new explosive?" Erikson asked suddenly. He had turned and walked to the window of the second-floor room and was standing with his hands clasped behind his back, looking out at the misty airfield. "It's why you were sent up here in the first place."

"I couldn't help noticing, sir," said Wingate, letting the palm of his left hand rest gently on the dressing covering the back of his skull.

"Did it impress you?"

"It impressed me."

"So it damn well should, the amount of work that's gone into producing it. You're going to be the first to give it its combat trial."

"In Naples?"

"You're not going anywhere near Naples, Wingate," said Erikson. "You're going to Greece."

"We were discussing Italy, sir . . ." Wingate protested.

"We're still discussing Italy," said Erikson, turning to face Wingate. He walked across to the table and tapped the map again.

Wingate could make out the name of a Greek town in the east of the country. "Larisa?" he asked.

Erikson nodded. "If we can't drive the bastards back in Italy, maybe we can pull them back. It worked in Sicily, it'll work again. We want to create so much trouble in the Balkans that they have to bring in reinforcements or withdraw. I can't see them withdrawing—not yet. And they certainly can't spare a single man from the Russian front. That only leaves them Italy. If we're lucky, they'll pull just enough men out of there to make a breakout from Salerno a real possibility. Anyway, ELAS is expecting you in seventy-two hours . . ."

"ELAS?" Wingate interrupted.

"The Greek Resistance army—or the part that matters . . ."

"I've worked with them before," said Wingate. "They're communists . . ."

"Wingate," said Erikson, irritably. "I don't give a damn if they're Martians. I need help. I'm prepared to take it wherever it's offered."

Wingate shrugged. He wasn't about to object. His sentiments, in any case, were the same as Erikson's.

"You'll cross the French coast west of Dieppe," Erikson was saying, tracing out the position with the ruler. "West of Paris, west of the Rhone, west of Marseilles. Stay on that course as far as here . . ." He indicated a spot in the Mediterranean, a little west of south-western Sardinia. "Then a direct course for Malta. The air crew has full particulars. So long as you have a general idea. In Malta you have a commando team waiting for you to join it. They'll put you into Greece by submarine. After that, you're on your own."

"Where do we pick up the explosives, sir?" asked Wingate. Now that he had an assignment that would get him out of this damp climate, he was anxious to be moving.

"You don't. That's the problem. You'll be flying the stuff out with you," said Erikson. There was worry on his face as he looked at Wingate. After a moment, he added, "Take care."

It was a very personal remark made with a good deal of genuine concern. Wingate was grateful for it. It gave him a new insight into Erikson. Of the two of them, Erikson had the lousier job. If the mission didn't make it back, it was Erikson who was going to have to live with the fact.

"I'll take care, sir," said Wingate.

"It's vital for your own security that you don't stick out like a sore thumb. You're just another member of a bombing crew, until you set that course down the Rhone. See the sergeant in the outside office. He'll kit you out—show you the ropes. And I've arranged for the navigator to keep an eye on you. He's an American as well—Brad Manganaro."

The briefing was over. Erikson was folding the map on the table and putting it into his briefcase. Wingate came to attention and saluted, then turned for the door.

"And Wingate," Erikson called. "What you risked for the boy—that was . . . brave."

Wingate turned. He found the word "brave" embarrassing. What else was he supposed to have done under the circumstances? He said, "Anybody who was human, sir . . ."

"His parents must be very grateful," Erikson cut in. "There are some occasions when parents just aren't around."

"I don't know about his mom, but his dad's with the 8th Army," said Wingate.

"Well—that's ironic," Erikson muttered, more to himself than Wingate. "And here we are trying to work out a way of helping him."

There was something more that Erikson wanted to say, but he couldn't quite bring himself to. Wingate waited, halfway between Erikson and the door. At last, Erikson said quietly, "Did I ever tell you, Wingate, that *I'm* a parent? Perhaps I ought to say 'was.' "

It was completely out of character for Erikson to open up like this. He was professional to the core. Something very dramatic must have happened to make him want to unburden himself, thought Wingate. He said, gently, " 'Was', sir?"

"They shot my son when he tried to run the Norwegian flag up again. It's me they were after, but I was down on the docks at the time and friends hid me till the SS had gone. I had a daughter. She was six years old—the last time I saw her." He paused for a moment to collect himself. Wingate had never heard Erikson mention a daughter. Finally, Erikson added, "I've had the underground trying to find out what they could ever since. I got this from their intelligence an hour ago." He groped in his pocket and took out the sheet of paper that had been lying on the table and thrust it at Wingate.

Wingate took it. It was in Norwegian scrawled on the back of an official signals sheet. It read: "Child cared for by relatives, Stavanger, 1942. July 1943, family accused of harboring patriots, shipped to Germany. Final destination believed to be Auschwitz. Regrets."

"I'm—sorry," said Wingate, automatically folding the signal before handing it back to Erikson. He'd never felt more inadequate in his life.

"Will you do something for me, Wingate?" Erikson asked. He'd drawn himself up now, and he looked very much in control of himself.

"Of course," said Wingate. He couldn't begin to imagine what Erikson was feeling. He admired the man for not breaking down altogether.

"When you next come face to face with some of those bastards—crucify them for me. Will you do that, Wingate?"

Wingate nodded. "I'll do that, sir," he said, quietly.